PROHIBITED MAGIC

PROHIBITED MAGIC

High Priestesses of Lemuria - Book 1

ANDREAS FARMANN

Chakra-Atelier

Contents

Copyright © 2023 by Andreas Farmann

All rights reserved. No part of this book may be reproduced in any manner whatsoever without written permission except in the case of brief quotations embodied in critical articles and reviews.

ISBN Trade Paperback: 978-3-907242-27-8
ISBN eBook: 978-3-907242-28-5
The German-language original of this book was published as "Gefährliche Magie" by Tredition, 2023
First English Language Edition published by Chakra-Atelier Publishers, Bernstrasse 7, 3600 Thun, Switzerland - www.chakra-atelier.ch
Translation & Illustrations:: Hau'oli, Chakra-Atelier
Cover created using Canva Pro. Image source: Getty Images Pro/bestdesigns
Maps: Created with Inkarnate

First Printing, 2023

For Eleonore. Thank you for reminding me of the fact that I hadn't wanted to just write non-fiction, back when I was a little boy. *Namaste.*

I

Prologue

Off the Danish West Coast,
In October of the Year 1863 A.B.

Still a few hundred feet away, yet close enough that she could almost feel fate breathing down her neck, an ice-cold wall of water and spray rushed towards the dark-skinned woman standing on the quarterdeck of the storm-tossed galleon. Drenched to the bone already, she struggled to keep her composure as she watched the vast, shimmering, green-grey expanse of water rise up in front of her. Life, she thought, was almost over.

Why couldn't this have happened in the familiar, tropical waters of her home? There, she could have contacted the water with a simple spell and would have been understood. Not so here, in the stormy waters of the European North Sea, and deprived of all her magical abilities.

The soft features of the woman, who stood just over five feet tall and still looked very young, took on a look of determination. She would not give up so easily. As long as she lived, there was hope.

Desperate cries echoed across the deck as the wet and exhausted sailors of the crew shimmied along the crisscrossing safety lines towards some kind of shelter.

The captain of the Swedish merchant galleon *Galileo*, the ship she had boarded in London a few days ago, stood motionless beside her. His name was Olge Sandershill, and he had already attached himself with a couple of well-practiced knots to the front railing as well.

"Check that your knots are still holding fast, Noble One!", he shouted, his voice almost drowned out by the whistling and howling of the wind. "This is going to get rough. Some men have already been washed overboard!"

The captain swallowed, visibly shaken. "I'm sorry it had to come to this. This hurricane hit us without warning, almost out of nowhere! I've never seen anything like it!"

The storm sails had long since been torn to shreds, their remnants fluttering from the rigging of the once-proud three-masted galleon.

Sandershill had urged his only passenger on this passage to her quarters two hours ago. But she had known that things were getting critical, and she wanted to at least face her fate with open eyes.

Only three months ago, she would have been able to calm the wind with a simple spell, or even open a portal and bring herself and the crew to safety. After all, they must have been only a few dozen miles from the safety of the shore, and a priestess of her abilities could bridge even such distances when it was truly a matter of life and death. Now, on the one hand, that possibility was so close that she could almost feel the Weave in her abdomen, and yet it was completely out of reach.

If only she hadn't... or, did she still have time? The Inquisitors would probably track her down within minutes and be waiting for her at the next port if she used the amulet now, months too early. She would be putting her mission in extreme danger.

But if she died now, the Temple would have to send someone else anyway. She might still be able to elude the enemies when she was in full possession of her powers again.

In a split second, she made up her mind.

A few seconds before the shining wall of water reached the ship, she pulled the small pendant in the shape of a fishhook from her neck and muttered the incantation that would bring back her magic and enable her to save the ship and its crew.

She breathed a sigh of relief, expecting the Source to appear before her, ready to serve. Yet, nothing happened. The spell evaporated into the salty air, without effect.

Shocked and uncomprehending, the woman stared at the object that should have secured her salvation and the success of her mission.

The amulet, having supposedly fulfilled its role, vanished into thin air. Her thoughts raced and blurred. A mistake? Betrayal? An insane joke of the Ix? This could not be happening, this could not be true! The amulet had been created in her presence by the most powerful and trusted of her sisters in the Temple of Ferns! She...

By force, she brought herself back to the present. The murderous wall was almost upon them. Not a second too soon, she took another deep breath and tasted the salt in her mouth, burning like chilli, but now just nauseating.

Then the wave broke over the ship with primal force. In the bubbling and roaring of the water around her, she felt more than heard the cracking and splintering of wood.

Huge forces tore at her, seeming to crush her body. Somewhere beside her, a shadow flew through the water.

"Someone's safety line broke," a thought flashed through her mind. The captain's? The helmsman's? There was nothing she could do but wait and hold her breath.

After what seemed like an eternity, the water finally drained away, and the woman's aching lungs, trembling with weakness and cold, breathed in the salty oxygen with relief.

She looked around with watery eyes, and only slowly could she make out anything through the dark streaks in her vision. She was the only person left on the quarterdeck. The mizzenmast was a stub, the bulwark splintered. The helmsman must have been swept away with the tiller. Her face was grim. Now all she could do was wait for the storm to come for her, too, the dark-skinned woman thought, her once elegant clothes hanging in rags from her slim body. Exhausted, she lost consciousness.

When the woman opened her eyes again, hanging limply in her self-applied restraints, the *Galileo* was still afloat.

The wind and the wild cross seas seemed to have subsided almost imperceptibly. That probably wouldn't help her much. She had no idea where her drifting wreck was, in what direction it was drifting, or how long it would be before she reached land or encountered another ship.

She jumped as an eerie sound rang out, a howling and yelping that drowned out the now noticeably diminished wind. It seemed to be coming from one of the aft deck compartments directly below her.

Then she remembered the Irish Shepherd puppy the captain had brought aboard as a gift for the shipowner's son. The animal had become everybody's undeniable favorite during the crossing, and had been spoiled by the entire crew.

"Poor fellow," she sighed, fiddling with the line that still joined her to the aft deck railing.

It was difficult to untie the tight, soaked knot, but she managed and staggered forward on aching legs. She struggled to keep her balance on the deck, which was still rocking violently in the heavy swell. She held on to the railing and waited for her strength to return, at least temporarily. Then she quickly descended the companionway.

When she opened the door to the captain's quarters, the frightened puppy almost jumped in her face.

"Okay, okay, calm down," she murmured, stroking its velvety forehead. The animal whimpered softly, but relaxed a little.

She thought hard. There had to be something she could do! This was not her world. On a ship of her native lands, she could have called for a rescue glider by means of an auroral distress signal, even if she had been robbed of all her natural abilities, as she was now.

She felt helpless and at a loss on this large sailing vessel, which was state of the art by the standards of most Earth nations, but completely archaic from a Lemurian or Atlantean point of view. She could only wait.

The woman dropped into the bolted chair at the captain's desk, not caring that water ran from her clothes onto the carpet, and looked at the young dog in her arms, now completely relaxed and snuggling up to her.

Suddenly, she was not sure who was comforting whom.

After minutes that seemed endless, she finally found the strength to go back on deck. She took the animal with her because the swell had continued to subside, and she didn't want to leave it alone. If this ship was going to sink, it should at least have the same chance of survival as she had.

She opened the bulkhead and looked out onto the main deck. There had to be something she could do. Perhaps there were other survivors, injured sailors? She was about to start searching the devastated deck before her when she lifted her head and stopped. A sound had caught her attention, a subtle change in the wind noise that she couldn't quite define. Cautiously, she poked her head out of the bulwark and looked out over the churning sea.

On the starboard side of the galleon, about twenty yards above the water's surface and so far hidden by the superstructure of the aft deck, a metallic thing was hovering. It resembled an equal-sided triangle about fifty feet long, and seemed completely unaffected by the wind even as the Galileo continued to sway and roll violently in the dying storm. She had seen these things before.

"An Atlantic hoverboat, of all things!" she muttered, quickly dropping back into cover. For a moment she wondered if she should make herself known. Was it wise to let the Atlanteans rescue her? Or would that only lead her out of the frying pan and into the fire, after all that had happened? Or did she still have friends on Atlantis? Which side were the pilots of this vehicle on?

A moment later, she was relieved of that decision. A blinding beam of light shot from the tip of the dull metal structure. It struck the *Galileo* amidships, causing another crack followed by a crash. The ship lurched violently to port. The woman lost her balance from the unexpected motion and hit her head on a spar protruding from the debris in front of her. Darkness followed.

After a moment of stupor—how long had she been unconscious?—she felt a rough, wet tongue against her face. The dog, she remembered darkly, and then awareness of her predicament returned.

Carefully, she half sat up. The young animal whimpered softly beside her. At first, she was not at all sure what had happened. There had been no explosion such as might have been caused by the firing of a cannonball or one of the modern grenades she had encountered during her journey through the Ottoman-controlled areas of the 'New World'. Nevertheless, she was certain that the ship had been hit. The Atlanteans had different weapons than the Europeans, and the Lemurians, her own people, knew of such devices of destruction only from the myths of the ancients.

She had had to learn quickly, since she had landed her outrigger boat on the shores of the Inca Empire, still besieged by the Spaniards. And each stage of her journey since then had brought new horrors to light.

Silently, she cursed the fact that her people had isolated themselves from the rest of the world for so many centuries, lost in their delirium of peace. They should have kept a closer eye on the Council of Seven. Who knew what the inhabitants of the double continent in the Atlantic Ocean had come up with now. But the Temple of Ferns had honestly believed that with the Treaty of Ilkarion everything would be settled, that the Crystal Priests had really understood. Naive they had been, gullible! With an effort she brought her attention back to the world around her. This was not the time to fret about things that could not be changed.

At first, everything happened in complete silence. The deck was slowly sinking down into a more inclined position. A few anxious seconds later, she heard the piercing hiss of evaporating seawater, followed by cracking and splintering noises. The ship's interior was probably on fire, and planks were splintering as seawater began pouring in through the leak.

The young woman froze for a moment, shocked. She quickly gathered her composure.

When she straightened and raised her head above the bulwark, the airship had disappeared. In all likelihood, she had not been seen at all.

She got up, thinking. Something was wrong. She couldn't put her finger on it, but it wasn't just the fact that she was on a sinking ship, that her life was in danger.

Then it went through her like a hot knife. She felt herself beginning to forget the existence of the Atlantean ship! That was it! The knowledge of her mission, and with it the few memories she still had, began to fade quickly.

For the second time in a short period of time, she had to use all her willpower to fight the panic that was rising within her.

This was not normal. Why...?

When she realized what was about to happen, everything inside her rebelled. She had to keep at least the most important thing! "I am Kaura Alenu'ala, High Priestess of..."

A sob ran through her tortured body. She couldn't remember! What was she doing here? And even her name began to fade away. "I have to open the portal and seek help!" she whispered. But which portal? Help from whom?

"My name is Kaura..." She fell silent, unable to recall.

She ran back to the captain's chamber, tore a page of heavy parchment from the log that lay open on the table, dipped the quill into the inkwell, and wrote her name on the paper with frantic strokes.

When she was done, she stared at the page, uncomprehending. What did this word mean? But she had obviously thought it important enough to write it down. Lost in thought, she turned the page back and forth in her hands. "Kaura," she murmured.

Outside the chamber, something cracked loudly, and she jumped. With great effort, the woman without memory forced herself back to the present. She was aboard a sinking ship! That was one of the few things she was still sure of. And the galleon was taking on water rapidly. If she wanted to survive, she had to act now.

Quickly, she shoved the parchment into one of the wax envelopes lying around and ran out onto the deck, where the little dog was now scurrying around, barking like mad.

At the edge of the ruined deck, she found a massive wooden grate. With unexpected strength, the delicate woman pushed and pulled the possibly lifesaving construct overboard. She watched as it landed with a splash in the waves. At least she would be able to hold on to it.

The deck was already tilting considerably. It would only be a matter of minutes before the sinking ship would mercilessly pull down whatever was still on it. She grabbed the puppy and stroked its head again.

"I guess we'll have to swim now, dear," she whispered. And jumped.

The water crashed over her.

As she surfaced, she hit her head on a piece of debris from underneath. She felt a sharp blow... then darkness enveloped her.

* * *

Meanwhile, the triangular metal boat was flying over the British island at high speed. With its cloaking shield turned on, of course, so as not to disturb the primitives. In its all-glass control room, a white-haired, hard-faced man in a yellow robe ran his finger over the holographic projection of the controls.

Then he spoke in a calm, almost bored voice.

"Log entry. Commander 2nd Class Elkin, 16 December 3285, 17:23 hours. Target was located in the Atlantic Ocean, heading northeast. As ordered, a storm force of 11 was generated, confined to quadrant 17-87-B, in combination with an anti-magic barrier field at one hundred percent capacity. The vessel was sunk. No survivors spotted, crew and passengers presumed lost in the storm. I placed a veil of forgetfulness over the site, just in case I missed anyone. No magical powers detected, so the barrier field was probably unnecessary. If there were any Gifted targets on board, they were already dead by the time I got close enough. The mission may be considered as accomplished. Heading back to Atlantia. A detailed report to the Council of Seven will follow. Period and close."

Sighing contentedly, the white-haired man enjoyed the view of the glittering Irish Sea that now emerged from the early evening haze before him. In a few minutes, he would reach the Eire peninsula at the easternmost tip of North Atlantis, and a short time later, he would fly across the mountain range separating the independent Irish provinces from his homeland.

The commander idly wondered who or what might have been on the galleon that had prompted his superiors to have it destroyed in taboo territory. The Lemurians would be furious if they ever found out. Though, whether the distant islanders still monitored the treaty at all, no one knew for sure.

After all, a little more than thirty years ago, even the Atlantic aid to the defense of the Aztec Empire against the Spanish conquistadors had gone unpunished. And that had been a war. A massacre.

Due to the technological superiority of the Atlanteans, a rather one-sided one, of course, Elkin thought with a disgusted twitch in the corner of his mouth. But the Spaniards had brought it upon themselves, after all. And they had still been able to grab enough territory from the continent that they called the New World to satisfy their greedy Sultan's hunger for gold.

Well, if his order should lead to any conflicts with the mythical overseers in distant Lemuria, Minister Ixkarel would have to take care of it. After all, Elkin himself had only carried out his orders.

He was looking forward to his evening off. The great Irkumseh had created a new entertainment pill, and the hoverboat commander had been able to secure tickets for himself and his wife to one of the previews in the noblest entertainment hall of all Atlantis.

The commander licked his lips at the thought of the multi-sensory delights awaiting him, then turned back to his instruments to contact Atlantia Hover Harbor Control and initiate his approach.

MAP OF
EUROPE &
ATLANTIS
NORTHERN
ATLANTIS
SOUTHERN
ATLANTIS
GULF OF
ATLANTIS
SPAN.-OTTOMAN
SULTANATE
MEDITERRANEAN
SEA
KINGDOM
OF SCOTLAND
EIRE
PENINSULA
Gothenburg
Inverness
Edinburgh
Copenhagen
Dublin
Oxford
Cork
London
Hamburg
Inmarsund
Paris
Venice
Rome
Constantinople
Athens
Rhodes
Alexandria
Pyrrha
Granada
Cadiz
Algiers
Agadir
Atlantia
Morania
Imelin
Axlin

2

Inquisitors in Inmarsund

It was freezing cold on this late December morning in the year 1868 after Buddha, or 1597 A.D., as at least some of the Spanish-Ottoman occupiers would have said. Frost glistened in the late-morning sun on alluvial logs polished by water into bizarre shapes, transforming the deserted Baltic beach into a gnarled fairyland. Ice floes creaked and cracked, pushed together by the gentle swell.

Just above the high tide line, on one of the remaining bands of dried reeds, flattened by past snowfalls, a thickly cloaked figure sat motionless, seemingly deep in meditation.

A great tit, also on the move despite the inhospitable weather, whizzed past the shape like a flash of yellow-black-gray, landing nearby and then hopping closer with a soft, almost questioning chirp.

A delicate hand slipped out of the thick, rust-brown cloak into the biting cold. The hand, darkly tanned even though it was winter, turned its palm slowly upward and waited.

After a moment's hesitation, the tit seemed to decide to trust the offer. It hopped closer still, then fluttered the last bit, and alighted on the outstretched hand.

The small creature snuggled into the inviting, warm hollow. Almost at the same time, a pleasant sigh of relaxation went through the two beings that were so different from each other.

Slowly, Kaura opened her eyes. She felt the small, beating heart of the little bird caressing her palm.

Her eyes scanned the horizon almost automatically as her vision adjusted to the cold but almost painfully bright winter light on the beach. Again, not a single sail. In the cold of this early winter's day, not even the fishermen were out on the water.

She sighed and looked at the small, feathered creature in her hand for a moment.

"What do you think, my dear? Will we finally see my aunt's ship one of these days?" she murmured, almost expecting an answer from the little bird. But of course, there was none. With a contented chirp, the bird closed its small eyes and snuggled even deeper into Kaura's palm.

Almost as soon as she had formulated the thought, she regretted it. After all, she could have enjoyed the quiet peace of her meditation for a while longer. Instead, she immediately thought of her worries.

"Oh, come on," she murmured to herself with a brief flash of annoyance. The uncertain fate of her best friend in this city was simply too close to her heart. No wonder she was worried.

The young woman's muscles must have tensed a little at the thought. In any case, her feathered friend was already fluttering off in the direction of a nearby tree that jutted bare and gnarled from the sandy ground at the edge of the deserted beach.

Kaura was considered very attractive by most of the young men in town. But she was also reserved and introverted.

Now, all that could be seen of her under the wide hood were her green-gray eyes, still watching the dancing waves with a touch of impatience.

"How can she do this to me?" she muttered. "First, she won't take me on the first trade mission for the *Kontor* to Atlantis, and now she dares to die in a storm or something!"

Well, it was probably just a delay, she soothed her concern. Due to the ongoing war activities of their rulers, it was not uncommon for merchant ships from the Spanish-Ottoman occupied territories to be detained in independent ports. Or—and this was also true of their friends from the 'free' countries—they were driven off course by the sometimes violent winter storms in the Atlantic. Even the modern, sleek, four-masted ships that served the transcontinental trade routes were dependent on the wind, and the North Sea between the warm Atlantean double continent and Northern Europe was notoriously unpredictable.

She interrupted her thoughts. Thinking about all sorts of difficulties would not help anyone, least of all herself.

Her timelessly beautiful deep brown face, with its delicate nose, twisted into a grim smile. No one knew exactly how old Kaura was, not even herself. She looked like an extremely attractive woman of about twenty-five, unusually mature for her age. But that had already been the case when she had first come to Inmarsund.

Almost exactly five years ago, she had been found and rescued as the only survivor among the wreckage of a merchant ship that had capsized in a winter storm.

Try as she might, she couldn't remember anything of what had passed before that moment. The passenger list had been destroyed in the sinking, and no one in the ports the ship had visited could remember her.

It had not even been possible to determine where she had boarded the vessel, and whether she had been a passenger or a crew member hired by the captain, though the quality of her clothes had suggested the former. Her rescuers had found a torn piece of parchment on her body, wrapped in wax, with the hastily scribbled word "Kaura" written on it, barely legible because of the water that had seeped in. No one knew what it meant or what language it came from, but in the absence of any other trace, it had become her name.

The merchant family to whose fleet the galleon that had rescued her belonged had taken her in, after a–futile–enquiry into the cause of the accident. They had given her work.

Kaura had become almost like a daughter to Aalyjah Leivenstein, the child-less matriarch of the clan, and her younger sister Resa, one of the most accomplished captains of Inmarsund's merchant fleet, did not allow the young woman to call her "Aunt" for nothing. They were the best family she could have ever asked for. And yet–where did she come from? What was her reason for being here in the north? Did she have another family somewhere? Did they miss her?

She looked a bit like the darker-skinned members of the Spanish-Ottoman "liberators", who had driven the Mongols out of some of the Western European territories still held by Genghis Khan some thirty years ago, but she spoke neither Spanish nor Arabic.

On the other hand, her mastery of Scottish and Atlantean, which, due to classical literature, served as a *lingua franca* throughout the known world despite the inaccessibility of its lands of origin, was so impeccable that either could have been her native tongue.

In the meantime, she had also learned Polish, the language of the natives of this cosmopolitan trading city. It had come so easily to her that her new family's language tutor had been baffled.

Aalyjah, however, found this completely normal. After all, she spoke nine languages fluently herself and had traveled much of the known world in her own youth.

The bright bark of a dog jolted Kaura from her reverie. Before she knew it, a strong blow hit her side. With a small scream, she fell to the sand with the blankets still wrapped around her. She laughed as the furry brown animal tried to lick her face, "Atam, no, leave me alone!"

Imar, the family secretary and scribe, joined them with deliberate steps and, as always, a serious expression on his face. His broad nose was deep red with cold, and his short red beard was white with frozen breath.

"I still don't understand how you can stand sitting outside at this time of year, Kaura," he puffed. "You always meditate on the frozen ground for hours. Any normal person would just freeze to death, or at least catch a fatal cold."

"Well, then I'm obviously not a normal person. Anyway, I don't freeze so easily."

Kaura smiled. She was always pleased when the serious, sometimes a little too serious secretary took the trouble to visit her out here.

He was like the good spirit of the family. Most likely, he was just coming to tell her that it was time for their morning meal.

"I'm having breakfast in town today," she said, before he could go on. "I'm going to meet with Joe Nelson. He arrived last night and sent a messenger right away. Maybe he'll know more about the situation in the Middle Ports. Resa just has to have been held up somewhere up there."

"Let me know if you learn anything useful," Imar replied. "For weeks now, we've only been hearing rumors, nothing solid to report. Anyway, the Atlanteans and our masters seem to be at odds again somehow. I wouldn't be surprised if the Middle Ports got involved as well. Even though they've always been politically neutral."

He lowered his deep bass voice a bit as Kaura stood up and brushed the sand from her skirts.

"Joe would be a pretty good match for you, don't you think? Attractive, intelligent, certainly obedient... you've been with us for a couple of years now and haven't had any relationships—at least as far as I know." He winked confidentially.

Kaura blushed.

"Hmm, I could think about that. He's a decent guy, and we get along well..."

In fact, it was unusual for a woman of her age in Inmarsund not to have at least one or two committed relationships. The occupiers from the distant Mediterranean might have found this a bit strange, but unlike in other European regions, matriarchy was still firmly established in the North, and it was not unusual for a woman to have five or more husbands. Whom she was usually perfectly willing to share with others.

After all, the Spanish-Ottoman patriarchs also had their harems, most notably Sultan Philip II in Granada. The Nordic women, however, would have hated to be compared to them. After all, no man could belong to another, and, with them, everything was based on free will.

Meanwhile, Atam was frolicking on the beach like an exuberant puppy, rolling in the sand and squealing with delight. Thanks to his thick, brown-gray fur, he probably didn't feel the cold at all.

Imar looked at him and smiled.

"It is hard to believe that your dog is already over five years old. At least his playfulness has hardly changed since we saved him from drowning in the wreck of the Galileo together with you."

He knew Kaura would not tell him more about her romantic intentions. She probably wasn't interested at all in the subject right now.

Silently, wrapped in their heavy winter furs, the slender woman and the stocky former sailor moved along the beach path, approaching the town with quick steps, circled by the joyfully barking animal.

Up on the dune, they could already see the walls of Inmarsund across the plains, the silhouettes of the town's tall stone buildings and massive red brick towers rising into the sky.

On the horizon behind the settlement, dark clouds slid into view like a black screen, bringing the sunlit buildings in front of them into even sharper focus. It was going to snow.

* * *

Barely twenty minutes later, Kaura stepped out of the damp cold of Market Street and into the warm dining room of the *Kawiarnia China*, where she had arranged to meet Joe.

The *China* was known as a popular meeting place for Asian merchants as well as the town's younger upper class. Located on the ground floor in one of the large company buildings that were lining most streets in the harbor district, it was quite different from the taverns usually found in the North. The pub had high ceilings and relatively bright interiors, and would probably not have been out of place in a large metropolis such as Constantinople, Valletta, or London.

Since Inmarsund, close to the new western border of Mongolia, had retained its importance as a trade center for goods of all kinds passing between Asia and Europe despite its occupation by the Ottomans a little over thirty years ago, there were plenty of customers on this chilly Tuesday morning, eager to enjoy a late breakfast, hold business meetings, or catch up with trading partners and friends.

As Kaura squeezed through the aisles in search of an empty table for two, she took in the distinctive blend of scents that permeated the place. The air smelled sweetly of the finest Arabic coffee, warm Swedish pastries, and the tart aroma of freshly brewed Chinese *Pu-Erh* tea. She sighed in satisfaction. Inmarsund offered its residents and guests an unparalleled standard of living, especially in view of this Baltic port's modest size.

In a somewhat quieter part of the main hall, she found a sitting area furnished with Japanese tatami mats, cushions, and a low wooden table. She beckoned to one of the busy waiters, ordered one of the exclusive autumn teas from the southern Mongolian province of Yunnan, and made herself comfortable.

The lead-framed stained-glass window beside her had a few clear panels through which she could see outside. Except for a few horses tethered to the building across the street, there was nothing to see. The animals' breath drifted as white steam in the cold wind that whistled through the alley.

Turning around the corner from Stralsund Boulevard, one of the new steam wagons was approaching. Three of the strange things had arrived in town a few weeks ago, and they were now competing with the horse-drawn carriages. Of course, only the wealthier residents of Inmarsund could afford the high fares. The alchemical machine was huffing and whistling loudly.

Kaura dreamed of the day when the steam engines invented by the Mongolian alchemists would be available everywhere. Perhaps they could even be built large enough to power ships... they would glide across the seas as if moved by magic.

Inadvertently, the young woman was frightened by her own thoughts. One was not even allowed to think about magic. It was one of the few things that could be dangerous in Inmarsund.

The occupiers had no love for sorcery. When they first came north with their great fleets of dhows, they had captured and taken away all the witches, energy alchemists, and herbalists who had not escaped in time - or so it was said more than thirty years later.

No one knew what had happened to them. Only that there were still large bounties paid for the extradition of magically gifted people. Of course, no one here would betray another; the occupiers and their brutal Inquisition were too unpopular for that. Still, she knew of no one who had anything to do with magic and still lived in freedom. Surely some had managed to escape to the far north, which would not have been very profitable as a colony for the economically minded imperialists, and where the Siberian witch tribes jealously guarded their territory.

Kaura hoped that some of the Inmarsund magicians had actually managed to get to safety. Without ever having met a witch or wizard, she found it strange that people were hunted down just because they were different. But the Spanish-Ottoman inquisitors were even said to have devices that could track down people with the "unnatural" talent by alchemical or even auroric means.

Emitting a loud hiss and with steam billowing out on all sides, the steam cab came to a stop in front of the entrance. With an elegant leap, a wiry, blond man in an expensive-looking fur coat alighted onto the cobblestones and bid the cabbie farewell with a few friendly words.

Kaura smiled. She might have guessed that Joe was not one of those who, fearing their speed and strangeness, shunned these new vehicles like demons avoided the prayer drums that could be found at almost every street corner in the town.

Surely, he had already charmingly coaxed all the secrets of how to operate this machine from the owner while they were traveling, and would probably soon tell her that he'd ordered one in Beijing.

He had the means to do it. John Horatio Nelson was the scion of one of London's richest merchant families. The Nelsons owed their fortune to exclusive contracts with the Atlantis-based steel-silk mills and, as co-founders of the East India Company, had only recently expanded their activities to include the trade of spices and tea from Asia.

Steel silk was a highly sought after commodity in all of the emerging industrial realms, as the fabrics spun from it were virtually indestructible and helped greatly to prolong the life of ships' sails.

It was also used to make high-quality clothing and other items for officers and the nobility.

Since no one but the mysterious Atlanteans had yet been able to produce this fabric, its prices were exorbitant.

Moreover, large quantities of the substance were currently being purchased by the Mongolian alchemist schools. They were probably working on another of the great discoveries for which the "nation of inventors" was known.

Joe often visited Inmarsund to maintain contact with the Mongolian Trans-Siberian caravans. Kaura had met him two years ago during a voyage to Copenhagen, where she was hoping to find clues to her origins. The thirty-one-year-old Scotsman had been very understanding, and even volunteered to make some inquiries with the Scottish Crown in London but had been unable to find out anything more.

The brief encounter had developed into a deep mutual sympathy that had even occasionally resulted in nights spent together. Which, of course, Kaura had never told her curious friend Imar.

Now, as Joe stepped through the thick wooden door into the room warmed by several fireplaces, she raised her arm and waved.

Her friend surveyed the entire hall in a few seconds with the alert eyes of a born fighter. The blond Scot smiled when he recognized her and was with her in a few measured steps.

"Good to see you, my dear," he commented as he slipped out of his heavy fur coat.

Kaura rose and hugged him, giving him a quick kiss on the lips. Immediately, however, she became serious again.

"I was glad to hear that you got through well. They say the shipping routes between Britain and the North are not as safe as they used to be."

Joe nodded and plopped down on a velvet chair next to Kaura's sitting area. Obviously, he didn't want to sit on the floor today.

"Yes, the Spanish-Ottoman Empire is still expanding and has stationed large naval units in the North Sea, which must be causing the Vikings some headaches as well. The Queen in Edinburgh has so far managed to stay out of it all. So, I would say our ships are still the safest from any incursions."

He sighed while Kaura pulled up a chair for herself and cleared the space on the tatami mats. "Of course, we still take precautions. For the past two months, we've only used armed ships on this route. What worries me more is that the Atlanteans have closed all their ports and won't let anyone in. The supply chain for steel silk has dried up. The prices offered for our remaining stock are rising astronomically. But we can no longer meet our obligations. The customers are displeased. I'm not looking forward to explaining the situation to the Mongolian representatives tomorrow.

Kaura frowned.

"Well, the Atlanteans have always been a mystery. Except for the few open ports and the Eire peninsula, which they practically left to themselves, they never allowed outsiders to enter their realm. And now you say they won't let anyone land at all?"

"Exactly. And no one knows why. Our ships were just intercepted about 20 nautical miles off the coast by Atlantean Coast Guard sloops and sent back. No reason given. Maybe they're having trouble with the Spanish. My grandfather sent an emissary to the Atlantean embassy in the imperial capital of Granada. Scotland, after all, they still don't think is important enough to maintain a representation with us. Granada, Beijing, Tenochtitlán. If you want something from them, you have to go there, even if it is just to obtain a permit to enter one of the open ports. We had not received a reply yet when I left London."

Joe sat up a little straighter and waved one of the bartenders over. "Coffee, please."

The bald man in his spotless white apron nodded and dis-appeared.

"But, enough of my troubles. How are you?"

Kaura fixed him with her clear green eyes.

"Resa is missing."

Joe sucked in a breath.

"I'm sorry to hear that. What happened?"

"Maybe it's just a minor delay. But the *Stralsund* was due to return a month ago. Resa should at least have been able to send a message to the Kontor through one of our branches. From what you just told me, she might have gotten stuck in Morániu, her final destination in West Atlantis. Maybe the Atlanteans won't allow anyone to leave either."

Kaura's Scottish friend breathed a sigh of relief.

"Yes, that is possible. At least then she would still be alive. I know how fond you are of her."

"If I could take over the command of a galleon already today, then I have only my aunt to thank for it. Not to mention the fact that she is also my best friend," Kaura replied.

Joe leaned back, turned a little, and dangled one leg over the armrest of his upholstered chair.

"Certainly not the best time to take up seafaring. Too much uncertainty."

With relish, he moved the cup of sweet, thick coffee under his nose and sniffed. The tart, mellow scent of the brew was clearly perceptible to Kaura as well.

"It never ceases to amaze me that you can get better coffee in this provincial town than even in London. This is as good as Constantinople or Granada."

Kaura laughed, a small flash of joy flickering across her striking, deeply tanned face.

"Yes, in Inmarsund we have a way of life. Perhaps you should settle down here..."

Her friend smiled back.

"The coffee is good, but the climate is even worse than in London. Much too cold. I was thinking more of an outpost in the Canary Islands, or maybe even the New World. The Spanish-Ottoman Sultanate still regards the Caribbean as a kind of private property to be exploited at will. I, on the other hand, believe there's still plenty of space there."

Kaura became angry.

"So you want to go over there and get rich, too? What the Spaniards and their Ottoman cronies have done there in the last hundred years or so is unbelievable. If the Aztecs hadn't been backed by the Atlanteans, probably all the inhabitants of the Colombian continent would be doing slave labor in some gold and silver mines today. As it is now, this is still what's happening to far too many of them."

Her eyes sparkled with indignation, and Joe leaned back a little. With a soothing wave of his hand, he signalled his agreement.

"You should know that's not what I meant, Kaura. There are ways to get along with the local civilizations. I firmly believe that we are all equally valuable as human beings. But I am aware that my countrymen are also making money from the slave trade. This is not just a Spanish problem, even though in Britain most people at least pretend to be good Buddhists and live non-violently.

Lost in thought, he peered out through the round, lead-framed glass. The sky had turned gray. An incipient snowfall drove white streaks across the rough cobblestones.

Then the conversation turned to more innocuous topics. Joe talked about his travels and shared the latest gossip from his city, and Kaura filled her friend in on what had happened in the time that had passed since his last visit to Inmarsund a few months ago.

It was not much. One of the things that made Inmarsund such a successful trade center was that it managed to keep out of most of the political turmoil that gripped the world in this late nineteenth century after the historical Buddha's enlightenment. The Spanish knew this, and for this reason they granted the town a relatively high degree of independence and self-determination, even after its occupation.

After a while, the Scot waved to the innkeeper to ask for the bill.

"I'm afraid I don't have much time. I have a business meeting with Orne in an hour. You remember Orne?"

Kaura thought for a moment.

"Wasn't she the merchant from St. Petersburg? The one you got the auroric floating crystals from? I thought you had never met her again."

"Yes, that's the one. When we moored at my family's dock last night, she had a message delivered to me. It seems she has something to tell me. Maybe it's about some new exotic trade item."

Kaura nodded and placed her hand confidentially on his thigh.

"Well, enjoy your date. I seem to remember she was quite attractive."

Joe grinned boyishly.

"I never mix business with pleasure. But you never know. Will you join me for dinner tonight? I'll be staying at our local *kontor* on Putgarden Street, as usual. Six o'clock?"

"Agreed."

They said goodbye and Joe left the room with an energetic stride.

Kaura, meanwhile, relaxed comfortably into the soft velvet cushions of her chair, letting the sounds of clinking china and chattering conversation wash over her, enjoying the inner silence that spread through her after having met her friend.

* * *

In the afternoon, Kaura worked at her adoptive family's counting house. She enjoyed the repetitive, simple actions of checking inventory and inbound and outbound deliveries. It gave her a chance to put her thoughts in order.

Should she suggest to Joe that they try a slightly closer kind of relationship?

She couldn't quite put her finger on why she was so reluctant to make a more committed connection with a man. But somehow, she felt that she could not settle down, not really. There was something that she had to do, a task that might mean that she would be away from Inmarsund and any potential lovers for a long time.

But what could that be? Was this premonition something that came from her past? Or was it just an expression of the fact that she still didn't feel like she fully belonged? She did not know.

It was still snowing when Kaura trudged up the gently sloping Putgarden Street toward the Nelson townhouse, slowly making her way through the gathering darkness.

By now the white splendor lay several inches deep, and the air had lost some of the piercing chill it had held earlier that morning.

Gentle snowflakes brushed against the nose and lips of the woman wrapped in her cape, melting instantly with the warmth of her body as she climbed toward the luxurious mansions of the foreign merchant clans.

When the weather was good, the city's noblest residences, which crowned Putgarden Hill, afforded their residents an unobstructed view of the city's sea of brick-red houses, which the region's former Asian rulers had christened the Pearl of the Baltic. Behind them stretched the seemingly endless expanse of the sea. Now, however, visibility was getting worse. Fog and driving snow obscured even the houses on either side of the steeply rising street.

When she reached Amber Square, Kaura immediately turned left. As she walked by, she gently caressed the outer skin of the large, leafless oak tree that grew in between the cobblestones at the edge of the square. Its branches stretched far up into the white mist.

She paused at the wall with the number six on it, and the words *Nelson Trading Co.* written in gilded letters. Mechanically, she reached for the big metal knocker when she noticed that the pedestrian gate was slightly ajar. Strange.

Quietly, she pushed the door open and carefully closed it behind her. It must have been an oversight. Inmarsund was a very quiet and safe town, but most residents still locked their doors out of habit, even when they were at home.

The driveway to the large private garden that belonged to the Nelson's local trading estate was already snow-covered. It looked like one of those winter stories her few friends who already had families told their children before they went to sleep.

In the evening there were not many people in the office. Only Mikhail Serunov, the Nelson clan's local representative in Inmarsund, had his private rooms in the mansion, as did his servant George and the cook, Mila. So, Kaura was not surprised to see light in only two windows. They were probably all waiting for her in the dining hall.

With an unpleasant shudder, she realized that the front door of the house itself stood half open as well. Something was wrong here. The fact that the front door was ajar could still have been a coincidence, but no one would leave the entrance to a heated room open in the middle of the winter without someone being nearby.

She suppressed the impulse to call out to Joe or George. First, she had to figure out what was going on. Maybe there were burglars in the house. Cold shivers ran up and down her spine as she imagined what could have happened here.

As a member of a family of traders, she was familiar with the customs of pirates and cutthroats through stories. In the city, however, one was usually safe from such attacks.

She gathered up her heavy skirts as she made her way as quietly as possible up the slippery stairs to the front door and tried to push the door open a little further with her elbow. When she did so, however, she was immediately met with gentle resistance.

Silently, she squeezed through the narrow opening and couldn't quite suppress a startled gasp when she spotted the lifeless body lying behind the door.

Bending down, Kaura flinched again. She recognized George's eyes, wide open in the dim light. Was the servant dead? Panicked, she searched for the pulse on his neck and breathed a sigh of relief when she felt it. The stocky, gray-haired man was only unconscious.

Since she had never seen an unconscious person before, she didn't know if open eyes were normal for someone who had been knocked out. Something seemed strange to her, however, because the body was completely rigid. It seemed that the man was aware of her but could not move a muscle to communicate in any way. She could not see any external injuries. He must have been put into this state as soon as he had opened the door.

"I will bring help," she whispered, hoping that George could hear her.

She knew that the only sensible thing to do right now would be to run down to the center of town as fast as she could and notify the City Guard.

But it would be at least half an hour before she could be back with the guards. Did she have that much time? Did Joe have that much time? As an important member of a wealthy family, he would certainly have been a suitable victim for an abduction. Maybe the criminals were still in the house, and she could do something to free him. Or had they simply killed him? That was another possibility, but not one she could bear to think about right now. Her thoughts raced and intermingled. Adrenaline coursed through her veins.

She shook herself. She wouldn't leave here until she knew what was going on and if there was anything she could do to help.

To the right of the large fireplace at the far wall of the entrance hall, where a fire was still flickering, she found a poker. She pulled it out of its holder with a low scraping sound and made her way up the wide, elegantly curved marble staircase to the living quarters.

Kaura had received combat training with all kinds of weapons as part of her training as a ship's commander in the Merchant Fleet. Aunt Resa had taught her herself.

The poker was not exactly a sword or a flintlock pistol. Still, she wouldn't be completely defenseless with it. Silently, she cursed herself for not bringing her rapier.

Foreign sailors sometimes did, and it was not forbidden, but the locals usually saw little reason to walk the streets carrying weapons.

Then she heard the voices. Men's voices, loud and threatening. One of them seemed to be Joe's. Unfortunately, she couldn't make out what was being said. The sounds seemed to be coming from the house library. She remembered the room well. Libraries had always been among her favorite places.

Quietly, she crept up the polished marble steps, staying close to the wall. She hoped they hadn't put guards elsewhere in the house. But she saw no one. Up in the great hall, the carpet, nearly an inch thick, swallowed the sound of her footsteps.

It was not until she had reached about the middle of the long hallway that she became fully aware of the risk she was about to take. Now she felt a little bit scared, and it became hard for her to breathe. But she would not leave her friend alone in this situation. The unconscious servant alone was proof enough that the inhabitants of the house were in danger.

Quietly, she slipped into the room next to the library and closed the door quietly behind her.

The hinges were well-oiled. Silently, she thanked all the

Bodhisattvas that Mikhail and George were keeping the house in such impeccable condition. Through the connecting door from the guest room to the library, she would be able to hear what was being said quite safely.

"...couldn't tell you more even if I wanted to," Joe's voice boomed.

The Scotsman was furious. "We've had no contact with our liaison in Atlantia for three months."

"I don't believe you, Nelson," a softer voice with a strong Spanish accent replied. "Don't think that I don't have other means at my disposal to get you and your friend to talk. We know you have been to Atlantis. That alone would be enough to have you brought before a court of the Inquisition of the Holy Church in Granada. You can imagine for yourself what would happen to you if that happened."

Joe seemed to have calmed down a bit, because his answer came in a softer voice, with a dangerous undertone.

"Don't think you can just carry off someone knighted by the Queen of the Scottish Realm. I have influential friends. The court would intervene."

The stranger sighed theatrically. "To do that, they would first have to know where you went, Nelson. You are in our territory. But very unfortunately, we do not have time to bring you to your just punishment as a heretic. So, we are going to make this short. My companion here will begin with your friend. He will tell us everything he knows. Unfortunately, he will not survive the procedure. Perhaps, after witnessing, you will reconsider speaking voluntarily."

There was a pause. Then a woman's whisper. Kaura could not make out what she was saying.

Then the stranger spoke again, in the same calm tone he had used to announce Mikhail's death.

"Ah, it looks like we have something else to attend to first. Sheka, bring in our guest."

At the same moment Kaura realized she was exposed, the

connecting door to the library exploded inward, as if hit by a hammer of air. Wood splinters flew in all directions, and Kaura was nearly deafened by the bursting noise that followed. Luckily, she had been standing a short distance away from the door to listen, or she would have been hurled across the room.

This was witchcraft, she thought numbly. But the man seemed to be a Southerner, a member of the Spanish-Ottoman Empire, where that word could not even be uttered without the risk of being brought before the Inquisition for torture. How did this fit together?

She had no time to think about it. The air around her body seemed to condense and she could no longer move. Still dazed from the shock of the explosion, she half unconsciously felt her feet lift off the ground.

Helpless, she floated through the doorway into the next room, where four pairs of eyes watched her expectantly.

Joe and Mikhail were tied with crude ropes to two of the library's cushioned reading chairs. Behind them, with his hands propped on the desk, a lean, goat-bearded man in a heavy black velvet coat watched her with intelligent eyes. It was obviously him who had spoken earlier. Kaura had never noticed this man before among the occupants of Inmarsund. He was probably from out of town.

Next to him, a tall, light-blonde woman of about forty leaned against a bookcase. She had a serene, almost friendly expression on her face, which now seemed extremely concentrated.

She was wrapped in a soft cloak of white silk and wore three belts with various small pockets and pendants. Undoubtedly, this was the woman who was holding Kaura in the air by some mysterious powers.

Around her neck, Kaura could make out the silver glint of a wide necklace or choker, connected to the goateed man's hand by a thin metal chain. What was the meaning of this? Did the Ottomans keep witches like pets?

Joe gave her a troubled look. "I was hoping you'd be a little later. We're having some minor complications here."

Kaura paid no attention to him. She couldn't take her eyes off the ice-blue ones of the mage—because that was what she was, she had to be. There was something there. Something she could almost sense. She felt it more than she saw it. She felt a kind of glowing thread that connected her to the other woman.

From the woman's forehead, another ribbon moved toward her, darker, winding like a snake, and somehow dangerous. Somehow, she knew that once this connection was in place, she would have no will of her own and would be completely defenseless.

More instinctively than consciously, Kaura flicked the glowing thread aside, but nothing happened, and she felt the glowing snake's probing head coming closer.

But her opponent's eyes widened slightly and she paled. "She's a Gifted one, Señor!" she murmured, "I can take her, I think."

The Ottoman drew in a deep breath of surprise.

"We have enough slaves, Sheka. But she could be dangerous. Kill her."

Kaura's insides turned to ice.

The glowing thread began to descend, now approaching her chest instead of her forehead.

Meanwhile, Joe tore at his bonds with almost superhuman strength. In the process, he fell to the floor along with the chair, but proved unable to loosen his restraints in the slightest.

"Don't touch her, you perverted fanatics!" he roared in a high-pitched voice.

Spellbound, Kaura watched the deadly energy tube approach. Now she could see it clearly, swirling and spinning, filled with semi-transparent, smoke-like feelers.

She knew she couldn't let that thing touch her, or she was doomed. Desperately she tried to move. But the air around her still held her in complete immobility.

Thoughts raced behind her forehead, memories she couldn't quite interpret. Images of an eerily beautiful, black-haired woman in a semi-transparent robe and wearing some kind of crown flashed through her mind.

She had to concentrate. There was something she could do, she knew, but she had no idea what. A single tear trickled from her left eye as the dark tube came closer and closer to the point between her breasts.

She tried to relax. If she was going to die, at least with the right mantra in her head. She had always enjoyed studying the Buddhist scriptures of the ancients, which were available in the central temple for those who were skilled in the art of reading and writing.

The thought of the temple and the ever friendly nuns in orange robes who lived there reassured her. Still, she struggled and screamed as the tube touched her skin with a sharp pain and she felt her life force begin to drain away.

In all this inner turmoil, there was suddenly an area just below her heart space that she had not noticed before. It seemed solid, inaccessible, and very stable. Like a drowning woman, she clung to this perception and prayed, "Great Mother, help me. I don't want to go like this.

With all her mental power, she pounded on the locked energy cluster in her solar plexus, gasping and groaning as she watched her golden glowing life force flow to the blonde woman whose still serenely smiling face now seemed like a mockery to her.

Suddenly, the space beneath Kaura's sternum opened. A glistening, bright, white beam of energy poured from it down into her belly and then on to the area between her legs.

There it felt as if a dam had burst and an immense jet of

something flowed up through her. The air around her liquefied, literally blasted away as if by a charge of black powder.

The serenity on the other woman's face had given way to immeasurable terror. The thread of energy between her and Kaura's chest swelled from one moment to the next as thick as her arm and glowed bright white.

Almost impassively, as if in slow motion, Kaura saw the Sultan's emissary let go of the leash, draw a curved blade, and charge toward her. Then there was only light.

* * *

When Kaura opened her eyes again, she smelled burnt flesh. She was down on the floor. Groaning, she rolled onto her side and tried to wipe the blood from her eyes. She had probably suffered a gash when she fell from her elevated position.

The realization that her enemies might still be there hit her like a cold chill.

With the greatest effort of will, she straightened up and fumbled for a weapon. But no, if the witch was still here, she probably wouldn't be alive now. The *other* witch. Kaura was trembling. She had to find out what had happened to the others.

As she sat up on her knees, she fought the rising nausea.

Then she saw Joe. He was still tied to the chair, half lying on his side under the desk.

Her friend smiled weakly at her.

"Thank you. That little issue is out of the way. Of course, we have a few bigger ones now. I didn't know you were one like those." He gestured to a large pile of charred ashes in which a few belt buckles and charred pieces of white silk could be seen.

Now Kaura could not hold back her rising nausea. When she was done, Joe cleared his throat.

"Could you please untie me when you're ready? Mikhail seems unconscious, I hope he's not badly hurt. And we have to look for George. I don't know what they've done to him. We all thought it was you when there was someone at the door."

"George is down at the entrance. He's alive, but in a strange state. He can't move," Kaura replied as she bent down to him and began to undo his restraints. "Did you see what happened to the Spaniard? Is he also...?

Joe made a face.

"When you suddenly started throwing flashes around, he was thrown all over the room. He was lying back there by the front door, I couldn't see him very well from where I was. Apparently he regained consciousness before you did and chose to disappear. I guess he doesn't feel so strong without his witch. We must expect him to return with reinforcements. At least he doesn't know who you are. That will buy us some time."

He rubbed his wrists while Kaura was already kneeling next to Mikhail, fumbling with his bonds. She breathed a sigh of relief when he started to move on his own.

"Mikhail! Mikhail!" she shook him by the shoulder, but let go immediately when she realized that the older man might have suffered some internal injuries. The trader looked at her for a moment, uncomprehending, before clarity returned to his eyes.

"That was close. You probably saved my life," he whispered, his voice shaking. "Still, I can't even imagine what I could have possibly told those two."

He moved his limbs carefully. "I think I'm okay. I hit my head when the chair flipped over."

Joe, meanwhile, rummaged through a hidden section of the library bookshelves, made of heavy, dark oak, and pulled out two books. Without comment, he slipped them into the deep pockets of the cloak he had pulled from a coat rack in the corner.

"There's an armory next to the master's living room," he commented. "We have no time to lose. And we shouldn't go out there unarmed. Once we're safe, we can figure out our next steps."

Kaura grabbed his arm as he tried to rush past her.

"Do you realize you're aiding a mage? Even without everything that happened here, that would be enough to put you on trial immediately - even here in Inmarsund, where the Iberians don't have such a firm foothold yet. Rumor has it that they have alchemical devices that immediately report the use of magic in the city to the magistrate."

Seriously, the Scot looked at her with his blue-gray eyes.

"That man was a direct emissary of the Sultanate in Granada. The very fact that he had the witch with him, working openly, shows me that he would not have let me live. Besides, we are friends, Kaura, and you got into this whole thing because you wanted to help me. Maybe it's more dangerous for you to be seen with me than it is for me to get involved with a mage."

"I'm not a real mage," she called after him, almost desperately. "At least then I'd know what I was doing and could help us somehow!"

Minutes later, Joe was back with three rapiers and a set of wheel-lock revolvers that looked brand-new. Unlike the flintlock pistols still used exclusively in most countries, these could fire multiple bullets without the need for laborious reloading. Only the rich and noble had such high-quality weapons.

Kaura hadn't even known that Joe could handle those things. Quickly, she strapped the rapier around her waist, checked the swivel of the pistol, and slid it into her belt on the other side of the sword.

Then she pulled her wide winter cloak over it, hiding the weapons at first glance.

"I never thought I would need these things here in the middle of the city. It is one thing to fight pirates at sea. But this..." she twisted her lips into a reluctant grimace.

Together they went downstairs, where Mikhail was already tending to George.

The grey-haired man, bent over his servant, looked up. He seemed relieved. "He's alive, but I don't know how to wake him.

Mikhail had already closed and locked the door and placed the unconscious man on his side. On the rough stone floor behind the entrance, the last snowflakes that had fallen were slowly evaporating.

Kaura breathed a sigh of relief. She had always liked the gangly, perpetually friendly servant.

"What do we do now?" she asked tonelessly, not addressing anyone in particular. "We should alert the city guard. But can we do that now?" -

Joe replied in the negative.

"Until we know what is really going on here and what these people want from us, we have to be careful. Don Alonso can probably put the Iberian soldiers on our trail–assuming his papers were real. Besides, the city guard is also under Spanish command, even though it is made up of locals."

Perplexed, he shook his head. "If it were just me, I might even be willing to confide in the authorities and pull some strings. I know some influential people in the city council. But we can't risk them investigating you. Once they know you're Gifted, no one will be able to save you."

He turned to Mikhail.

"We have to leave George here. I have heard of this condition. Some people who opposed the Inquisition or criticized the Spanish Sultan were found like this. But so far I suspected poison, not witchcraft. Anyway, he will wake up on his own in a while. So no one should be able to blame him, I suppose. Unlike us."

Mikhail's face turned into a grimace.

"I don't like leaving him here, even if we can send help later. Let me try with some snow."

Meanwhile, Kaura had climbed a few steps to the large stairwell window and peered out.

"Too late," she called. "There's a whole group of people approaching out there. I can barely make them out through the blowing snow. But two of them seem to be wearing red cloaks."

An icy chill ran through her as she realized what that meant. Her knees threatened to buckle. Red cloaks. They must be High Inquisitors, the dreaded emissaries from the headquarters of the Holy Inquisition in Granada itself. And there were even two of them! They had never appeared in Inmarsund before. But she had once seen their local representative, Don Marquez de Melilla y Aragon, the administrative chief inquisitor of the Spanish Baltic provinces. He had attended an execution in the viewing gallery beside the governor. The man had worn an aura of absolute implacability and toughness around himself like a cloak.

It was only when the condemned woman had fallen through the trapdoor to her death that an almost cheerful smile had appeared on the face of the churchman, who was supposedly personally appointed by the Sultan of the Empire. She had hoped never to see this man again. Not to mention his employers from faraway Iberia.

Joe grabbed her hand and pulled her away from the window.

"We can't risk a conflict here. Let's make for the back exit! Follow me! And be quiet!"

Gathering their coats, the two men and Kaura ran to the back, leaving George. The fire in the kitchen now consisted only of smoldering orange coals, occasionally flickering with a tail of flame.

With a pang of nostalgia, Kaura thought that on a normal evening, George would probably be standing here right now, preparing their meal. Mila, the main cook, was obviously not in tonight. She was probably staying with her old mother in Ustka, a fishing village outside the city near the Mongolian border. She was glad that the woman had not had to witness the events of this unfortunate evening.

As quietly as he could, Mikhail unlocked the door to the backyard. There was a small gate in the wall opening onto the alley that led from the back of the estate down to the city center and the port. Urgently, he waved the two companions through before carefully closing the door behind him.

"That probably won't hold them off for long," he whispered. "And our tracks are easy to see in the fresh snow. Hopefully there'll be some traffic in the alley. Then we won't be so easy to follow."

Joe nodded. His face was barely visible in the dark. But the rawness in his voice betrayed his determination.

"We'll make straight for the harbor. The *Pride of Edinburgh*, the ship that brought me here, is still moored there. She wasn't supposed to take on her cargo until tomorrow. I'll have her cast off immediately, before a warrant can be issued for our arrest. The captain will not be happy to leave Inmarsund without his trade goods destined for Scotland. But he will, of course, do as I tell him."

The Scotsman began to trudge down the alley at a brisk pace, with the other two following behind him.

The wind whipped large snowflakes into his face. With his left hand, he pulled the hood of his cloak forward a bit, while with his right, he gripped the handle of the pistol under his cloak.

In the glow of the sparse lighting of the alley, the far-flung torches flickering in covered iron baskets, his face looked as expressionless as a mask.

A few quick steps brought Kaura to his side. She was pale but calm, although she knew now that it was only by chance that she had not been discovered and taken away by the Sultan's henchmen long ago, with all the years she had spent in Inmarsund.

"If they didn't recognize me, maybe we could stay with my family," she considered before contradicting herself right away. "No, it's common knowledge that we're close. We probably wouldn't be safe there for long. Still, I can't just disappear. I have to at least send a message to Aalyjah.

Joe nodded seriously as he glanced back behind them.

"Now we're already in Algiers Alley. The snow here is full of boot and hoof prints. They will not know for sure which way we turned. But I am afraid they will figure out very quickly that we are attempting to take refuge aboard the Pride. So we have no time to lose."

Kaura's face, hidden under the heavy hood of the woollen cloak, took on a look of determination.

"The Leivenstein's kontor is just around the corner. From there it is only a couple of minutes to the port. You two go ahead. It will take some time to get the ship ready for casting off anyway. Have you considered the possibility that the crew might be on shore leave?"

Mikhail, panting a little behind Joe as he tried to keep up with the two younger people, interjected, "Sir Elias was worried because he had heard rumors of tension between some foreign crews and the local population. Anyway, when I was on the ship this morning with the cargo lists, he wanted to keep most of the crew on board to be prepared for anything."

Kaura smiled grimly.

"Then it should be okay. I'll see you on the ship in half an hour. Tell the guards I'm coming, so we don't cause a stir by calling out."

She disappeared into a side alley and was instantly consumed by snow and darkness, even before Joe could offer her one more admonition to be careful.

3

Escape

Panting with exertion, Kaura hurried through the dark, making her way through the drifting snows of the night. Two more alleys, one more... she turned left between the familiar facades of the large commercial offices lining Shanghai Street. The dark, rectangular buildings were decorated with stone ornaments, and, in the case of the houses of the wealthier merchants, also with Greek columns and scantily clad statues that seemed to leer mockingly at the passing woman out of the frosty twilight.

A home for five years, a family that had welcomed her, a complete stranger, with a warmth that perhaps not even biological children would have experienced in other places.

Involuntarily, the thought crossed her mind that she might never see this place again.

A single tear trickled from the corner of her left eye. As a Gifted person, she would be a hunted creature in much of the known world. At least, her talent didn't seem to be all too obvious.

Otherwise, the Inquisition would certainly have found her out and put her on trial long ago .

In the five years she had been here, she had never tried to gather information about magic. She had seen no reason to do so. In the Spanish-Ottoman Empire, sorcery was not a subject to be discussed lightly. Magic was against the will of the Highest. Period. And against human law as well. The Ottomans, unlike the Scots, Hellenes, and Atlanteans, were closely tied to the Sacred Congregation that had formed after the Peace of Lepanto, unifying the great patriarchal religions of the Arabs, Romans, and Armenians, while the people of the traditionally Buddhist northlands were much more tolerant in their thinking, accepting views that differed from their own with relative ease.

Routinely, Kaura wiped the snow from the doorstep of the kontor's side entrance, which led to the kitchen and the family's private living quarters.

When she opened the heavy wooden door, a warm rush of air hit her, a heady mixture of smells. Fried fish, spices from the nearby storerooms, and incense that told of the evening meditation that had probably just ended.

Reile, the cook, looked up from her stove as Kaura hurried past.

"Back already? I thought you were off for dinner?"

"I won't be staying long. Where is Aalyjah?"

She hurried past without waiting for an answer. Arriving in the main hallway, she slowed her pace. She didn't want to worry her adoptive mother by rushing in like a madwoman.

The matriarch looked up and smiled as Kaura entered the sitting room with its blazing fireplace.

"Hello my dear, back already? I thought you were having dinner at the Nelson Mansion?"

She frowned.

"What's the matter with you? You've been running. Sit down and have a bowl of tea. It will calm you down."

Aalyjah took a second bowl from the small, perfectly aligned stack on the table, placed it on the wooden tea tray, and poured.

The contrast between the events of the last hour and this carpeted room with its red wallpaper, warmed by the fireplace, where this serene woman, unshakeably, was devoting all her attention to pouring a cup of tea, was so great that Kaura began to cry, despite her determination. But she quickly pulled herself together. Now was not the time for a breakdown.

She sat down and accepted the cup. The steam rising from it condensed on her still cold face and mixed with the moisture of the tears on her cheeks.

Aaliyah handed her a small linen cloth and watched her attentively. She waited until the younger woman had dried her cheeks and was ready to speak.

Kaura took a sip of tea and cleared her throat.

"I don't have much time. I want to tell you what happened. I just hope I'm not putting you in danger by being here."

She recounted in short words what had transpired in the house on Putgarden Hill.

Aalyjah listened in silence. When Kaura finished, there was a long pause.

Then the gray-haired matriarch, mistress of nearly seventy ocean-going ships and offices around the world, leaned forward and patted her adopted daughter's hand.

"So, you're a witch. I almost thought so when you arrived here, the unlikely sole survivor of a shipwreck in the dead of winter. Yet you've never shown any signs of being supernaturally gifted."

She smiled reassuringly as Kaura's face contorted almost painfully at her words. "Don't worry, I have no prejudice against the use of magic. It's a normal characteristic of us humans, if you ask me. Some can learn it, some can't. Then, it's all about if you use it responsibly, as with any other talent. However, our friends from the south are known to be less than enthusiastic about it, and that means your life is in grave danger here."

She thought. "I am particularly surprised that the Spaniard himself had a magician with him. A Russian energy witch, if I'm not mistaken. From the dark side, probably, or she wouldn't have treated you like that. I met one of her lighter counterparts once, years ago, before the occupiers either took them all away or drove them far out into the Northlands. Joe is right. You must leave Inmarsund, and fast. I can't help you if you stay here."

Then she sighed and shook her head.

"Too bad. I had hoped to see you commanding one of our ships soon. You have talent. Well, what isn't now yet can be. And I have a feeling that these events will bring you closer to your origins. If you survive. Which is what I wish for you with all my heart."

Her eyebrows knitted together in concentration.

"I have something for you."

The older woman rose, went to one of the large wall shelves and rummaged through it.

"It is said that all magically gifted people must be initiated by a witch or wizard as soon as the ability shows itself, usually sometime between the ages of thirteen and sixteen," she said as she pulled various books and boxes from the shelf and put them back after a quick glance. "Otherwise, the Gift will destroy them within a short time, burn them out. The poor people just go mad. Well, since you're obviously not crazy, I'll assume you're an initiated magician."

Kaura shook her head.

"But shouldn't I still feel something from it? I don't even know what I did back there at Joe's house!"

Aalyjah had now found what she had been looking for. She took a flat wooden box disguised as a book from the shelf, placed it carefully on the small table in front of the fireplace, and opened it. Inside was a pendant. She took it out.

Hanging from two artfully knotted lengths of bi-colored string was what looked at first glance like a simple fisherman's hook. The hook was made from a piece of white bone and covered with carved spiral symbols that seemed both strange and almost painfully familiar to Kaura.

"Do you know what this is?" the older woman asked.

There was a slight disappointment in the matriarch's features when Kaura answered in the negative.

But she quickly collected herself and explained.

"I don't know what it's called either. It belonged to my great-grandmother. She was a witch. In her youth, she traveled to the land of the Ottomans, quite far southeast of the Mediterranean. She stayed there for many years. No one knows exactly what she did there, although she returned with many stories about the magic of the Orient and the Djinns, which my grandmother would tell me from time to time. What exactly happened to her there, though, she never told anyone, as far as I know.

"Nevertheless, when she returned, her energy field was so intense that all the local magicians spoke of her only with great reverence. Unfortunately, none of her descendants had the gift. But what she did bring back were trade contracts with many trading houses in North Africa and among the Hellenes. It is on this foundation that our family's fortune has been built."

She sighed. "I talk too much, and we have no time. This belonged to her. It was passed down to my grandmother, to my mother, and finally to me, with the instruction to give it to whoever in our family would show magical abilities again. You are one of us now, so I want you to have it. Maybe it will help you find out where you came from."

Almost reverently, she placed the pendant around Kaura's neck.

"Thank you, Mother." Kaura was still confused. For a moment, she felt completely disoriented.

Aalyjah gave her adoptive daughter a firm hug and looked her sternly in the eyes.

"Go now, my dear. Pack only what you need and hurry. I can send the rest of your things to London. The Nelsons will take you in, and I'm sure Joe can arrange for a secret courier to get them past the controls of the Spanish Protectorate. Let me hear from you!"

The matriarch pushed the younger woman vigorously toward the door.

Outside, she almost tripped over Atam, who was lying in front of the door. The dog immediately jumped up and barked happily.

"You'll probably want to take him with you," Aalyjah called after her. "We'll miss him here."

Breathless, and followed by her four-legged companion, Kaura arrived at her rooms. Without thinking, she threw her seafaring clothes into a bag, followed by a more socially appropriate dress and a pair of spare boots. Looking around her bedroom, she was at a complete loss. What else should she take? She couldn't really imagine that she might never return to this house that had been her home for the past few years. Everything was happening too fast!

The young woman shrugged. She would manage somehow, even without her other belongings. Five years ago, she had arrived here with nothing.

Without looking back, she left the room and stormed down the stairs to the first floor.

Downstairs, she met Imar, who was just putting on his cloak.

"The mistress told me you were in trouble," the red-bearded man growled. "I'm to escort you to the harbor."

Kaura frowned.

"Did she also tell you that it might be dangerous? Maybe the city guard is already looking for me."

He laughed grimly. "The city guard—or someone else, that's what she said! Let's go. At worst, maybe I can distract them from you."

Like two shadows, they slipped out the side door into the driving snow of the Nordic night.

At first, everything seemed to go well. The streets were not particularly busy, but they were not deserted either. All the passersby wore heavy winter clothing and hoods that made them completely unrecognizable in the flickering light of the streetlamps. Kaura and Imar did not stand out.

Once they saw a City Guard patrol checking people in one of the boulevards. They immediately turned into a side alley without being seen.

As they approached the dock, Imar suddenly stopped dead. He grabbed Kaura's arm and pulled her into the shadow of a warehouse entrance.

"Look, there!" he pointed into the shadows at the edge of the open area of the quay, where goods were stacked and loaded during daytime. "See them?"

She narrowed her eyes.

"Yes. Three lone hooded figures. It appears as if they're trying hard not to be seen. So, it's not the City Guard. They'd be more conspicuous with their helmets and halberds."

Imar nodded.

"I think so, too. No guards. Maybe the Spaniards. All the more reason to be cautious."

Kaura pointed to the four larger ships moored at the foreign merchant's pier. There were two galleons of the type sailed by most of the northern European and Scottish merchants, an Algerian zebec, and a Dutch fluyt.

"Those ships have large crews. There must be sailors who return to their vessels from time to time. Perhaps we can use them as cover. The *Pride* is the third one from the left. If we go around that storage shed," she pointed to a large building at the edge of the dock, "we should be able to get very close to the ship without being seen."

She scowled, concentrating. "Imar, do you also see a bluish glow around these three figures?"

Imar shook his head.

"I don't see anything, just these dark, almost motionless outlines. Maybe you're just imagining it."

Kaura said nothing more, though she was certain of her observation.

At that moment, she heard loud shouting and singing in a melodic, unfamiliar language from a side alley.

"Dutchmen!" muttered Imar. "They must be on their way to the fluyt over there. That's your chance! When we get to that corner over there, you just walk over to the *Pride* like you're part of the crew. Hopefully, the drunkards will distract the watchers."

They ran to be behind the warehouse at the right time.

Around the corner, she hugged the secretary.

"See you soon, old friend. I'll be back. This matter must be cleared up somehow." She was anything but sure of that, but she had to believe it. Otherwise, it would have been too painful to say goodbye to her confidant.

The Dutch were now close by and moved out of the alley onto the pier. They were yelling, shouting crude jokes at each other, and generally made a lot of noise.

Determined, Kaura started to move as well. Atam stayed close on her heels like a big shadow. The dog seemed to sense that she did not want to attract attention now.

On the galleon she was heading for, light shone from some windows in the stern, drawing golden streaks in the fog like little lighthouses. A sentry stood at the gangway, apparently bored, looking out into the driving snow. The ship was at most a hundred yards away.

Kaura suppressed the urge to run. It wouldn't do if her pursuers knew she was on the ship. Nevertheless, she quickened her pace a bit.

The sentry had become aware of her by now and was looking over at her, but did not call out. Fifty more yards. Forty more...

Suddenly a shadow rose up in front of her, seemingly out of nowhere. Atam growled and moved up beside her. The hairs on his neck bristled under her fingers. She had not even seen the figure approach! Under the dark hood she could not make out a face. But now she was certain that the man's silhouette was surrounded by a bluish, fluorescent glow.

"This is an inspection by the Imperial Inquisition," the figure whispered in Spanish, which everyone in Inmarsund understood reasonably well by now. The Inquisitor had a high-pitched, almost childlike voice that sent a shiver of fear down Kaura's spine. "Where are you headed?"

Kaura pulled herself together and answered in as broad a Scottish accent as she could.

"I'm a deckhand on that ship over there," she pointed to the *Pride*.

"Name?"

Kaura's mind raced. Did they already know who they were looking for?

"Jane Smith. What do you want from me? I've never heard of harmless sailors being questioned here. Has something happened? And what is this anyway, the Imperial Inquisition?" Kaura tried to buy some time.

"I'll know in a moment if you're telling the truth," the eerie voice whispered. "Then you may proceed to your ship." The figure grabbed Kaura's wrist with an iron grip.

The growl in Atam's throat deepened, but he contained himself. The dog would not strike without Kaura's command, unless she was clearly under attack.

The blue aura surrounding the Inquisitor moved, forming a kind of protrusion that now approached Kaura's forehead.

She realized that she had to act now, otherwise she would surely be recognized. Either because she fought back with magic, or because this being was stronger than she was and learned what it wanted to know.

But it was already too late. With a smacking, sucking sensation, the strand connected to her forehead. But this time there was no energy flowing between her and the creature. She felt completely normal. Only the pendant between her breasts had suddenly become very warm.

The Inquisitor sighed.

"Well, it seems you speak the truth, girl. You seem quite stupid. Not very readable thought strands."

She tore herself away forcefully and raised her voice.

"I don't have to put up with this. We're all properly registered with the harbormaster and allowed to move about the city freely. Do you even have the authority to stop people here? I'm going to my ship now," she shouted angrily and ran off without looking back.

A second figure had appeared at the *Pride's* bulwark and was talking to the guard, who seemed to be explaining what had happened.

The group of drunken Dutchmen had also noticed and approached the figure behind her.

"Hey, buddy, you need some help? What does he want from you?" one of them shouted over to Kaura in heavily accented Scottish, his strong voice somewhat slowed by the alcohol.

By now, she had reached the gangway of the Pride, breathing heavily.

"He tried to stop me from getting back to my ship!" she yelled back over her shoulder. "Now they start harassing innocent sailors. Besides, he was trying to touch me because I'm a woman!"

The leader of the Dutch group grabbed the figure firmly by the shoulder.

"Is that right? Who are you, anyway? You don't look like a member of the City Guard!"

Meanwhile, the newly arrived man at the bulwark waved Kaura aboard. The dog bounded ahead, moving nimbly across the snow-covered plank.

"I am the captain, Elias McGregor. And you must be Kaura. We've been expecting you," he greeted them in a whisper.

The ship's master had a very strong country accent. He must be from somewhere in the far north of the island, Kaura thought.

He pointed to the scene in the harbor.

"Inconvenient. We must leave quickly before they try to search the ship by force. For the time being, go to the quarterdeck. Joe is in the officer's mess. I'll try to salvage what can be salvaged here.

Whispered orders rang out across the deck. The crew was obviously already preparing the galleon for casting off. Fortunately, the wind at least seemed to be favorable. White streaks of freshly fallen snow blew out to sea in the light of the stern lantern.

From outside the ship she heard a muffled scream. She stopped at the bulkhead leading into the stern and peered through the shrouds.

The burly Dutchman who had earlier grabbed the Inquisitor by the shoulder rubbed his right hand and had backed away a few paces. The cloaked figure, meanwhile, turned to the sailors and whispered something Kaura could not understand. Then it raised its gloved hands to its hood and slowly lowered it.

In the half-light of the harbor, Kaura could see almost nothing. Only the blue aura of the figure—could she really be the only one to see that glow?—seemed to intensify a bit. Something seemed to have happened, though, because the Dutchmen retreated as one. The leader stammered an excuse. He was visibly distraught.

"I'm sorry, we didn't mean to disturb you, *Mijnheer*. We have to get back to our ship, our captain is expecting us."

He turned and almost tripped over one of his companions in his haste. Staggering and running, the Western Europeans hurried back to their fluyt.

Meanwhile, the dark figure pulled its hood back over its face. Slowly, seemingly in no hurry, it turned and approached the *Pride*.

A few steps before it reached the plank leading up to the small opening in the bulwark of the great Scottish four-masted galleon, it stopped.

"I am Kraik, envoy of the Imperial Inquisition," the figure whispered, loud enough for Kaura in the stern to hear. "We are looking for three fugitives. Wanted by the crown. Let me speak to your captain."

"I am the captain. Elias McGregor is my name. I'm sorry, I can't help you. We only have our crew on board at the moment. All bona fide subjects of the Scottish realm. Some of my people are on shore leave. I hope they haven't caused any trouble?"

A growl came from the dark hood.

"I will come aboard. If the ones we're seeking are hiding on board, I'll find them quickly." Kraik leaned forward a bit. "One of the subjects is suspected of using magic. Do you know what that means?"

"The resentments of your Sultan and his congregation against the supernatural do not interest me," the captain replied calmly. "You will know that magic is not illegal in the Scottish Empire. But I can reassure you. I would put my hand in the fire for every member of my crew. We know of your follies and would not take any Gifted ones into Spanish territory."

The figure hissed something incomprehensible. The sound was like that of an angry snake.

McGregor seemed to have understood the Inquisitor, and his voice grew hard.

"Listen, I don't like your kind. Don't think you can make trouble for us, Señor. We've done nothing wrong. Paddy!"

He nodded to the anchor watch, who immediately began hauling in the plank. Shadowy figures, hardly visible in the fog, had already seen to untying the mooring lines and now returned to the ship by way of rope ladders thrown over the bulwark.

Kraik stood motionless on the pier.

"You do realize that your attempt to escape is an admission of guilt. You are sentencing yourself and your entire crew to death. We will not allow you to escape." Still that unnerving, monotonous whisper.

"Cast off," a voice cried. "Set sail."

Suddenly the deck and shrouds were full of men, shadows scurrying about in the driving snow. Fluttering, the sails unfurled and filled with wind. The ship began to drift away from the pier, picking up speed.

Kaura looked back, transfixed, at the small but strangely terrifying figure in the dark red hood, whose color was now becoming visible in the dim light of the stern lantern. Because of this, she was able to watch as the blue glow around Kraik began to expand, like a giant soap bubble. The bubble grew larger and larger until it caught up with the ship and slowly enveloped it.

When the bubble of light reached the mizzen mast at the stern of the ship, its sail suddenly collapsed in on itself. The ship's speed decreased. Kraik's bubble continued to expand and now reached the main mast. Suddenly the sails there had no wind either.

Excited shouts went up from the Scottish crew. No one understood what was happening.

Meanwhile, an entire company of Iberian port soldiers arrived on the pier at a run from a main alley and aimed their muskets at the ship.

A shadow emerged from the darkness of the main deck. Sir Elias quickly moved past her, climbing the stairs leading up to the quarterdeck.

Almost at the top, he turned to Kaura. His face, barely visible in the dim light, was worried.

"Joe told me what happened and what you did to the Spanish witch. Is there anything you can do for us? If that warlock can cripple us here, we'll probably all end up together before the Spanish executioner."

Kaura shivered with cold and excitement.

"I will try. It's just that I don't know what I'm doing myself!"

The captain nodded darkly at her and disappeared with an urgent, "Do anything! It'll have to work."

Desperately, she tried to relax and breathe calmly. She could not - she was too excited.

Suddenly, she remembered an exercise that the old abbot of the Buddhist monastery outside of town had taught her years ago. It had served her well in swordfighting when, after hours of sparring with Resa, her concentration had faltered and she had begun to let her guard down.

With a pang of desperation, she brought the candle flame into her consciousness.

Meanwhile, the blue bubble had enveloped the entire ship and its speed had slowed to almost zero. The bow wave collapsed more and more.

Kaura fed everything she felt at the moment into the flame of the candle within her mind. Mortal fear, uncertainty, shame that she should know what to do and didn't, disappointment that her escape seemed to be failing....

And then there was just the flame, burning steadily in the

middle of the void. She realized she had closed her eyes. The excited shouts of the crew around her rolled off her like raindrops from a lotus blossom. She could still see the blue bubble around the ship in this inner space, though.

With all her might, she imagined the bubble bursting, just like a real soap bubble. But it only billowed slightly, deformed.

Above her, the topsail filled with wind, flapped for a moment, and immediately collapsed as the bubble regained its stability.

Sweat ran down Kaura's face despite the cold. Again and again she relaxed, letting all the tension flow into the candle flame in her mind, and watched almost unconcernedly as the flame burned brighter and brighter.

Then, she realized that she could see two blue bubbles: the large one around both Kraik and the ship, and a smaller, paler one that probably surrounded Kraik himself. The centerpoints of the two bubbles were connected to each other by a thin, faintly fluorescent tube, which she had not noticed before because of her concentration on the ship.

Now, she was just following her intuition. The candle flame inside her transformed, almost as if by itself, into a red-yellow glowing sword. She felt herself leaving her body, grabbing the long sword hilt with both hands and lunging forward. With all her might, she struck the blue glowing cord.

At first, the energetic structure stretched only slightly downward, seeming to yield elastically - but then, the red blade slid smoothly through the tube. The bubble around the ship wavered wildly, then burst completely.

With a bang, the canvas of the galleon filled with wind, just as the candle flame inside Kaura was extinguished as if blown out by a strong gust of air.

She swayed, close to fainting for a moment, and Atam, sitting next to her, whimpered softly.

She opened her eyes and looked back at the pier. There, the dark figure was slumped on its knees, holding its head. Two other hooded figures were moving toward it. The soldiers meanwhile didn't seem to know whether to open fire or not and waited for orders.

A feeling of satisfaction flashed through the young woman. Then she had to hold on to the bulwark to keep from collapsing from weakness.

Suddenly, Joe appeared at her right side and slid his arm under her shoulder. He nodded to McGregor, who had reappeared behind the aft deck railing and was looking down at them.

"I'll take care of her. Make sure you get us out of the harbor in one piece, Elias. It will take them some time to get the Coastal Patrol ships ready to follow us. They'll never find us in this fog and darkness."

Joe still supported her as he shouldered open the bulkhead that led to the aft deck compartments. He pulled her into a heated chamber that smelled of charcoal fire, followed by Atam.

Kaura softly pushed her friend away and began to shrug off the heavy cloak. She was annoyed at her own weakness.

"Thanks, I'm fine. I'm just very tired all of a sudden. I need to sit down somewhere. But what if the other two Inquisitors do something now? They are probably Gifted as well."

"Elias would send for you if something strange happened again. What the hell was going on out there? Suddenly the wind died, just around the ship. Then it came back and you had that fainting spell. Was it another one of those magical attacks?"

She nodded weakly.

"That Kraik put some kind of light bubble around the ship. At least it looked like a light bubble to me. Apparently you can only see these effects if you're Gifted?"

Joe shrugged.

"Probably. Anyway, it looks like we owe you our lives. At the very least we've gained some space to breathe. The *Pride* is a fast ship. Maybe we can cross the Skagerrak before the Iberians turn the Vikings against us . That will not be easy for them anyway. Scotland upholds very good relations with the Norsemen, and they are mainly interested in tolls and less in politics. I still don't know exactly what to do. But once we get to London, you won't have to worry about extradition, at least for now. And we can do some research."

He pulled up an upholstered chair for her and, with a sigh, slid into the recliner behind the large desk that was firmly bolted to the floor in the center of the owner's cabin.

"Fortunately Inmarsund is not fortified. Otherwise our Spanish friends might get the idea to shoot at us despite the fog. Here, have some wine. I'll see that we get something to eat soon." He poured and pushed the large silver cup over to her.

Kaura drank and wiped her mouth with her wrist, half-consciously adjusting her manners to the familiar maritime environment.

"What did that Spaniard want from you? Something must have been very important to him if he threatened to kill Mikhail on the spot. How is he, by the way?"

"He's sleeping. Exhausted. The whole thing took a lot out of him, and he's worried about George. We sent a sailor ashore to inform the few crewmen who were still on shore leave and couldn't be reached in time. They will also try to take care of George, without exposing themselves to any retribution measures by the occupiers. But I don't think he's important enough for the Spaniards to take him prisoner. He's just a servant. The Inquisitors are unlikely to give him much trouble."

With a thoughtful expression on his face, the Scotsman leaned back and sipped the tasty wine, which Kaura thought was surely from the Iberian Peninsula, just like their pursuers.

"Regarding your first question, the Imperial Sultanate apparently intends to take military action against Atlantis. The fact that the Atlanteans thwarted their conquest of the Aztec Empire in 1548 A.D., as the Ottomans now count their years, still gives the ruler in Granada no peace, that is widely known. They seemed to think I had a key to opening a portal that supposedly led directly from the eastern Mediterranean to Atlantis."

"A portal?" asked Kaura. "You mean underground or something? That would be a long tunnel. And under the sea, of all things."

He shrugged.

"I just don't know," he muttered tiredly. "I've been racking my brain ever since that guy was talking about it. I really don't think I've ever heard of anything like that. I would have to remember something about it if I had."

Suddenly he gave a start. "Ah, but there are the books. Fortunately, I remembered to pack them when we left the villa in such a hurry. Since the Ottomans were so interested in Atlantis, I didn't want to leave them in their hands. After all, my late great-uncle and former agent for the Nelson family in Inmarsund had gotten them there. His wife was originally from Atlantis. It was to her that we owe the contracts for the supply of the silk steel that, within a few decades, turned us from a small river shipping company into the most successful trading house in Scotland. Genuine Atlantic books are hard to find outside of university libraries, even though most European academics are writing in Atlantic and there are many copies around. The island has sealed itself off from the outside world very successfully for centuries, yet their classical texts are still one of our main sources of higher knowledge."

Joe made a move to stand up. "I'll go get them..."

Kaura put a hand on his forearm to stop him.

"Let's look at your books later. You must be exhausted as well. And we should talk with Sir Elias to see about our next steps."

Joe sank back into the chair and nodded. He looked relieved.

"I'm sure he'll be joining us soon."

By now the ship was rolling and pitching steadily through moderate swells. It was clear that they had already left the coastal waters and were on the open sea. Kaura closed her eyes for a moment, giving in to her exhaustion.

A knock on the bulkhead of the chamber brought her back to the present. Accompanied by a gust of cold sea air, the captain entered, and Kaura could see him more clearly for the first time in the light of the oil lamps.

Sir Elias McGregor was a red-haired giant. Kaura could vividly imagine the man throwing huge logs around to prove his strength at archaic warrior gatherings in the Highlands. With a bearish growl, and without being prompted, he dropped onto the couch that stood against the back wall of the cabin. The bolted piece of furniture cracked and creaked precariously as he turned to Joe.

"You've managed to get us into quite a bit of trouble, my young friend. We probably can't show ourselves in the entire Spanish-Ottoman Empire anymore! Your family will not be pleased."

Joe nodded.

"No, they won't. But at least they'll be happy about the fact that I didn't end up on the executioner's block, I imagine. Without Kaura's help, that might have been quite possible. Even likely. Now we'll have to deal with the consequences. Shit happens, as my old great-great-grandfather Jamie Nelson said when he slipped on a banana peel at the top of the mast.

The captain did not smile. Seriously, he leaned forward.

"In three days we can reach the Skagerrak and from there push on to the North Sea. It will be almost impossible for the Spanish to catch up with us in their ships. The *Pride* is a fast vessel, and the winds are on our side. Only if they send horse messengers to Denmark might they be able to get the Vikings to stop us in time.

Joe shook his head.

"The Vikings will be reluctant to search a Scottish ship. If

Elizabeth learns of it, they could lose their trade privileges with her realm. They won't risk provoking the ire of the Queen. Especially not on a flimsy accusation from the Spanish. And besides, we have no choice."

Kaura shook her head.

"Well, we could disembark in Lübeck and head overland to the North Sea. I'm sure there's a ship in Hamburg that could take us to London. The two city-states are still independent and are unlikely to hand us over to the Southlanders," she interjected.

Joe made a face.

"Sure, that would be something of a last resort. But I don't think we'll have to use it. I feel safer here on the ship. We're among friends, and we have our own guns if we need them."

The four-masted galleon was superbly armed for a merchantman, with ten fourteen-pounders of the latest design on each side, straight from the royal foundries of Glasgow.

Joe often boasted that even most of the ships in the Imperial Navy were equipped with less powerful cannons than the average vessel in the Nelson fleet. With their merchant galleons sailing all over the known world, and even in the Spanish-Ottoman dominated Caribbean, this was a necessity. Besides, Kaura suspected that at least some of the Nelson ships were also engaged in privateering. Though Joe never spoke of it, the Spanish gold convoys sailing between the 'New World' and Europe were certainly a tempting prey for well-armed ships of a nation not exactly friendly with the Sultan, and it was known that Elizabeth, Queen of Scotland, did not hesitate to issue letters of marque to her captains, protecting them from prosecution for piracy, at least in her own realm.

"I agree with Joe," Captain McGregor interrupted. "We can negotiate with the Danes, even if they stop us and inspect the *Pride*. After all, we are allies. Still, it's important that we get out of the Baltic as soon as possible. I don't like the fact that the Inquisition wants something from you. That makes you outlaws in all Spanish-controlled territories. At least, it does if they feel you are important enough to have drawings made and distributed to the colonial troops."

Silence fell over the chamber, dimly lit by two oil lamps. All three men were lost in their own thoughts for a moment.

Then the captain got to his feet with a sigh.

"I'll check the situation on the quarterdeck. Get some rest. To-morrow we'll be able to think more clearly. Kaura, you can use the passenger compartment next door. I will send the ship's boy with bedding."

The bulkhead closed silently behind the giant.

When they were alone, Joe gave Kaura an almost shy look.

"Even in London, there are some people now who condemn magic as dangerous and unnatural. They do not yet have enough influence at court to do any real damage, and the Scottish mage guilds are still in good standing with the Queen. Besides, there are many in Greater Scotland who believe that these people are being stirred up by Granada." He took a deep breath and let it out. "Any-way, I want you to know that I have no prejudices in this regard. Neither does my family. Now that you know you're Gifted, maybe you'll finally find out where you come from."

Kaura nodded wearily.

"Thank you. I know I can count on you. That means a lot to me."

He smiled.

"Let's go to the galley and get something to eat. And then we'll sleep. If you want, we can share a bed. We don't have to..."

She stood up, swaying slightly in the constantly moving room. It would take her a few hours to get used to the constant rocking and pitching of the big wooden hull.

"Yes, I think some company would be good for me tonight," she replied, "Let's go talk to the cook and see what he has for us."

Together, the tall Scot and the petite, brown-skinned witch left the chamber and made their way through the ship's narrow corridors to the galley, from which, even at this late hour, firelight and steam were still emanating.

* * *

Less than two days later, off the Swedish south coast

Kaura stood on the quarterdeck, leaning against the forward railing. She narrowed her eyes against the biting cold sea wind. It had stopped snowing long ago, and the sea was choppy, not stormy. The gray sky on the horizon merged almost invisibly with the equally gray surface of the sea. Visibility had improved over the past two days. No pursuers had been sighted.

The *Pride* trudged relentlessly northwest, toward the main passage leading from the Baltic to the North Sea.

Despite the cold, Kaura enjoyed the freshness and salty smell of the open waters. Behind her, Captain McGregor barked his orders. Down on the main deck, Atam let the wind blow around his snout and snatched at the occasional drops of spray that splashed over the bulwark.

Joe and Mikhail had retired to the shipowner's son's luxurious cabin hours ago. They were conferring.

Soon they would reach the strait between Copenhagen and Malmö.

They all still hoped that any messengers on horseback sent from Inmarsund would have to travel too far to notify the Spanish-Ottoman Baltic fleets stationed in Flensburg and Rostock in time. As long as no one there knew of their escape, no warships could be sent to intercept the *Pride* before it reached the North Sea, where they would be much harder to find.

"We still must be prepared for all eventualities, but we probably gave them the slip," McGregor had rumbled, and both Kaura and Joe had agreed with him.

She brushed a strand of her long black hair out of her face. It crunched slightly under her fingers and she felt the wetness of rapidly melting ice crystals. Her eyebrows were probably white with frozen moisture as well.

Half an hour later, the sailor manning the topmast lookout called out, "Land in sight!" The men up there were relieved every half hour because of the biting cold. The captain handed Kaura his scope and pointed to starboard, where a flat strip of land emerged from the hazy gray winter light.

"The Falsterbo Peninsula. Soon we will see the island of Saltholm. The way the wind goes, we will sail through the strait between Helsingborg and Elsinore just before dark, where the Viking customs boats will be waiting to inspect us."

Joe and Mikhail had meanwhile climbed on deck as well. Both men were wrapped in thick winter coats.

Kaura set the scope down and smiled at the old Russian.

"Hello Mikhail, good to see you up and about. I was getting worried. The whole thing must have taken a lot out of you!"

The addressed man laughed boisterously, and Kaura suppressed a pang of pity. Mikhail was often in a good mood and a cheerful demeanor was normal for him. Today, however, there was a strained quality to it. He seemed to be trying to hide his insecurity.

"Weeds don't die, Kaura. Honestly, I don't know what's been going on with me these past two days! Maybe that strange woman had already started to do something to me. Anyway, I'm glad nothing worse happened."

He scratched his beard thoughtfully.

"But, now the Nelsons will have to appoint a new representative for Inmarsund. I don't think I can show my face there again so soon after our somewhat hasty departure. Maybe I should have stayed. After all, I didn't really know anything. And I'm still worried about George."

Kaura shook her head.

"There were too many uncertainties. I think you did the right thing by coming with us."

She paused.

"Wait a minute. You *didn't* know anything? Are you saying you found out what the Ottomans wanted from the two of you now?"

Joe, now leaning casually against the balustrade beside her, grinned smugly.

"You know, we've spent most of the last two days studying the two Atlantean books. Not easy, since they are written in an old dialect. Together we were able to decipher most of it. Well, today Mikhail came across a very interesting passage in the *Travels of Mila Intan*. The edition is quite old, about five hundred years, and the Atlantean version contains several additional chapters not found in the commercial editions—at least not in the Scottish ones we normally get to read. One of these is about a trade caravan between Hellas and the Arabian Peninsula. The southern route was apparently still passable at that time. Mila speaks of a forbidden city with man-made mountains in a desert valley. The mountains, according to some caravan leaders, were a link to the "Worlds of the Ancients". Apparently, the locals prevented Mila from approaching the place. Even then, the caravans seemed to avoid it by a fair margin. However, she suspects that the city may be identical to the island of the Rainbow Bridge, called Pyrrhan, which is legendary even to the Atlanteans. After that, twenty pages have been ripped out. But here's the thing..." he leaned a little closer to her and lowered his voice. "The margins of this last page are densely covered with writing. Most of it seems to be just numbers and location information that we can't make sense of yet. However, there are references to portals in the notes."

Kaura's green eyes flashed with interest.

"I want to see that. Let's go down there once we are past Copenhagen. Maybe we'll find out more."

To starboard, the landscape was now slowly changing, and the multitude of columns of smoke rising in the distance and dissipating in the wind revealed that they were approaching Malmö, with the Viking metropolis of Copenhagen just beyond on the opposite shore.

The Inmarsundian felt a pang of regret at the thought of not landing in the great city this time.

Less than an hour later, the four of them stood around one of the books salvaged by Joe, which lay open on the map table of the captain's chamber. McGregor had joined them.

"These are not coordinates," the *Pride's* commander said thoughtfully, running one of his chubby fingers over the old parchment. "At least not in any system I know of. Still, they seem to be clues to finding other places, namely these portals."

Kaura also bent over the small notes written on the paper in immaculate handwriting. She thought hard.

She couldn't even decipher some of the symbols. They did not look like any script she was familiar with. Nor did they resemble the Arabic syllabary or the graphic characters used by the Mongolians and in Cipangu. As far as was known, the Atlanteans were exclusively writing in the Latin script of the ancient Romans. Some also claimed that the Romans had adopted it from them.

At the end of the chapter came the page they were most curious about. The note was written in microscopic, Atlantean Latin handwriting:

Portal Sectors Pyrrha. Can be enabled (?)
Sect. 1 Port. A LEM. Z. 17-63-5D Key 759380#
Sect. 1 Port. A LEM. East 17-69-1 Key 780001# (Alt.)

Sect. 9 Port A ATL. 18-89-XP Open. Ctr. reqrd
Sect. 3 Port C ARK. 20-00-A1 18.3.1463 P.8956P
Sect. 7 Port E ILL. 00-13-7C avoid.!!! Dang. def. trsm.
Alt. 00-18-7C? blocked. Attn. Gods!!! Cn. Rgn.?
Sect. 10 Temp. - Core Earth, West. Taboo(??)
Ask Celia. Passc. "Wanderer". Vega 4 E/F?

Next to the third line was the drawing of two double intertwined spirals. Somehow the symbol looked familiar to Kaura. She just couldn't remember where she had seen it before.

"Hmm, well, there seem to be several of these portals," she mused aloud. "And Pyrrhan or Pyrrha seems to actually exist, at least according to the person who wrote these notes. I think if we were there, it would probably become clearer what is meant by the numbers. But we still don't have a clue about the key. Why "Attention Gods"? And who is Celia?"

She pointed to the mark scribbled next to the Sect. 1 note.

"That double spiral looks familiar. Have any of you seen anything like it before?"

All three men shook their heads.

Several minutes of silence followed.

Then the Captain pointed to the pendant between Kaura's breasts.

"It looks like the engraving on your hook."

She lifted it up to her eyes. Indeed, the two double spirals engraved on it were identical to those in Joe's book.

"Yes, you are right. And Aalyjah's great-grandmother, from whom the amulet came, seems to have traveled a lot in the Mediterranean. So, there could be a connection."

She thought some more, then shook her head.

"Let's go to London and try to find out more about this

mysterious portal city," she said. If the Spaniards are so interested in the book, you should probably hide it well, Joe."

She gave the Scottish adventurer a curious look. "You seem pensive. Do you have any intention of seeking out this portal yourself?"

He shrugged.

"I would like to. But it would be an unnecessary risk."

Captain McGregor gave a stifled laugh, then coughed.

"When has that ever stopped you, my boy? The more unnecessary the risk, the more fun it is, hasn't that always been your creed?"

A momentary grin flashed across the young Scotsman's face, then he lowered his gaze.

"I don't think the Atlanteans would be pleased to see me on their island," he said quietly. "For various reasons I can't tell you more about. But perhaps we should send them a warning. After all, our Spanish friends seem to be seriously out to get them."

* * *

A few hours later, the Pride sailed past Helsingør. Arne, a slim deckhand originally from Sweden, was at the helm of the galleon while Sir Elias calmly faced the Viking guard sloop.

The sloop came toward them with a foaming bow wave. In the bow, standing motionless and tall, was a watch officer in the uniform of the Nordic Crown with a shining golden helmet. When he was within shouting distance, he called out to the Scottish tall ship.

"What ship? Going to which port? Cargo?"

Sir Elias leaned over the bulwark. "*Pride of Edinburgh*, Captain McGregor. We're bound for London. No cargo, just passengers."

The lieutenant saluted.

"Scottish ship? Have a good trip. Be careful. We hear of major Ottoman fleet movements in the North Sea!"

The sloop turned away and headed back toward the shore in the dim light, where the first lights in the windows were already on.

Kaura breathed a sigh of relief. Finally, something that did not give them any unexpected trouble.

* * *

The next morning, Kaura, Joe, and Mikhail had breakfast in the mess with the captain and the boatswain, Gary. They were all hungrily helping themselves from the round platter of eggs with ham and freshly baked bread that had been placed in the middle of the table when the cook came over to talk to Sir Elias.

"I strongly suggest that we call at Gothenburg to take on water and provisions, Sir. We haven't even been able to replenish our drinking water supply due to our hasty departure from Inmarsund. It would still last us as far as London. However, I would prefer to be prepared for unforeseen delays."

The captain was an experienced sailor and knew that his cook was a good planner. In addition, the Nelson ships' officers were widely known to take excellent care of the physical well-being of their crews. The Nelson family believed that only happy people could deliver the performance and loyalty they demanded of all their employees, down to the lowest deck hand.

Sir Elias nodded.

"All right, Roger, I concur. We can be in Gothenburg by to-morrow morning. Be ready to get the supplies as soon as we arrive and have them loaded in the afternoon. We want to get to London as soon as possible and not give the Spaniards a chance to still intercept us in the North Sea."

He turned to his passengers.

"Roger is right. It will take us at least five more days to reach

London against the prevalent winds, and the North Sea is unpredictable. I don't think we'll encounter any problems in Gothenburg."

No one objected, and they all turned back to their breakfast. The food was still hot.

4

The Consul of the Witches

Around noon on January 3, the *Pride* passed between the flat, rounded islands and granite headlands off the coast of Gothenburg.

The sun had reappeared, sending its golden rays through the crisp winter air, in which the small, brightly painted wooden huts of the fisherfolk were clearly visible in every detail. The light brown triangular sails of the small fishing and coastal boats glowed warmly in the Nordic light, and only a few patches of snow could be seen on land.

It almost made you forget that it was still the dead of winter, Kaura thought as she leaned lazily against the bulwark of the main deck.

The crew members of the Scottish ship were perfectly attuned to one another. Though Kaura had offered her assistance, the provost, Edgar Bell, had merely pointed out with a friendly grin that, as the only woman on the ship, she would be enough of a distraction for the men even if she didn't move from the quarterdeck.

She didn't hold it against him. After all, everyone on board had been extremely gallant and polite to her. She knew that men liked to look at her, and sailors didn't often have the opportunity to make unobjectionable female acquaintances in ports. With her pitch-black hair down to her waist, her clear face, and her velvety brown skin even with the northern lack of sunshine, she also liked seeing herself when she was a guest in one of the more distinguished houses that had mirrors. By now, almost all of the rich and noble had some of the sleek, floor-to-ceiling things made of polished glass that had been leaving the secret Mongolian factories on Hangzhou's West Lake for the past few years, making their costly way to Europe.

She stroked Atam's broad head and looked out beyond one of the small harbor sloops that was just crossing their course to the towering spires and square stone buildings of Gothenburg, already visible in the clear winter air.

"Strange people, these Westerners and Southerners," she murmured to the dog, who wagged his tail idly in response. It still filled her with disbelief to think that the ships of most nations today were commanded and manned primarily by men. This would never have happened on the ships of the liberal Baltic cities. There, all ships were sailed by mixed crews. In most cases, women outnumbered men, and male captains were a rarity. It was said that the matriarchal culture that had come from the East with the Tantric-Buddhist conquerors more than a millennium ago had survived virtually unchanged in those areas.

In the lands of the original Celtic population of Western Europe, the balance of power between men and women had remained somewhat more balanced even after the Great Migration. It was said that even some people in the north of the Scottish Empire still did not simply bequeath their lands to the eldest child, but only to the eldest son. And in the realm of the Sultan of Granada, this was not a question anyway, as everyone knew by now.

Kaura rolled her eyes inwardly, then her attention was captured by the port facilities that were now drawing nearer.

Gothenburg was by no means the size of a metropolis like Copenhagen or London, but there was still a lot going on here at the main gateway to the largely unexplored northern parts of the Viking Empire. People scurried about, wrapped in colorful, heavy cloaks. Merchants shouted their wares and prices to the crowd, carts hauled heavy barrels and jute sacks across the piers. Every now and then a helmet or a musket flashed in the sun, where patrols of the city guard were on the move.

Wafts of steam rose into the dry winter air from stalls selling all manner of culinary delights. In the fishermen's area at the edge of the harbor, large sloping wooden racks had been erected, on which freshly caught and salted fish could be seen drying in the sun.

Kaura smiled and touched the fishhook pendant dangling freely between her breasts through the fabric of her heavy wool cloak. She hadn't found the time to really think about it yet. But now she remembered how strangely the little thing had reacted during her encounter with the High Inquisitor. Since then, she had wondered if she owed her narrow escape in Inmarsund to that amulet. She believed she did.

The young woman had been, at least in the five years her memory stretched back, an extremely rational and not very superstitious person. What she could not see, touch or experience held little interest for her. After all, anyone could make up anything, and if it didn't turn into concrete experiences, into visible and tangible effects in her life, it was a waste of energy in Kaura's view. Now, things had happened, and they were real - at least for her. She saw things no one else could see.

And these things had an effect that was clearly perceptible even to the people around her.

An unwelcome image of the burnt, reeking pile of ashes that had once been the Siberian witch popped into her mind, and she almost felt nauseous again. Visible effects.

Her logical mind could not deny it. Still, she could not bring herself to really think about it, even now, several days after the event. The others had accepted her silence and had not pushed her further. In the end, she was simply afraid, she bluntly admitted to herself. Afraid of not belonging anywhere..

She had found a new family, friends. And now she had discovered that she probably had abilities that were frightening to most people, even in the few countries where they were not considered a capital offense. And that made her an outcast in her new home, a pariah, a forsaken woman. Could she handle that? What did it mean for her life?

A hard thump on the galleon's hull jolted her from her brooding thoughts. A port captain's sloop had already guided the *Pride* to her berth. Two dockworkers on the mole picked up the ropes thrown by the crew and tied them to the massive metal bollards firmly anchored in the stone.

Sir Elias was already talking to the cook and the two crew members who were to accompany him as porters on his shopping trip.

Then he turned to Kaura.

"We will be heading out in four hours, if everything goes according to plan. If you want to go ashore, report to the sentry. If you wish, I can assign someone from the crew to accompany you as a bodyguard."

"No need," Kaura replied with a smile. "By human standards, it's almost impossible that our pursuers are here in Gothenburg. Besides, I can defend myself if that should be necessary."

She placed a hand on the hilt of her rapier, which protruded from a fold in her cloak.

The red-bearded captain twisted his wrinkled face into an agreeable grin.

"I don't doubt it. Have a good time, then. And stay out of those dodgy taverns in the harbor."

Shortly after the cook and his companions, Kaura left the ship via the gangway, exchanged a few friendly words with the guard, and then, closely followed by Atam, ducked into the hustle and bustle of the Scandinavian port.

Joe would probably want to visit the city as well. At the moment, however, she didn't feel like company. There was little room on the ship for the solitary meditations the young woman used to keep her energy up, and she needed some space to herself.

She didn't know exactly where she was going, but she would soon find out.

In Gothenburg lived a consul of the Siberian Witch Nations, she had heard once from the trappers who sometimes passed through Inmarsund, a paid agent who could also issue letters of transit and make contacts if necessary. This was the person she wanted to meet.

She imagined the Witch Nations might help someone in her situation. After all, they were Gifted too - and would probably at least not be antagonistic towards a sister.

Even if they could not offer any direct support, she thought, the Consul had to know what the situation was like for magically gifted people in the Western European territories, and where she could go if she encountered any more problems.

Furthermore, she still did not even know the exact nature of her talents nor whether she was in danger because of them. After all, Aalyjah had told her that all untrained mages and wizards died, went mad, or burned out soon after the first signs of their gift, unless they learned to control the powers flowing through them in time. That bothered her. Maybe she was just a late bloomer and needed help. This thought made her feel a little dizzy.

"Or," a small, hopeful voice whispered inside her, "you belong to the witches. Maybe this is your family..."

Determined, she turned into one of the alleys that, she guessed, led from the port to the city center. The tantalizing smell of oriental spices and roasted chicken wafted toward her from the long line of mobile market stalls selling fruit, roasted meat skewers, fresh flatbreads, and all manner of other goods. Kaura's stomach growled.

Involuntarily, she looked up, searching for the source of the smell. One of the market women raised her voice slightly when she noticed the slender Inmarsundian's searching gaze.

"Curry, vegetable, tofu, yellow, red," she called out, alternating between Viking, Atlantic and Scottish. Apparently, visitors of all nationalities were not uncommon in Gothenburg.

Smiling, Kaura approached.

"How much for a yellow curry?"

"Three coppers," was the answer, and she nodded in agreement.

The older woman began scooping rice and vegetables out of her steaming pots. A pair of intelligent, ice-blue eyes blinked at the dark-skinned woman.

"You're from the Island, right? Britain?"

Kaura shook her head.

"Inmarsund. On the Baltic Sea."

She had started the conversation in Scottish, so it was clear that the woman would probably think she was from there.

She fished three copper coins out of her leather pouch in exchange for a wooden bowl containing a yellowish mixture of rice and vegetables that smelled of peanuts and chili. While she fished out a piece of carrot with the bamboo chopsticks she always carried and put it in her mouth, the old woman studied her curiously.

Kaura decided to take advantage of the opportunity. Maybe she could learn something about where the consul lived.

She clicked her tongue appreciatively.

"Excellent. Real Ceylonese spices?"

The woman nodded.

"Since the Scots entered the trade with the eastern empires, crossing Russia with their steam caravans, these luxuries have also become available to us here in the north. In the old days, the Spaniards and their Arab friends controlled practically all the world's trade in spices, and it all ended up in their fat pots in the southern lands."

She blushed.

"Sorry, girl. Inmarsund is also a Spanish port, and you look like you have Arab roots. I didn't mean to offend you."

"Don't mention it. I belong to one of the local merchant families. We are not particularly happy about the occupiers, even though they have freed us from the supposedly bad association with the Mongol Empire."

Kaura spooned the curry and continued to chat with the market woman, while Atam curiously eyed a cat that was enjoying what was probably the first sunny day in a long time on a wall not far from them. The cat showed no fear of the big dog. It just stretched its body and yawned.

When the bowl was almost empty and Kaura raised it to her mouth to slurp the last of the sauce, the old woman beamed.

Slurping was apparently considered a sign of enjoyment here too, even so far north. It was said that some of the Asian immigrants who came to Europe with the conquerors more than a thousand years ago had started this custom.

With a satiated feeling in her stomach, Kaura returned the wooden bowl. She leaned a little closer.

"Where can I find the Consul of the Witch Nations, would you know?"

The old woman's smile faded abruptly. She lowered her voice.

"What do you want with him? Nice man, Melkar Bellin, but dangerous company. Many people here don't want to have anything to do with the witches, even though the Viking king has good connections to them. Many also believe that it will not stay that way for long. The Spaniards have already sent several delegations to convince him of their views. There is one in town right now."

Kaura shrugged her shoulders and lied brazenly.

"I have nothing against the witches. In fact, I just want to inquire if they have any trade goods to offer. Amulets and sculptures from the Witch Lands are very rare. They would certainly sell well in Inmarsund. Below the counter."

The woman nodded and pulled her red headscarf slightly forward.

"Just keep walking down the alley. At the second square you'll find a large fountain decorated with the sculpture of a nude flute player. You cannot miss it. Turn right into the alley. It is the house at number seven or eight, I think. Bellin runs a bookstore called *The Reading Phoenix* as his main profession.

Kaura thanked her and continued on her way.

A short time later she found the place.

A large metal sign swung above the door in the light, now almost spring-like breeze. It showed a bird half made of flames, holding an open book in its feet which were equipped with large claws.

The shield was elaborately carved in relief, and the outlines of the phoenix and the book were gilded, making the moving emblem glitter intensely in the sunlight.

Next to the door was a small metal plaquette with some words engraved on it:

Melkar Bellin
Honorary Consul
Republic of Siberian Witches
Clan Representative: Viranuk, E'ki, Manuk

With determination, Kaura pushed open the heavy wooden door, flinching for a moment when the loud sound of a heavy gong rang out. Atam slipped in behind her.

Surprised, she paused as the door clicked shut behind her. She had expected to find one of the usual, dark and cramped shops, with dim leaded windows that let in little light, and poorly lit high shelves. Now, however, she found herself in a place that might as well have been a reception hall in Inmarsund Castle.

The room behind the gate was two stories high. A heavy green carpet covered most of the marble floor. Large, beige-painted bookshelves were evenly spaced around the hall.

Between them stood several round, white wooden tables and comfortable-looking upholstered chairs. The entire room was lit by a golden glowing sphere suspended from the ceiling, with silver reflections scattered across it at irregular intervals, like clouds on the surface of the earth. To the left and right, winding staircases led to other rooms. Through doorless gothic doorways she could see more bookshelves, the aisles between them leading off into the far distance.

There was not a single human being to be seen.

Kaura wondered how these huge halls managed to fit into such a seemingly small and unassuming building. Somehow the neighboring houses must have been hollowed out and included in the creation of this place. But no, she thought she had seen open shops on both sides of the entrance to Bellin's store.

Confused, she shook her head. Yes, she was absolutely certain. When she had entered the *Reading Phoenix*, a blacksmith had been busy making horseshoes just to her right. She had been able to overlook the entire forge, which had been open to the outside.

A deep, melodious voice pulled her out of her thoughts.

"Welcome to the Reading Phoenix. I am Melkar Bellin. How can I help you?"

A man descended the stairs to her right with long-practiced dignity. Bellin immediately captured her with his charisma.

First she noticed his clear, ice-blue eyes, which seemed to glow from within and, despite their intensity, had an unmistakable glimmer of human warmth and friendliness in them. His white beard was divided into two long plaits that fell back over his shoulders on either side, where they appeared to intertwine with his equally white, braided hair.

Bellin's robe was made of fine, dark blue silk and reached almost to the floor, so that he seemed to float down the stairs rather than walk. He was even shorter than Kaura, and of stockier build.

"I have books on any subject you might be interested in, in any language, from any era!" He spoke in Atlantean, but mistook her hesitation for incomprehension and continued in Spanish.

"Where are you from, my dear? Let me guess, you are an escaped Oriental princess from the Spanish harem, señorita? Is that it? Do you need a book on Scandinavian love customs?" He winked at her mischievously.

Then he glanced sideways at Atam, who was sitting patiently by the door. "Or maybe a book on dog training?"

She had to laugh. Then she answered him in Atlantean.

"Thank you, no need. I live in Inmarsund. And I'll be happy to take a look at your books sometime. But right now I'd like to talk to you in your capacity as consul."

A warm smile appeared on Bellin's face. "Then welcome again, friend. Call me Melkar. There is no room for formality when it comes to sisterly matters. Let's sit in the back."

He grew serious as he led her up one of the staircases to a comfortably furnished office and gestured for her to sit down.

"You are aware that you have probably already been spotted by the henchmen of the Inquisition when you entered this shop?"

Kaura shook her head.

"I didn't know that the Inquisition is also active here in the free North. Very surprising."

"They've even started harassing my regular customers. Bad for the business," he continued. "Since the Spaniards have gained control of the Skagerrak with their fleet, hardly any witches are passing through these parts anymore. The Viking king, Rogan, has to tolerate it if he wants to keep his independence. Those who still need to travel today take the northern route through Bergen or leave the nations via the Black Sea and Asian routes. The Mongols do not like magic very much either. But fortunately, they don't enforce their laws, unlike their southern neighbors."

He snorted angrily. "Who do they think they are, those snotty Spaniards? They think they own the world! But they have no idea! They don't have a clue! Don't worry. I'll get you out of the house unseen. Now, what is it that I can do for you two?"

He looked at her attentively with his intense blue eyes and stroked Atam's head, which the dog acknowledged with a satisfied grunt.

It was then that Kaura decided to speak openly to Bellin. She trusted her intuition, and it told her clearly that she could be honest with the old man.

In short words she told him what had happened to her. She also told him everything about the mystery of her origin.

The consul proved to be an attentive and sympathetic listener.

When she had finished, he leaned back in his massive chair, looked at the young woman thoughtfully, and was silent for a long moment. His right forefinger tapped his high cheekbone repeatedly.

Then he leaned forward.

"Do you have a tattoo between your breasts?" he asked Kaura.

When she answered in the negative, he looked slightly disappointed.

"Then you do not belong to the northern witch nations. Every witch and every sorcerer bears the mark of their clan indelibly over their heart from the moment of their initiation. And you are initiated. Your adoptive mother was right. With almost one hundred percent certainty, you were introduced to magic as a girl by someone, somewhere. The only question is by whom. The history books tell us that many centuries ago there were isolated so-called naturals among the Gifted - women and men who brought their awakening power under control on their own, because for some reason they had no access to anyone who could teach them. But even then, it was believed that out of a thousand untrained magicians, only one would survive unaccompanied without losing his or her reason."

He gave her a questioning look. "Judging by your appearance and your dark skin, I suspect you belong to a southern or eastern school - perhaps the Arabian dancing witches, Indian Aalid descendants - or you come from the Himalayan cities. Most of them use tattoos as well, though. But I'm not sure that applies to all clans.

Bellin explained to Kaura that there were also shamanic magician nations on the Asian subcontinent. What was significant about Kaura's situation was that she did not seem to possess her powers in everyday life, and only found access to them in emergencies and under great pressure. This was highly unusual. Normally, a witch should have mastered her art as naturally as language or the ability to use her hands.

The consul, who was already several hundred years old, had never heard of the ability to use magic being affected by memory loss. In his opinion, there had to be something else behind it.

"It sounds to me like someone has placed a magical block in your aura," he concluded. "That's the kind of thing the clans in the north usually do to the worst criminals. You don't look like that to me, though."

Gratefully, Kaura put her hand on the white-bearded man's arm. The prospect of possibly being a criminal suffering from the effects of her punishment did not cheer her up at all. But at least now she knew a little better where she stood.

"Could the witches help me remove the block?" she asked.

The old man tugged at one of his beard plaits.

"That depends. There are certainly some master witches who might be able to. But the witch nations are very closed to outsiders, and the initiation rituals are hard. You'd have to prove yourself worthy in ways that could just as easily cost you your life."

Bellin hesitated. "If I were you, I would start somewhere else. There is a sort of central library of all initiated magicians on Earth, where all are registered with their own signature. This registry is located in the eastern Mediterranean, in a city called Pyrrha, which cannot be found on any map. The journey to Pyrrha has become an adventure in recent centuries, as I have learned from my connections among the witches. Many, even the magically gifted, return without having found the city. Other travelers disappear without a trace, and no one knows exactly why or what happened to them. Anyway, maybe this is where you can find out where you've come from and who can help you find this block and remove it if possible. Access to Pyrrha is only granted to the Gifted. There are also said to be permanent embassies from all the magic clans of the world and some other planets.

He sighed. "Of course, the Inquisition has wanted to wipe out this city ever since they were created, and the reports of the Gifted refugees from the Mediterranean who have been traveling north in small numbers via Gothenburg for the past few years do not bode well for it. Personally, I believe that the isolation and conquest of Pyrrha is one of the main reasons for the Sultan's expansionist efforts and alliance negotiations in North Africa and the Mediterranean."

Kaura nodded. Her head was spinning, but she was glad to receive so many new clues.

"My ship will be leaving soon. I can't tell you how grateful I am,

Melkar. If there is ever anything I can do for you, please do not hesitate to contact me. I should be reachable through the Nelsons in London."

She hugged the old bookseller warmly.

He was about to open the door to an adjoining room where, as he said, the tunnel to the secret exit was located when the air in the chamber began to shimmer.

Kaura's eyes widened even as the consul reassured her.

"No danger, all is well!"

Still, they both took a step back.

From a blurry smudge in the middle of the room, a dark silhouette began to emerge and solidify.

Dressed in a black linen skirt, the blonde woman appeared to be around forty years old. Heavy silver chains and amulets hung from her forearms. She wore a loose-fitting cloak, actually much too thin for winter, with a generous neckline that revealed a complex, branching tattoo between her breasts.

The woman immediately turned her stern, ice-gray eyes on Kaura.

"Am I interrupting, Melkar?"

Her voice was harsh and commanding. Kaura could imagine how the crew of an entire ship would have stood in awe of her commands and been eager to obey them.

"No, Lara, on the contrary. This young lady was just about to leave. But now that you're here, maybe you could take a look at her. Because she's got a problem there."

The consul explained in a few words. The witch stared at Kaura with a piercing gaze without even looking at him.

"I am Lara, head of the Viranuk clan," she introduced herself when Bellin had finished. "So, you are a sister, I understand. That is strange, I should be able to see that in your field of light. If you have a block, it is unlike anything I've ever seen. May I put my hand on your forehead?"

Kaura immediately felt as if she could trust this woman with her life - even without knowing her at all. She nodded and approached.

Lara placed her hand on her forehead.

The touch was cool and firm, and Kaura breathed a little deeper as she felt the connection entering her.

"Hmm. Yes, there is something. Like a soft shell in your heart brain. Soft and pliable, yet completely impenetrable. I can't see what's behind it. Maybe a Circle of Twelve or a male energy mage could make something of it."

She looked at Kaura intently. "I don't know what this is. Not any form of magic I know of, and I've traveled a long way. Besides, what still puzzles me is that I can't see your talent. The block proves it's there, but no matter what's been done to it, I should be able to tell from your aura that you're a sister."

Now something occurred to Kaura. She pulled the fishhook pendant out of her neckline and showed it to Lara.

"When I first met a mage, I didn't have this and she recognized me immediately. After I got this amulet from my stepmother, that seems not to be possible anymore".

She pulled the pendant over her head and placed it on the desk next to her.

Lara's eyes opened wide.

"Indeed. Now I recognize your gift. Impressive. May I?"

Without waiting for Kaura's nod, she grabbed the hook almost greedily, twirling it between her fingers while whispering a few soft words.

"'Supreme craftsmanship," she murmured then. "I have never seen anything like it. To hide a witch's talent from a sister or brother is considered an impossibility. Not even the mystic Kerfe Miwala could do it." She handed the pendant back to Kaura who quickly slipped it back over her head.

Lara took her hand.

"This pendant can probably do much more than protect you from being discovered by other Gifted people. What it is exactly, you'll have to find out for yourself. I don't know who or what you are. Only one thing is certain: you are not who you appear to be. Your energy is great, extraordinarily great. You are older than you look. And there is something else, something I can't quite put my finger on. But I see much good in you. Know, sister, that you are welcome in the Viranuk clan if you ever need shelter.

She pulled one of the silver bracelets from her wrist and gave it to Kaura.

"With this, you will receive free passage through all lands associated with us and the support of all allies of the Siberian Witch Nations. Use it wisely. Now you must go. And be careful. I hear there are High Inquisitors in the city. They also use magic, although they don't call it that. Those beings are dangerous."

Kaura bowed and let herself be shown out by Bellin. Atam trotted silently behind her.

The consul led them through a long maze of corridors lit by lamps floating in mid-air. The last corridor ended at a rough wooden door. The old man pushed it open, looked around warily for a moment, then shook her hand firmly in farewell.

As the heavy wooden door closed behind Kaura, she and Atam found themselves in a passageway between two market stalls, amidst the colorful hustle and bustle of the covered bazaar.

Deep in thought, she began to make her way back to the harbor. The sun was already hanging low over the rooftops. She had just under an hour until the fifth bell, when Captain McGregor planned to depart.

Five minutes later, she was back on the same main boulevard she had taken earlier.

Kaura recognized the statue of the naked flute player, around which fountains of bubbling water played and gurgled. Quickly, she crossed the square, determined to reach the *Pride* as soon as possible.

But apparently she had been observed, for a hand grabbed her roughly from behind. It belonged to a man dressed in a light green robe. He had a black, slicked back hair, a tonsure and a piercing stare.

"Stop, in the name of the Holy Inquisition!" he hissed. "You have been found entering the house of the witch heretic. What do you have to say for yourself, woman?"

Kaura remained calm this time.

"This is a free city where you have nothing to say, Spaniard. I go where I want to go. Now let go of me, or I'm going to call the City Guard."

The green-cloaked man waved his free hand wildly. He seemed to be calling for reinforcements.

"I am a servant of the High Inquisitor. He will examine you, wretched sinner! Maybe you are one of them dirty witches!"

Now Kaura had had enough. She grabbed the little finger of the hand holding her arm and bent it back with all her strength.

The monk let go with a shriek and tried to strike her with his other hand. Snarling, Atam grabbed the hem of his robe with his teeth and pulled, causing the man to lose his balance and fall to the ground in a tangle of green cloth. Some people looked over at them curiously, but none made a move to intervene in any way. Kaura simply turned and walked away. Inside, she was shaking. She had never been physically attacked before, and now they seemed to follow her everywhere.

"Come, Atam!" she ordered.

Only when she was several dozen feet away did she turn her head and look back. Beside the monk, who was slowly getting back to his feet, stood three other men. Two of them were armed with pistols—

and the third, two heads shorter than the others, wore a ruby red robe. She cursed softly, turned a corner, and then started running.

After hastily crossing several labyrinthine alleys and market streets, she was reasonably sure that no one was following her, and she slowed her pace.

She asked a cloth merchant for directions to the harbor and made it to the *Pride of Edinburgh* without further incident. Still breathing heavily, she boarded and reported herself and Atam back to the sentry.

"We're only waiting for Joe, then we can cast off. The goods are already loaded," the man informed her cheerfully.

In the officers' mess, she found Mikhail and Sir Elias, two mugs filled to the brim with rum on the table in front of them.

"Pour me one too," she demanded as she dropped into one of the heavy wooden chairs.

Mikhail readily obliged. In turn, she told them her story.

Sir Elias tilted his head in concern.

"You should not be seen outside again until we have left the harbor. Better safe than sorry. Soon half of Europe will be after you if this keeps up."

Mikhail grinned faintly.

"You really are very popular, Kaura. Hopefully you'll be less conspicuous in London."

The young woman made a face at the good-natured grin he gave her.

"Let's hope so. It hasn't been under my control so far. I'm just kind of hard to overlook, as it seems."

A few minutes later, the trampling of bare feet could be heard on the main deck. Something slapped audibly against the outside wall of the ship.

Then a sailor appeared in the mess hall and reported that Joe had returned and that the first mate had already begun preparations for leaving port, as ordered.

Sir Elias rose, gave a friendly nod to his two passengers, and went upstairs to supervise the casting-off maneuver.

A little later, Joe appeared. He looked rather battered. A thin trail of blood trickled from a small cut on his forehead.

"A more dangerous place than I thought it would be, Gothenburg," he joked weakly.

Kaura got to her feet anxiously and pushed him down onto a chair.

"Let me see that."

She breathed a sigh of relief. The wound was not deep nor otherwise serious and would heal quickly.

"What happened?" she asked.

Joe explained that three hooded men had ambushed him on his way back to the ship. According to his account, the three assailants now looked much worse than he did.

"Still, it didn't feel like it was just a street mugging," he said. "Certainly not in broad daylight! And the three of them were too well dressed. Possibly a kidnapping attempt. Sadly, I couldn't question any of them. I was just glad to get away with my skin on my back. Three against one. Got pretty close. I think they didn't want to hurt me seriously and held back a bit. That probably saved me."

* * *

In the Palace of the Spanish Legation, Gothenburg

A few miles from the departing galleon, which was now slowly gaining speed, two very different men faced each other. Don José de Gutierrez y Alariva was officially a special envoy of the Casa de Contratación, the imperial authority responsible for exploiting the conquered territories and bringing the stolen treasures to the Mediterranean.

Unofficially, however, he had a second role: he was one of the most important men in the Red Wing, a non-religious branch of the Inquisition that reported directly to the Sultan and aimed to extend Spanish-Ottoman power to world domination.

A stocky and somewhat chubby Andalusian, he made a jovial and always friendly impression on most people who met him for the first time. His direct subordinates had a different story to tell. Don José did not hesitate to go over dead bodies to achieve his goals. And that included even his closest associates—if they dared to disappoint his expectations.

Now the heavy man, dressed in the best purple brocade silk, leaned back against his desk, took a sip from the bejeweled wine goblet in his hand, and glared wickedly at his counterpart.

"So, you're telling me that Nelson got away from you, Señor. Escaped again, we must assume. As before, we have no word from the people you sent to Inmarsund to arrest and interrogate him."

The figure in the red robe stood completely still. There was no face to be seen under the all-concealing garment. Don José could not help but think that it was grinning maliciously at him from the darkness, as was always the case when he had to deal with the magical sector of the Holy Inquisition. He did not like these people. Neither the humans, nor those strange blue-skinned beings hiding under the robes.

They were using methods that they themselves outwardly condemned as diabolical. But they were useful. Very useful, in fact. And the end justified all means, as everybody knew, long live the Sultan!

"We were surprised by Nelson's presence in Gothenburg and had no time for lengthy planning," the Inquisitor whispered in his childish high-pitched voice. "We almost had him. He was lucky to escape our grasp. If he spends the night in town, we will have him tonight. Our men are checking all the inns and ships in the harbor."

Don José puffed excitedly.

"If he has already met our agents in Inmarsund, he will be warned and leave the city as soon as possible. Since we cannot reveal ourselves openly in Gothenburg and jeopardize the diplomatic pretense with the Viking government, we cannot have the harbor blocked. Perhaps we should declare him a criminal and put a bounty on him."

The Inquisitor shook his head. All his movements were excessively slow, a habit that nearly drove Don José to the point of hysteria at times.

"Then he will soon find out and be even more cautious. Besides, that way his family and the Scottish queen will know whom to thank when we finally find him. It would be better if he disappeared without a trace."

There was a pause. "Besides, it could be that my people in Inmarsund already have the key and only the Scotsman escaped. Then we can let him go."

Don José nodded.

"We'll see about that. The key is the most important thing. Using the key, our spies and later troops could finally be smuggled into Atlantis. Then we will be only a small step away from obtaining the Atlantean knowledge of the *devices*."

With piercing eyes, he looked at the Church envoy, who was a head shorter than himself. "No one will be able to resist the Spanish Empire once we have their war machines! They showed us enough of what they can do in the battle of Tenochtitlan. But we will have fewer qualms about using them than those white-haired weaklings who always seemed to try to spare the lives of our soldiers. We will finish off the Atlanteans and bring the treasures of their rich continent to Granada, to increase the glory of our Lord! And thanks to the Atlanteans' flying machines, we will also finally learn what is located in the white sector between the New World and the Philippines - God save the Sultan!"

His watery eyes blazed fanatically and he laughed softly. "Plenty of new sheep for your church, my friend, I suppose. And loads of gold for our Ruler."

He grinned broadly at the thought. "Well, let's see what your people report. You're dismissed."

Graciously he waved his hand.

The Inquisitor turned without a word and seemed to float away without a single visible footstep. In two hours he would be back with the report that the wanted man had left the harbor aboard a ship of the Nelson fleet before the Spanish agents had arrived.

Don José would have a fit of raging madness and then move quickly to make new plans.

* * *

North Sea, January 4, 1869 A.B..

By daybreak, the *Pride* was sailing through the Skagerrak between Kristiansand and the open North Sea. Land was nowhere in sight, and the sky was hazy, with a high, even cloud cover under which the horizon stood out sharply between the light gray sky and the dark gray sea.

Kaura had woken early and was standing next to Aran on the quarterdeck, chatting casually about the dangers of the ocean between Scandinavia and Britain.

"If the weather stays like this, we can count ourselves lucky," the first mate said. "With a good wind, we will reach the east coast of the Scottish mainland in a few days. Once we're in the Thames estuary, we'll have made it. But now is the time of winter storms. And this calm gives me the feeling that something is brewing, as it were.

Kaura nodded absently, trying to follow the whitecaps swirling in their wake until they disappeared into the wave troughs behind them.

Then the yell of the man in the lookout echoed down to the deck.

"Masttops ahead on the horizon! I can't make out any details yet. It seems to be a whole squadron. At least ten or eleven masts. Three to four ships, that is."

The first mate listened and turned to Kaura.

"Could you go knock on the master's door and ask him to come up? If it's Vikings, we have nothing to worry about. But as the customs officer in Helsingør has warned us, there do seem to be units of the Armada Fleet hanging around this area again of late."

She nodded and went down the companionway.

McGregor was already on his way. He seemed to have an infallible instinct and always knew at once when something unusual happened on deck.

When he was told what had happened, his scrunched face behind the red beard turned into a worried pile of wrinkles.

"Vikings don't usually come here with entire fleets," he grumbled. "We'll try to avoid them. Better safe than sorry. But they have the better winds. It will not be easy. Pyotr, drop two points to starboard," he shouted to the helmsman as he stepped onto the quarterdeck.

"Aye, aye, sir, two points north," the black-haired man confirmed.

Two hours later, it became clear that the evasive maneuver would not succeed. The sails on the horizon grew larger and larger. The captain had climbed up the main mast himself and watched the approaching formation through his spyglass. When he rejoined the group on the quarterdeck - Joe and Mikhail had also come up by then - he wore a somber expression.

"Spaniards," he said, cursing. "The crucifixes on the sails are unmistakable. Official ships of the Armada. We must assume they are looking for us. Mounted messengers could easily have reached Kristiansand from Inmarsund by now."

He turned to Aran.

"Bring the free watch on deck. We'll prepare for battle, but keep the gunports closed for now. I won't let the chestnut-eaters get close enough to trouble us, even at the risk of making them more suspicious. Not before we know if they're here for us."

Another hour later, the ships drew closer. They were a heavily armed war galleon and three smaller, maneuverable caravels. Even before they were within range, the *Pride's* crew was relieved of any doubt that the Spaniards were up to no good. There was a flash in the bow of the galleon. Thunderously, the shot from a fourteen-pounder cannon discharged, creating a huge fountain of spray about a hundred yards off the side of the Scottish galleon.

"That was the declaration of war," the burly captain grumbled between clenched teeth. "The caravels have already spread out. That's how they're going to attack us! We shall spoil their soup."

He bore away further so that the galleon was now speeding away from the enemy formation at a sharp angle. In this way, he hoped to gain more distance, but gave up the windward position, which would have been an invaluable advantage in the coming battle.

But neither he nor Kaura nor any of the other seafaring men aboard were deluding themselves. They would be lucky to survive this encounter unscathed. The four enemy ships vastly outnumbered and outgunned them, even if Sir Elias' crew had a reputation throughout the Nelson fleet as fighters who could even rival the Royal Navy.

The outermost of the ascending caravels was now almost within range. Then they made a mistake. The Spanish captain seemed to have either lost his nerve or miscalculated. He luffed, causing the caravel to turn broadside on the departing galleon. Then he gave the order to fire, which, distorted by the wind, was heard faintly on the Pride. About thirty yards behind the galleon, fountains of spray rose in a long line.

"Ha, missed!" yelled Aran, shaking his fist.

On the enemy caravel, the gun crews were already hard at work, cleaning and reloading the barrels while the ship turned back into the wind. The heavy, sooty stench of burnt black powder mingled with the fresh sea air that wafted across the deck of the Pride.

In the meantime, Sir Elias had already sent for the three crew members who were capable of handling the large, solid Scottish longbows made of oak that they had on board.

The Scots, all three of them from the Orkney Islands far to the north, all sporting wild red beards and eyes glittering with ferocity, had placed a basin of glowing charcoal between them to light the fuses of the fire arrows.

With a narrow trail of black smoke, the first of the arrows soared toward the caravel, which by now had resumed its pursuit. Immediately, a small flame blazed in the mainsail. Two Spaniards climbed into the rigging with a bucket to extinguish the fire. But now the arrows came almost every second.

One of the Scots picked up one of the special arrows with a powder-filled shaft. The Spaniards jumped wildly as the first of these projectiles hit the deck of the caravel and exploded with a primeval crack.

Soon the caravel was in a mess. Two sails were ablaze, and the crew had their hands full trying to put out the fires that flared up everywhere. The ship was rapidly falling behind.

Sir Elias heaved a sigh of relief.

"Now there are three left."

"Two," Aran corrected him. "The heavy hauler won't catch us anymore. Now it's paying off that we had to leave Inmarsund without cargo. We probably wouldn't have made it against that fire-breathing fortress. We stand a good chance against the caravels, though."

The captain nodded in agreement. Indeed, the Spanish-Ottoman war galleon, with cannons of the heaviest caliber protruding from her gunports spread over two battery decks, was falling farther and farther behind, even though the men in the glittering helmets on the quarterdeck had set every available scrap of cloth.

The two caravels, on the other hand, continued to catch up, but kept a wary distance. The fate of their sister ship had probably made them more cautious.

Nevertheless, they continued to close in on the galleon from both sides. The bowmen on the quarterdeck made another attempt. Indeed, a few arrows struck the enemy sailing to leeward. This time, however, the Spaniards were prepared and quickly extinguished the fires.

The caravel, on the other hand, sailing upwind, was still safe from the arrow fire, as the incendiaries had to fight the force of the breeze. The *Pride's* gun crews lurked behind the fourteen-pounders, eagerly awaiting the order to fire. But they knew they were still too far away for that.

Sir Elias had three of the guns loaded with higher-dose powder cartridges. This was a risk, as the tubes could burst and injure or kill the operators if they made a mistake.

However, the Galleon's gunner was an expert in his field. If anyone could assess the risk correctly, it was him.

The caravel to windward now sailed out of range, almost parallel to the *Pride*. It would not be long before the Spanish captain would pull in and open fire. Sir Elias would have to beat him to it.

"Ed, open fire at your discretion," he called to the gunner who was purposefully moving around the gun deck between his crews. "Shave off his mainstay if you can."

The brown-haired man from Liverpool in southwest Scotland nodded his assent and made the final adjustments to the three cannons prepared with larger gunpowder charges. He estimated the distance and the speed of the ship's rising and falling motion through the waves.

Then he lowered the fuse on the first cannon, and the gun discharged with a primeval boom. Ed was already at the next gunport, not caring about the success or failure of his shot. He lowered the firing pin again. Meanwhile it cracked and splintered in the distance.

Kaura narrowed her eyes. A direct hit in the side of the ship, just above the waterline.

The caravel was now approaching its own firing range. The *Pride's* second cannon boomed dully, then immediately the third.

The sound mingled with the crash of the enemy caravel's broadside.

Involuntarily, Kaura ducked behind the bulwark. Bursting and splintering sounds told her that the Spaniard had scored a hit. At the same time, she heard the howl of triumph down on the gundeck as the Scottish cannoneers watched the caravel's mainmast slowly topple and finally fall into the water with a huge splash on the starboard side of the ship.

The Spaniard immediately ran off course as the men scurried around trying to cut the rigging and keep the ship from tipping over. The caravel fell back quickly.

"You did it, Ed!" the men shouted, enthusiastically slapping the modestly smiling piecemaster's shoulders with their calloused hands.

Meanwhile, the captain just laughed grimly.

"Another clean job, Ed! Now let's get the other one so he doesn't follow us all the way to London."

He luffed further, putting the Pride in an excellent firing position, with the Spaniard in the target area of his starboard broadside, while the latter could not reach him with his own without slowing down himself.

The captain of the third caravel reacted quickly, but not quickly enough. Four bullets from the Scotsman punched a neat row of bullet holes right in the waterline of the Spanish ship. It immediately took on water and began to list. Further pursuit was out of the question.

"They'll have to go into their boats soon, Captain," Aran commented.

Sir Elias shrugged.

"Leave them to it. Those guys have started shooting first, after all. And their friends over there can pick them up."

He pointed to the big man-of-war, which was plowing heavily through the sea and had caught up a bit by now, but was still far out of firing range. The *Pride* would be able to shake it off easily if they bore away northwest with the wind.

If necessary, they would reach Scotland a little further north than planned and follow the coast all the way to the Thames estuary. The Spanish would certainly not dare follow the merchantman into waters controlled by Queen Elizabeth's troops.

The ship's carpenter had already examined the damage and reported that nothing of importance had been destroyed.

The damage to the bulwark, the bowsprit and one of the sails, where an enemy bullet had punched a frayed hole, could be repaired in a short time with onboard resources.

The Spanish war galleon followed the Pride's wake for some time, falling farther and farther behind, until, after about two hours, it bore away toward the Danish coast.

5

Lockwood College

Six stormy days on the North Sea later, even the most hardened crew members were glad to see the tip of Scotland's east coast emerge from the haze. Kaura and McGregor were among the few who weren't at least a little pale.

The sun stood as a white-yellow halo behind the banks of high fog.

Behind the galleon, to the northwest, the black storm clouds with which the ship and its crew had become intimately acquainted over the past few days still loomed.

Now the winter wind sang evenly in the billowing sails, and even the creaking of the ship's rigging had a soothing rather than alarming effect on the exhausted souls aboard, who had barely had time to sleep during the past few days.

Joe and Kaura stood side by side on the quarterdeck, Atam at their feet. The petite woman in her heavy winter furs had an arm around the tall Scot's waist, enjoying the moment of peace.

For the time being, no one had anything to do. That would soon change when they passed the tip of the headland and had to sail against the wind in the direction of the Thames estuary.

Joe pointed to the left.

"See that lighter spot on the shore? That's Margate. As a child, I often spent months at a time on our nearby country estate when my parents felt I shouldn't be constantly exposed to London's pollution. I would often wander the woods alone for hours, talking to the squirrels and hugging the trees.

Kaura chuckled as she imagined the muscled fighter Joe hugging trees.

"And, did they answer? The squirrels? Or even the trees?"

She looked at him from under half lowered eyelids. An attractive man. Under other circumstances, she might have proposed to him long ago. But the Scots were mostly monogamous and had little understanding for the need for freedom of Nordic women. Well, she could talk to him about it sometime.

A pleasant warmth spread through her lower abdomen at the thought.

He gave her a serious look.

"Maybe you'll laugh, but they did. Sometimes. There are more things between heaven and earth than we can imagine. And even those of us who are not Gifted have ways of perceiving more things in the world than if we were walking around with our eyes closed."

She nodded in agreement, watching the blurry white patches of sail that stood out sharply against the slightly darker background of the coastline. Probably fishing boats.

"Tell me more about your conversations with the trees some day. I would like that. When do you think we will reach London?"

"We should be there by tomorrow afternoon. We'll dock at Southend tonight and wait for the tide to turn. "

His face took on a dreamy expression.

"Your first time, right? At least, as far as your memory goes. I think you'll like it. One of the world's great cities, up there with Granada, Constantinople and mystical Bombay. A grimy behemoth, unfortunately, but the entire world meets here. Our real capital, Edinburgh, to the north, is much prettier. Nevertheless, all the threads come together here in the south. That's why Queen Elizabeth usually resides at her palace in Westminster."

Kaura did not answer. Her eyes were fixed on something far away in the distance.

Joe looked at her from the side. Her soft features and full, soft lips would never give away what a tough woman she could be at times. And at the same time, what a warm and fluid lover she was when she opened up to him.

This being was full of contrasts, he thought. And that was what fascinated him about her. Under her heavy winter coat, she wore simple wool-lined trousers of waxed canvas, on her feet simple sailor boots. In profile, with her slightly rounded, delicate nose and her black eyebrows, each tiny hair perfectly in place, she looked exactly as he had always imagined an Oriental princess from India or Arabia to be like.

In his still short but eventful life, he had met a few women who had been that. None of them had fit the cliché as perfectly as Kaura, however. And even the clear, dark green patterned eyes did not disrupt the impression in any way. Moreover, she seemed almost ageless. At first glance, she seemed to be somewhere in her mid-twenties, a determined young woman. And she acted the part. But sometimes, when Joe looked into her eyes for more than a moment, he thought he saw more experience there than could be accumulated in a human lifetime. Even the Queen herself, old Lissy, didn't have that much depth in her gaze.

When Kaura caught his gaze, she smiled.

"Who do you see, the woman or the witch?" she asked.

"Both," he replied. "And a few others more. You are an extremely complex person, Kaura. More than you realize yourself, I think."

To port, the south bank of the Thames estuary began to emerge more clearly from the haze. Kaura looked with interest at the small fishing villages of gray, brick-built stone houses that dotted the shore at regular intervals.

"Densely populated," she muttered.

Joe nodded.

"Scotland will probably want to expand beyond the British Isle at some point. I just hope our government will do a better job of it than the Spanish-Ottoman Empire. It's not a solution to just annex territories, enslave the natives because you think they're inferior beings, and then ship all the wealth home to balance your own national budget."

Kaura took a deep breath. The subject was particularly upsetting to her because she had spent the last five years in a colony ruled by the Spanish Sultan.

"True, they did not enslave us. But imperialism is never a reasonable solution. And what happened to me alone shows that the Spaniards are slowly taking over our culture and trying to impose theirs on us. Next they'll abolish matriarchy and polyamory, you'll see! By merging with the Ottoman Empire after the Battle of Lepanto, the Iberians have become even more male-dominated. They would have tried it long ago if they hadn't known that it would cause a revolution!"

She had unconsciously raised her voice and shouted the words into the wind. Some of the men in the crew gave her openly admiring glances, while others seemed more uncertain.

The short adopted Immarsundian took a deep breath and tried to calm herself. A little more quietly she continued.

"I still don't understand why the Atlanteans don't intervene and just tolerate the Spanish expansion for decades. Only when they attacked the Aztecs, who are directly related to them, did the Crystal Princes deign to stop them. And then they just walked away. They don't seem to care about the rest of the world. As long as they don't have to let anyone onto their glorious islands!"

She looked directly into Joe's eyes as he stood next to her. "That reminds me of something. The Spaniard in Inmarsund said they knew that you had been to Atlantis. Does that mean you were really there? And I don't mean in the trading zones of Imelin and Moraniu. Really inside the country?"

He sighed.

"It took you a long time to remember. Mikhail asked me about it days ago. Yes, I was there. In Atlantia. And in the Misty Mountains. I had to take an oath not to tell anyone what I saw. I'm sorry." He looked away.

Kaura looked at him carefully. She knew how serious Joe was about his promises. She wouldn't be able to make him break an oath. And of course she didn't want to.

"Just tell me this," she pleaded with him. "Is there anything among the things you are not supposed to tell me that might shed some light on my heritage?"

She swallowed. Despite the warm welcome she had received from the Leivenstein family, the feeling of not belonging anywhere still weighed on her beyond all reason.

Sometimes she would wake up in the middle of the night, drenched in sweat, remembering dreams where she was attending crowded dances and no one even noticed her, everyone was turning away. Somehow that felt even worse than the dreams of her struggling to survive on the grate in the waves before the Leivensteins' ship had found her and Atam and taken them aboard.

Joe thought for a moment. Then he shook his head.

"I've had the same question in my mind. I don't see any direct connection between you and my experiences in Atlantis. I also don't believe that you are originally Atlantean, even though you speak the language so perfectly. Their mages look, well, very different. At least the ones I've seen."

She nodded and left it at that.

Two hours later, they docked at Southend, where they called to register with the local authorities and to wait for the next incoming tide to sail up the River Thames. The mood among the crew was one of joy and anticipation as they approached their home port.

Shortly after the mooring maneuver, an officer of the Scottish Crown dressed in a red tunic came aboard with some soldiers to inspect the ship's cargo and question the crew.

The reason he gave for the unusually sharp inspection was that a ship carrying Spanish spies had entered London without being spotted just the week before. Three of the men had been arrested when they tried to attach a barrel of gunpowder to the Tower Pier. It was still unclear how many passengers had been on the ship. As a result, the entire kingdom was on high alert.

The officer was duly impressed by Joe Nelson's presence. With the assurance that the ship would be allowed to proceed unhindered to the Nelsons' docks in London, he and his companions departed.

Despite the uncertainty, much of the crew was given shore leave that evening.

Kaura stayed aboard with her companions. However, she asked the first mate to make some discreet inquiries about Pyrrha. Near the river ferry pier of the small town at the mouth of the Thames was a tavern called *The Happy Hedgehog*, which was known as a trading post for all sorts of information by sailors and locals alike.

Aran agreed and left the ship with fifteen men. They were happily chatting and laughing.

"Some proper Scottish beer at last," she overheard.

And "Have you ever met Lisa, the waitress at the Golden Sheep?

I hear she's almost as beautiful as our passenger. Only she has bigger breasts. And she is said to be much more approachable..."

Silence fell over the docks as the sailors disappeared into a side alley.

For a while, the only sound was the gurgling and sloshing of water against the side of the ship, drifting in small eddies towards the North Sea with the still outgoing tide. A dog barked in the distance. The mooring lines that secured the galleon to the pier creaked softly.

In the gathering darkness, Kaura could make out the sails of several coastal ships as whitish shadows, all following the same course to the northeast.

It was an image of profound peace. She would miss this serenity once they arrived in London.

In her mind, Kaura went through the list of things she wanted to tackle in the great city.

She needed to learn more about Pyrrha and how to get there. She also had to find out how to control her gift. She no longer wanted to leave it to chance and experiment to decide if she'd survive her next encounter with the Inquisitors, which was bound to happen sooner or later.

Her delicate fingers touched the silver bracelet the Siberian witch had given her. Maybe she should have tried to reach the nations in the north directly from Gothenburg. No matter how dangerous their initiation rituals might be. Maybe the hoop Lara had given her would have made it easier to get to the important people without having to go through the usual paths...

Annoyed at herself, she shook her head.

"Could have, would have, should have - you can't make anything out of that," she muttered. "No, I'm in the right place. It'll all work out."

By the afternoon of the next day, London was coming into view in front of the tall ship's bowsprit. Thousands of columns of smoke, rising almost straight into the cloudless winter sky from the chimneys, foundries, tanneries, and all the other proofs of human industry and entrepreneurship found here, formed a brownish-yellow cloud over the city, visible for miles around.

Aran had returned late in the evening. He had learned little of value about Pyrrha. It had turned out that even many of the sailors who had traveled far and wide in the Mediterranean considered the city a mere legend. The others, for the most part, were merely passing on rumors. There were said to be triangular stone buildings several miles high. Others spoke of talking animals, floating galleons, and entrances to the bowels of the earth. The rumors also agreed that no one had ever entered the city and returned, though no one could explain then how the "eyewitness" accounts of the strange city's peculiarities had reached the outside world.

Kaura dismissed most of what she heard as the exaggerated stories of imaginative yarn spinners. She knew, however, that even such stories were usually based on a more or less large kernel of truth.

Now she was on deck with the crew, watching as they approached the unofficial capital of the Caledonian Empire.

London left no one indifferent. The sounds of the city surrounded the ship like a humming cloud of human activity. Metal clanged against metal. Steam hissed. Merchants shouted. Sails fluttered in the wind as they were hoisted or lowered.

A distorted trumpet sounded from the castle ahead on the ship's starboard side as the galleon glided slowly upriver toward the Nelson family's Quays. The Tower of London had been the Queen's former city residence before Westminster Palace was built.

Street urchins waved from the shore, noblemen in colored silks glanced at the *Pride* before turning back to their businesses. Smells of smoke, tanned hides, feces, roasted meat, and oriental spices drifted over to the ship and blended together in a mixture that was difficult to describe, sometimes inspiring, sometimes nauseating.

Civilization, Kaura thought. It smelled like civilization.

The smell brought back premonitions, memories like islands far beyond the horizon, invisible but so palpable that there was no doubt they were there.

Had she been here before? Or in another settlement of comparable size? She did not know. Something here seemed familiar, though.

Joe noticed her thoughtfulness. Full of verve, he bounced toward her. His enthusiasm was plain to see.

"Home!" He sighed happily. "Look at this! The greatest city in the world! Okay, Cuzco, the Inca capital, is supposed to be even bigger. And Atlantia has no competition anyway. But no place *smells* like London!"

He gleefully inhaled the air, which had just taken on the pungent smell of mixed sewage that was flowing from a nearby drainage canal into the Thames, leaving a dark stain that stood out clearly against the muddy brown river water.

The Scotsman made a face.

"Well, not just pleasant, of course. But this intensity! Feel it! The vibration of humanity. Here you get everything! You can experience everything! Meet everyone! Find ships that will take you anywhere! You can see the latest inventions from all the countries of the world! The Ottomans may think they are the masters of the world with their conquests. But *we* have the best connections!"

On the shore, there were now more and more warehouses, indicating that they were approaching the docks and offices of the large trading companies.

The galleon luffed and glided in an elegant arc to port, toward a large cluster of massive red-brick buildings.

Only a short distance upstream, the city seemed to have grown over the river. On about twenty irregularly shaped stone arches stood houses, each of which in Inmarsund would have been matched at most by the largest of the merchant's kontors.

Joe made an all-encompassing hand gesture.

"The London Bridge! Shortly after the Romans founded the city over a thousand years ago, there was a bridge here. Grown a bit since then, of course. Over a hundred shops. Homes. Mills. Of course, you can also use it to get across the river. Between the houses there is a tunnel-like passage. Unfortunately it is constantly jammed. Too many people. Those who can afford it take one of the many ferryboats."

With a slight jerk, the Pride of Edinburgh touched the dock. Thick loops made of rope had been placed across the bulwark to cushion the ship's grinding against the rough-hewn stone. The galleon had already been spied, and longshoremen were on hand to take up the mooring lines that had been thrown ashore.

Shouts of welcome rang out.

From a doorway on the side of one of the brick houses, a well-dressed woman in her thirties stepped out with a measured stride and raised her hand in greeting. She was blonde, blue-eyed, and a line of freckles ran across her pale nose, clearly visible in the light of the winter sun.

"Abigail Andrews, the administrator of the Nelson port facilities," Mikhail remarked, standing on the quarterdeck with the other passengers and the ship's command, watching the maneuver. "A capable woman. Good to see her again."

And with an appraising sideways glance at Kaura, he added, "I think you'll like her. You're quite similar in many ways, I'd say."

With a rumble, the plank leading from the deck of the galleon down to the breakwater was laid and secured.

The steward approached with a few energetic steps and called to the captain.

"Hello, Elias! Good to see you. Can I come aboard?"

Even as he finished his inviting gesture, the soles of her leather boots already touched the deck with a hard clack, and she clambered up the companionway to the quarterdeck.

A friendly smile appeared on her freckled face.

"You're back early." With a fluid motion, she slid closer to Joe and kissed him on the mouth.

Kaura looked at her in surprise. After a few long moments, the Scottish woman pulled away.

"Not that I'm unhappy about it," she added before turning to Kaura.

"I am Abigail. Responsible for everything that goes on here at the Nelson *Kontor*. Welcome."

Joe slid in between them, still with a slightly dreamy expression on his face. He put his hand on Kaura's arm and winked at the port administrator.

"This is my friend Kaura from Inmarsund. Abigail has already introduced herself. We've known each other a long time."

It wasn't quite clear if he meant Kaura or Abigail.

Kaura smiled warmly and took both of the Scotswoman's hands in hers.

"Any friend of Joe's is a friend of mine," she said.

Abigail's gray-blue eyes lit up with amusement.

"I've heard a lot about the customs of the Baltic matriarchy. We should have a woman-to-woman talk sometime. I'd be interested."

She turned back to Joe, and her expression went from friendly-intimate to businesslike-professional in a matter of seconds.

Kaura wondered how she did it. All of a sudden she was transformed, a completely different woman.

"Have you received the shipment of Northern Mongolian wool bales in Inmarsund? My buyer is eagerly awaiting them. Our farms in the Highlands can no longer meet the demand. Since the Atlantic steel silk producers have stopped delivering, even higher quality garments are again being ordered from ordinary wool. The spinning mills..."

"You'll have to find another solution for that," Joe interrupted gravely. "We had to leave Inmarsund with no cargo. The Spaniards have caused us some unforeseen problems."

Abigail's eyes darkened.

"I was afraid of such a thing. It was bound to happen sooner or later. With Scottish corsairs causing more and more trouble for the Spanish gold convoys in the Atlantic, and apparently now in the Caribbean as well, countermeasures are only too understandable. The privateer galleons are not official ships of the crown, but they do have letters of marque from the Queen. The Sultan in Granada will be unhappy about that."

Joe nodded in agreement.

"Yes. But that's not it - at least not yet. They're after me personally, it seems. We'll tell you more about that later. For now, let's go to the office. Do you have a carriage across the river that can take us to Nelson House?"

"Yes. Whenever you're ready."

After a fond farewell to Sir Elias and Aran, the three companions who had escaped from Inmarsund followed the Scotswoman through the docks. Atam trotted behind them, his broad head held high, sniffing in all directions.

Joe carried his duffel bag by himself over his shoulder.

Kaura smiled.

That was typical for this man. Anyone else of his standing would probably have brought a couple of huge sea chests, carried by half a dozen servants. After all, as a member of one of the most influential families in the country, he was something like a nobleman, and he had been knighted by the Queen. Surely he had access to the highest circles.

And here he was, leisurely strolling through a busy port area, greeting some of the dockworkers personally here and there, and discussing business with the port administrator - with whom he probably also slept as a matter of course.

Idly trotting behind Mikhail, Kaura wondered how many playmates the handsome merchant's son had. She would ask him if the opportunity arose. She laughed softly. It was a good thing the people of Inmarsund didn't think much of exclusive one-on-one relationships, she thought to herself. Otherwise she would have probably been jealous right now. Well. Was she really not jealous?

She considered for a moment.

No, obviously not. It was too clear to her how much he valued his freedom - she was exactly the same and didn't want to limit herself. And when they were together, it couldn't have been better.

Half an hour later, everything had been arranged. Kaura and Joe hugged Mikhail goodbye, as he had relatives in the city and wanted to stay with them until he was assigned a new task within the "Company".

Joe had generously compensated him for the inconveniences he had suffered, and also offered to have a ship sailing under another flag pick up his personal belongings from Inmarsund.

Mikhail had smiled, thanked him, and remarked that if a position opened up at a Nelson trading post in the Caribbean, he would be interested. Life on the Baltic coast had been getting too cold for him anyway, he said.

At the pier there was a small harbor sloop that would take the travelers across the Thames to the center of the city.

Carefully, Kaura climbed down into the rocking boat and let Joe pass Atam down to her. The dog allowed him to do so with astonishing equanimity.

As soon as the young Scotsman had followed, the watermen pushed off from the small pier, weaving vigorously through the dense boat traffic to the other shore. There, a sleek black carriage awaited them.

The driver was already standing on the bank as they landed, taking their luggage from the boaters.

"Welcome back, Mr. Nelson," he said with a slight bow. "Straight to Nelson House, sir?"

Joe nodded and thanked the man before they both climbed into the back of the vehicle.

Atam followed with a bold leap and Joe closed the door behind him.

To the snorting of the horses and the creaking of the leather wheel suspensions, the carriage lurched upstream along the banks of the river, in the direction of Westminster.

Kaura's teeth chattered; the thick, plush upholstery of the bench seat absorbed only a fraction of the vibrations as the metal-covered wooden wheels bounced and swayed over the cobblestones, and with each larger bump, the dog sitting on the bench beside her was thrown against her.

"Well, there are more comfortable ways to get around," she grumbled. "Couldn't we have gone on horseback? Or just walk?"

Joe grinned.

"Sure. We could have taken a direct boat, as well. We've got a backyard where we can dock. I just like to feel the city in my butt when I haven't been here for a while. Don't worry, it's not far."

He pointed out the window.

"Look, these are the headquarters of the big trading corporations –the Muscovy Company, the Turkey Company, and over there, the big house, the East India Company. Founded only last year. My grandfather is on its board of directors."

Kaura leaned out of the window. The carriage was now passing through the most densely populated areas of the medieval city center. The hustle and bustle of people, animals and companions was breathtaking.

In fact, the whole world seemed to converge here. Arab merchants in long white robes. Indian men in colorful turbans and women in long, glittering saris of bright silk.

Atlantean travelers in their simple, mostly beige or brown linen dresses and with short white hair. Tanned Mongolian envoys with their distinctive almond-shaped eyes.

At an intersection, a palanquin with an armed, red-robed escort made its way. The crowd gave way respectfully.

"The Queen?" asked Kaura with a curious sideways glance at the scene.

"No, just a high-ranking member of Parliament, I think," Joe replied. "The Queen would cause more of a stir."

Fifteen minutes later, the street were becoming less crowded. Some of the houses were set back about a hundred feet from the street, and behind the walls one could glimpse gardens with mature trees whose tops gave the residents of the stately homes some privacy in the midst of the bustling city.

As the carriage turned left into a courtyard, Joe pointed further down the street.

"That's Westminster over there. It's where the Queen lives when she's in town."

A gatekeeper armed with a musket and dressed in black and gold livery raised his hand in greeting as the carriage thundered past, and then slowed down sharply. They came to a shuddering halt in a large yard paved with multicolored cobblestones. The pavement bore the Nelson family crest—a roaring lion in red on a green and white background.

Behind it rose a house that would undoubtedly have been called a palace in Inmarsund, but here could be considered one of the smaller mansions. Its facade was lavishly decorated with finely carved stone work and gleaming white marble statues, which represented Hellenic and Asian deities. To the left and right of the sweeping stairs leading up to the front gate, two mighty oaks, now completely leafless, towered up into the sunny winter sky.

Joe didn't wait for the coachman to dismount, but unlocked the door from the inside and swung out onto the pavement with an elegant leap.

He gallantly held out his hand to Kaura, and she accepted it with a slightly ironic smile.

"Thank you for offering your strong arm to a weak woman, my good man."

He almost choked. Cackling, he replied, still half laughing,

"Welcome to the humble little house of the Nelsons, noble lady of the weaker sex. My house is your house, or so it would seem. Of course, I don't really own it. Ah, there's Jane."

An elegantly dressed, gray-haired woman of about fifty came toward them. Joe gave her a tumultuous hug.

"Mother, may I present Kaura. A dear friend from Inmarsund. She's run into some trouble with the Spaniards and decided to come along. Kaura, this is Jane Olivia Nelson, my mother, and the good spirit of the house. Even though the men are officially the head of the family in our clan, nothing happens in the wide world of Nelson Enterprises that this woman doesn't know about and play a major role in shaping.

Jane laughed.

"Joe is exaggerating, as usual. Our company has grown far too large for any one person to keep track of it all. Still, it's true, we're all one big family here. And my dear son here is doing his part to hold it all together.

She winked. "And not just with his amorous escapades."

Joe pretended to be insulted.

"Mother! What will Kaura think of me?"

Jane laughed, a bell-bright, carefree sound, and stroked the head of Atam, who sniffed at her curiously.

"As far as I know, the Baltic cities basically invented open marriage, so to speak. At the very least, an active love life shouldn't frighten someone from these parts too much. Come in. You must be hungry. I'll have something prepared for you. And there's hot water for a bath today, too."

She beckoned Kaura to follow her and disappeared into the Gothic archway with a rustle of her blue silk robe.

It took Kaura a moment to collect herself. At least now she knew where Joe got his easygoing ways. Back in Inmarsund, the family of the town clerk was more pretentious than any of these people.

She wondered how that would work out at the Scottish Royal Court. Maybe they behaved differently there, probably surrounded by a hundred snooty old nobles, all vying for Queen Elizabeth's favor. Perhaps.

In the foyer, which was also opulently decorated with Buddha statues and black marble with gold trim, a servant met her and showed her to her guest suite. The suite consisted of a bedroom and a drawing room.

Floor-to-ceiling windows opened onto a narrow terrace from which she could look out over the riverside natural garden. Here, above the main part of the city, the Thames was still a silvery blue ribbon, seeming almost untouched by the filth that was dumped into it further downriver.

When she had unloaded her few belongings, the servant, dressed in the black and gold of the Nelson's house, led her to the bath-house. The facilities were available to all residents of the house. That was where she also found Joe. Her boyfriend was already lounging comfortably in a huge marble tub filled with steaming water.

He gestured to a row of sinks where soap bars and white linen rags were carefully stacked in neat piles.

"You can clean yourself there. And then you can warm up in the hot pot. We are lucky. The water is heated like this only twice a week, even in winter. Or on request. Normally, there's just the little jugs of hot and cold water to rinse off."

He went underwater for a moment, and when he surfaced, he continued talking. A curtain of glistening water threads flowed from his long blond hair.

"The idea for the hot water pool came to my great-granduncle George after he returned from a trade mission to Cipangu, beyond Mongolia. Apparently, they pipe hot water directly into the pools from thermal springs in the ground. Here we have to heat it with fire.

He grunted with pleasure while Kaura also stripped off her clothes and doused herself with warm water from one of the jugs set up next to the fire.

"You can just leave the clothes on the bench there. The servants will wash them and bring them to your rooms. There are bathrobes in the closet."

When Kaura had rinsed off the foaming, jasmine scented soap with lukewarm water, she padded over to the hot water basin, which could have comfortably held five or six people.

At first she contorted her face in pain as she felt the hot water, then she let herself slide all the way in with a soft moan and gave in to the intoxicating sensation of being properly warmed for the first time in weeks.

* * *

At the same time in the Palace of the Holy Inquisition, Granada

The headquarters of the Holy Inquisition was located on Calle Pagés in Granada, the capital of the Spanish Ottoman Empire. It was a short walk from the Alhambra, where Sultan Philip II directed the affairs of his sprawling empire.

Eleven figures in ruby robes sat cross-legged in a circle on the floor of the large, dimly lit hall deep inside the building.

None spoke.

The dark oak panels on the walls and the plain, grey marble floor conveyed an oppressive heaviness.

The only bit of light was a glimmer of the winter sun, feeble now for these latitudes, which filtered through a large skylight three stories above the silent group, revealing only the outline of their hoods.

One of the figures raised a hand.

"The circle is open," she whispered.

"It is open!" rang out from ten childlike, high-pitched throats.

"Let us now close the circuit and send out the call," murmured the being who obviously had some sort of leadership position in this group, though outwardly he was no different from the others.

The breathing of those present deepened, became audible. Fiery red columns of light rose from the open palms of the eleven cowl-wearers, joining together to form a glowing, billowing circle that lit up the somber, blue-skinned faces under the hoods with an eerie glow.

Eleven columns of light wound their way toward the center of the circle like the undulating spokes of a wagon wheel. As they converged, a sound resembling the droning of a heavy gong rang out.

In the red glow of the center of the circle, a shadow began to solidify.

"We live to serve you, Master," the eleven voices whispered in unison. Now the figure in the center was becoming clearly visible.

There stood an elderly man of slender build, in an upright, almost arrogant posture. He wore a yellow cloak of silky shimmering fabric, draped around him like one of the togas that ancient Roman statues wore. His hair was silvery white and fell behind him to just above his waist. His face was pale, and he had pale blue eyes, with no visible iris, but completely filled, like those of a seal.

The stranger wore a mask-like, slightly condescending smile on his face, which grew a little deeper as he looked around.

"Well, we haven't made much progress so far." His voice was deep and melodious, revealing that this man - this being - was used to giving orders. "So, you would do well to improve your serving skills a bit more. I will have to take care of everything myself again."

He paused. "The Inquisitors who were supposed to take over the key-bearer have failed."

A murmur of surprise went through the circle as the man continued unperturbed.

"One of the *Sareitha* slaves was drawn back to me through the inner field and could be interrogated while she was waiting for her new host body. She was defeated by a northern witch whose name we do not yet know. This witch saved the Keyholder and helped him escape. Unfortunately, we do not know where they are now. We must assume that the bearer is back in Scotland."

The leader bowed until his forehead touched the ground.

"We will inform our spies in London immediately. We live to serve you, Master!"

The white-haired man nodded.

"Good. One more thing. I need more *Sareitha'alan*. We no longer have enough Gifted females. We're going through them faster than expected, since the extractable essence is getting weaker. Send me a hundred new candidates in two weeks, through the usual channels."

The face under the ruby robe swallowed.

"My lord, we have already had several searches of the areas under our control. All the Gifted have either been captured or escaped."

The man in the middle glared at the speaker with his large, watery-blue eyes.

"Then send troops into the border areas. There must be enough shamans among the Incas and in Central Africa to take. Or try the Scots. Our spy in Lockwood might be able to help. Be creative. I'll punish you first if you don't deliver."

"Yes, Lord. We live to serve you," murmured the one so rebuked.

"Also, make sure there is still a great deal of interest in the conquest of Atlantis at court and in the imperial administration," the white-haired man continued. "The Sultan must be absolutely certain that only the alchemical devices available there can assure him of complete world domination. The Atlanteans must be kept on the defensive to distract them from figuring out our true plans."

The pale figure turned away. "I expect unconditional and immediate success. When you have the key-bearer, put him on a ship to Alexandria immediately and notify me in the usual way."

Suddenly he disappeared, and the air of the room filled the place where he had just been with a loud swoosh.

The Inquisitors were silent. They were thinking. Then they rose and left the room without a word, one after the other. Each one knew what he had to do.

Outside, the wintry afternoon sun lay low over the snow-capped peaks of the Sierra Nevada. The hustle and bustle of the Spanish-Ottoman capital took its colorful course, with no one suspecting what dark machinations were being hatched in the gloomy building on Calle Pagés.

* * *

London, January 18, 1869 A.B.

Kaura used her elbows and shoulders to push her way through the crowd. One hand clutched her purse, which was tucked into the front of her belt under her cape. London Bridge was prime territory for pickpockets and bag thieves of all stripes. The narrow tunnel under the overhanging wooden buildings was always crowded with people shoving in both directions.

On top of that, a flock of sheep was just being driven into the city. The bleating, stressed animals were heading in the same direction as she was. They probably sensed that their end was near in one of the city's many slaughterhouses.

Sighing, Kaura vowed never to take that route across the Thames again. In the future, she would always hire one of the watermen to take her across in comfort.

She had gone to the famous Globe Theatre over in Southwark to see the new play by the most fashionable playwright at the moment, Shakespeare. It was a tragedy about Julius Caesar, the Roman emperor and main antagonist of the first Buddhist conquerors.

Now she was exhausted, inspired, happy and sad at the same time. She wondered if drama really was, really had to be, an inescapable component of human life. She herself did not feel that her life was a drama, although it was not without its dark moments. Things happened, she dealt with them, life went on. It was that simple.

Sometimes she thought that all suffering in life came from resenting things that had already happened, or from the fear that the future would not turn out the way she wanted it to. Well, of course, she wasn't immune to that either.

Still, she was proud of herself for being able to simply enjoy the beauties of life for the most part, instead of getting lost in thoughts of what could have been, what she should have done, what would be the right course to take.

All of a sudden, she felt a hard shove on her shoulder that almost knocked her to the ground. She had been distracted and bumped into someone.

A woman in front of her had stopped to avoid a tangle of sheep being forcibly pushed one by one by a shepherd through a narrow gap on the sidewalk, created by a wheelbarrow.

The woman–the girl, Kaura corrected herself, since her counterpart was hardly more than seventeen years old–looked at her out of wise hazel eyes, without a hint of reproach in her gaze. Her brunette hair formed a tangled quiff across her forehead, giving her an air of lively sass.

"Sorry," Kaura muttered, looking away and wanting to keep walking.

Then she turned around when she felt the girl tug gently on her sleeve.

"You're one of us, aren't you? I'm Loren. Forgive me for approaching you like this. But one doesn't often meet other witches outside of Oxford!"

Kaura smiled back. She liked the other woman right away.

"I am not from here. Yes, I am also Gifted. My name is Kaura. How did you know that, by the way?"

Loren raised her eyebrows.

"Can't you tell? She smiled smugly. "My master says I'm better at it than any witch she's ever known. True, your glow is quite weak and probably hard for others to see. That means you're probably more spiritually endowed than with terrestrial magic. But it is there. So, you are one of us."

Kaura stared at her. Then she gave herself a jolt. The tunnel in front of her was now clear again, passers-by pushing past them on all sides and showering the two women who had stopped in their tracks with hefty curses.

"I'd like to talk to you sometime, Loren. Where can I find you?"

"I won't be in town much longer. My internship in London is almost over. I'm going back to Oxford the day after tomorrow to continue my studies. Until then, I'm staying at the Westminster branch of the Lockwood Society. Come and see me tomorrow at noon! We can have lunch together."

Loren smiled at her and disappeared into the crowd.

Back at the Nelson house, Kaura was almost swept off her feet by Atam, who was enthusiastically wagging his tail. The dog had made himself at home in the house and especially in the adjoining garden, forming an almost inseparable team with the house's three cats.

Kaura had sent a short letter to Aalyjah on the next ship to Inmarsund via the Leivensteins' London office. It basically said no more than that she was fine. Although she was quite sure that the letter would not be intercepted, she had refrained from giving any details about her whereabouts. She would send a messenger to the branch office from time to time to find out if a reply had arrived.

In the drawing room, she met Jane and her father, Mercurio, the official head of the Nelson clan. The old man was a real roughneck, having spent half his life at sea himself. He was friendly towards her, but rather reserved. Kaura had the impression that the many women in his grandson's life worried him. But he would never admit that directly, being an old sailor. Her guess was that he, too, had once had a lover in every port.

Jane's welcoming hug nearly squeezed the air out of her lungs.

Kaura immediately asked what they knew about Oxford and the Lockwood Guild, and she told them both about her encounter with Loren.

"Witches!" grumbled old Nelson. "Nice gals, aging well, but far too full of themselves! I knew one once..."

His daughter interrupted him firmly.

"Your adventures with the love-struck Welsh mountain witch are probably not what the girl is expecting us to tell her right now."

She shot Kaura an apologetic sideways glance. "That Welsh sorceress made quite an impression on him back then. Once he starts talking about it, he can't stop for hours."

She sighed and gave her patriarch an indulgent look. "So, the witches and wizards. Until a little over a thousand years ago, the south of Britain was said to be ruled entirely, or at least in part, by Gifted ones. This ruling clan around the immortal Merlin Silvercloak then left England for reasons unknown, and the Scottish monarchs extended their kingdom to include us here in the south. Where Merlin went, nobody knows. Some say he originally came from Atlantis and returned there. Others believe he and his people left Britain because of a lost conflict with the Atlanteans. In any case, the present-day magical societies of Greater Scotland are, as far as I know, the descendants of the Druidic tribal shamans of the Caledonians, who practiced a somewhat different kind of sorcery than the ancient High Mages, and in particular, traditionally belonged to the priestly rather than the ruling class. The Druids organized themselves into so-called *septims*, a kind of family that shared the same master—male or female - across clans," she added, smiling at Kaura. "Some of these septims later joined together and evolved into two of Oxford's most famous colleges, Easing and Lockwood, when the Great Royal University was formed. As a result, the mages are nowadays more of an academic guild than a political force in our realm. They are also very careful not to influence the court or the affairs of the government—or at least not to give the appearance of doing so".

"I'll be damned if I believe that!" grumbled Malcolm, laughing grumpily.

"Exactly," Jane agreed. "Still, they go to great lengths to remain inconspicuous and not step on anyone's toes. I suppose what happened to the Gifted in Spain a hundred years ago, when the Court surprisingly approved the merging of religious organizations in the Empire and the creation of the Inquisition as a political power, has made some people very cautious here as well. Many now see mages as nothing more than quirky alchemists with potions and gadgets, trying to figure out how to make the world more efficient and convenient, and they do everything they can to solidify that image in the public mind. Personally, I'm not so sure. There's a lot more going on behind closed doors than we realize out here."

She leaned forward in her padded chair and looked at Kaura. "It's a good thing that we're talking about this anyway. Ever since you told me about your experiences, I've wanted to suggest that you contact one of the colleges. I'm sure you can find out more about your talent there; at worst, you'll at least find some like-minded people. Unless you want to take a job here at the counting house and forget about it for the time being. You would be a suitable candidate."

The younger woman nodded in agreement, then shook her head in response to Jane's second suggestion.

"I keep thinking about where I came from. If I have a chance to shed more light on it, I will. This is the first real lead I've had in years!"

Her gaze was lost in the distance. "And I'm worried about Joe. The whole thing with him and the Atlantean key is something else entirely. If the Spanish went to the trouble of intercepting him in Inmarsund, with four High Inquisitors to boot, there's more to it than that. The fact that they also caused problems for me seems to be more of a happenstance than anything else. Maybe I can find out something about that as well."

* * *

Around noon the next day, Kaura made her way to Westminster. She had decided to walk. The clouds hung low, and the temperature, which had risen over the past few days, had dipped below freezing again during the night. Scattered snowflakes blew across the slush-covered streets.

It took her less than half an hour to walk along the busy

boulevard of the *Strand* from Nelson House to Westminster Abbey, past the sprawling palace of Whitehall.

The impressive Westminster Abbey was the main bastion of Scottish Spiritualism. The priestly caste of the Spanish Ottoman Empire condescendingly referred to it as a religion of "heretics," ostensibly because the Scots sought to integrate the influences of the various religious views present in Europe and rejected the dogmas of the Granada-based Sacred Congregation. The shrine was an uplifting sight, with its high windows and light, almost floating Gothic stone arches.

Only lightly touched by the Buddhist wave that had swept most of northern and central Europe over a thousand years ago, the Caledonians had maintained a great religious tolerance, where Buddhists, Christians, and Celtic Druids lived and worked together in peace.

The island was considered one of the most diverse sanctuaries of different religions and worldviews, which Kaura thought was one of the main reasons for the impressive economic success of Scottish merchants and entrepreneurs. They were simply less prejudiced than most other people in the known world.

But the Scots also used the Buddhist calendar. Only in the Spanish Ottoman Empire were different calendars used depending on the region. In the western regions of the realm they used one based on the birth of Jesus Christ, according to which they wrote only the year 1598, while in most of the world people took it to be 1869 after Buddha's enlightenment.

Of course, no one could say exactly when these two gentlemen had lived. At least that's what the adopted Inmarsundian, who was not particularly interested in ecclesiastical matters, thought. Probably there were other calendars outside the Mongol-European civilizations, as well. Kaura sometimes wondered how the Atlanteans counted their years. No one really knew. They were reclusive folk, the islanders.

The young woman asked a passerby, elegantly dressed in a blue dressing gown and a brown velvet hat rounded at the top, for directions to the Lockwood Society residence. The man readily provided the information before turning around and quickly disappearing into one of the adjacent government buildings.

She turned right, walked a few steps into Abbey Orchard Street, and then turned left into St. Ann's Street.

The London branch of the Lockwood Society was housed in a nondescript three-story stone building, no different from the other houses in the alley.

One wing of the gate was open. Behind it, a most unusual sight in the middle of winter, was a courtyard with a garden full of blooming rhododendron bushes.

Kaura stepped through the archway and looked around curiously. The first thing she noticed was the change in temperature. In one step, she had gone from the slushy, cold London winter to a warm spring climate. Dry, balmy, with a faint scent of blooming roses and jasmine in the air.

Involuntarily, a vision appeared in her mind. She was standing on a soft green meadow. In front of her, deep green palm fronds swayed in the breeze, and behind them stretched a vast expanse of turquoise water. She was about to sniff an intensely fragrant jasmine blossom that lured down from a dense, leafy shrub among thousands of its sisters. Far away, beyond the glittering surface of water, lightning flickered silently around a lush island of sharp cliffs and jagged mountains, now only visible as a dark shadow.

She tried desperately to hold on to the image, to pull herself into some memory of her past life. This had to be a memory! It seemed far too real to be a mere product of her imagination!

Almost in panic, she felt the image begin to slip from her grasp and disappear. She slumped a little, so great was the disappointment. She still had no idea who had seen this fairytale scene. Who was she? Where did she belong?

A dry sob formed in her throat. Suddenly, there seemed to be a heavy knot in her stomach.

A thin voice cleared its throat behind her.

Surprised, she spun around. Hovering at about head level was some sort of miniature creature, its shimmering purple, translucent wings making a faint buzzing sound, like one of the dragonflies that bred in the many ponds in the woods around Inmarsund during summers. The wings were attached to the back of an almost surreal, beautiful blonde woman who measured no more than five or six inches from head to toe, just a little beyond the length of Kaura's hand. She wore only a short, irregularly shaped skirt and a strip of cloth over her bosom, which was very large for her small size.

"Sorry, I didn't mean to startle you."

The creature had a bright, cheerful voice.

"Welcome to Lockwood House. May I help you? The reception hall for non-Gifted supplicants is over there. I'm Ariane, the guard fairy on duty."

Grinning, she fluttered a little closer to Kaura's ear and lowered her voice slightly.

"I know I don't look terribly dangerous. But I do know how to box."

Again the bell-like laughter. "Just kidding. Of course, I have plenty of other ways to deal with unwanted intruders. So, are you coming?" She gave an inviting wave with a perfectly manicured miniature hand. Its fingernails were painted purple to match the color of the fairy's wings and eyes.

Kaura was still staring at her, fascinated.

"Sorry. I've never met a fairy before - I think."

"You *think*?"

Ariane's voice went up an octave. "I can tell you that if you had ever met one of my kind, you would be sure of it! We fairies are not that easy to forget. Some say it's because of our ethereal beauty. Personally, I think it's because of our charming personalities and our vast vocabulary of profanities! Want to hear a dirty joke? Well, a nun was presented with a bicycle... Do you even know what a bicycle is? Recently invented by some guy outside of London, everybody likes it! Doesn't come in my size yet. But I can fly, so I guess it doesn't matter. Anyway, one of the latest jokes! So..."

Kaura caught up with the fairy in two quick steps and interrupted her.

"I'd love to hear this, but later, Ariane. Actually, I'm just meeting someone. Loren, from Oxford. Can you tell me where I might find her?"

"Ah, why didn't you say so! The other way, totally the other way! The quarters of the sublime are over there. Sublime, my ass! They don't believe it themselves, these ladies and gentlemen. But tradition has to be upheld, right?"

She winked at Kaura as she dove into an elegant, screwed loop and changed direction, waving at her to follow. "I'm glad to see the girl is getting some sensible company. Having to deal with old witches and wizards every day is not the best thing in the world, I tell you. Nice people, all right. But they're a special breed. Somehow they all think the same way. Spells, levitating gnomes, turning lead into gold, reading minds, training phoenixes... some of it may be quite practical. But you can get a little over-the-top. Lift off, I mean. In my case, you can take that literally..."

Kaura had gotten over her initial bewilderment and was beginning to enjoy the fairy guard's barrage of words.

Chattering nonstop, Ariane led her up two flights of stairs, past ancient looking paintings that were highly detailed and whose contents seemed to rise out of the paintings almost like sculptures.

At one point, Kaura tried to touch one of the images to see if it was really just a flat canvas or a three-dimensional model.

The subject of the painting, a young blonde witch with a pointy red hat and an owl on her shoulder, leaned back a little, away from her groping hand.

"Hey, paws off!" the image shouted, and the owl cawed harshly.

Kaura nodded and mumbled an excuse.

Ariane giggled.

"Yes, yes, our paintings are a bit sensitive. They're not really alive, you know. They have been charged with some of the essence of the person or historical scene they portray, so they can give you certain information. If you ask them nicely. If you're more of a touchy-feely girl, there's a picture of a young cat on the third floor. It loves to be petted."

The fairy stopped in front of a heavy wooden door with iron fittings.

She nonchalantly waved her tiny hand, and the wooden panel slid noiselessly aside, disappearing into the wall.

"So, here we are. Guest quarters lounge. Make yourself at home. I'll tell Loren you're here."

The fairy fluttered away.

Carefully, Kaura lowered herself into the largest of the thickly upholstered red velvet chairs.

The chair sighed comfortably as she leaned against it and began to massage her back. Kaura shrugged and grinned to herself. Nothing here really surprised her anymore.

A little later, a door in the back of the room opened and Loren came to meet her with a friendly smile. The two women embraced.

The girl pointed to the chair.

"I see you've met Oscar. You can also tell him right away what kind of massage you prefer. He can do anything from pressure points to feather light strokes. Just not an oil massage, of course. You'll have to ask one of the tantric spirits on the fourth floor for that."

Her features took on a dreamy expression for a fleeting moment. "Are you hungry? I know a good Indic tavern around the corner. They make really delicious *Dal*, and the place is not too noisy. Good for quiet conversation. Agreed?"

Kaura nodded, and Loren flashed a bright smile. "Before we go, let me show you the Mediterranean Gardens in the courtyard. One of my favorite spots in all of London."

The young woman took her cloak from a massive wardrobe in the corner that leaned helpfully toward her, thanked the piece of furniture, and then motioned for Kaura to follow.

The Mediterranean garden was indeed a sight to behold. It was located in the second inner court of the building. In the center of the circular space, which was about two hundred feet in diameter, floated a gleaming artificial sun. It flooded the entire garden with a warm, early summer light, which made the bushes and trees that bloomed in all colors seem even more intense.

Kaura inhaled the all-pervading floral scent with relish.

Loren was visibly proud.

"Hard to believe it's snowing outside, isn't it?"

She playfully hopped over a couple of round granite boulders jutting out of the small pond in the center, deftly dodging the jets of water whizzing through the air out of the oriental fountains installed at its edges.

"Everything is fully automated by spells anchored in the general field. Sun, irrigation, humidity... At night, you even have an artificial starry sky up there"–she pointed to the skylight where the small sun seemed to float without any suspension–"Complete with the Milky Way and everything. I studied here for my astronomy exam."

She plopped down contentedly on a curved stone bench that

overlooked a small waterfall nestled between black rocks and jasmine bushes.

"Magical," Kaura sighed, sitting down next to Loren. The latter just nodded. The two women sank into contemplation of the falling water.

After a while, Kaura noticed Loren looking at her curiously from the side.

"Where exactly did you get initiated?" the girl asked. She blushed slightly. "I know some mage guilds are a bit secretive about that. Of course, you don't have to tell me if you don't want to. You're probably not from Britain, even though you speak Scottish without an accent. You look too exotic. However, we have a professor at Oxford who is originally from the north of the "New World". Her name is Eagle. Very kind. She was previously a resident of Atlantis, too, after losing her entire tribe in the battles of Tenochtitlán. They, like many others, had moved south to help defend the Aztec Empire. The Atlanteans erased all her memories as she moved on. Or so she says."

Loren blinked at her expectantly.

Kaura thought for a moment. What should she say?

"It's a long story. In short, I don't know where or by whom I was initiated. Just as little do I know about my Gift. My memory goes back only five years, when I almost died in a shipwreck. I've only known that I have the Gift for less than a month. And yet, as far as I've been told, the very fact that I'm mentally and physically healthy proves that I must have been initiated somewhere.

Loren's brown eyes had taken on a sympathetic expression as Kaura spoke.

Gently, she put her hand on her forearm and squeezed it lightly.

"Well, at least you have a hint now. And friends. If you like, you can come with me to Oxford. The High Council at Lockwood should be interested in your problem. They'll probably even give you a scholarship. Even if you're not very strong, you should at least know what you're doing."

She thought. "It could also be that the weakness of your power saved you. Maybe it just wasn't strong enough to drive your brain crazy when the connection to the magic source opened without the help of another magician."

Now Kaura thought of something. She nestled the fishhook out from between her breasts and showed it to Loren.

"I got this in Inmarsund. It seems to hide my ability from the outside world. That's why I was so surprised that you recognized me at all."

She lifted the pendant above her head and placed it on the bench next to her.

"Do you see me differently now?"

Then she gave a start at seeing Lorens reaction.

Her companion's eyes had widened in surprise. The girl seemed to struggle for words for a moment.

"Yes, I really think the High Council would like to meet you," she breathed. "I've only seen someone with such an aureole once before, and that was the High Priest of Atlantis, who was here on a state visit a few years ago, just after I'd been admitted. Not even the Headmaster has such a powerful aura."

Loren swallowed. "Whoever you really are, you are—or were—very, very powerful."

Then she grinned weakly. "Well, after that little surprise, I need something to eat. Will you buy me a drink? And you better put that thing back on." She pointed to the pendant lying on the bench next to Kaura, shining like mother of pearl in the light of the artificial sun. "Otherwise they will all be kneeling before you if we meet any-one on the way out."

6

The Ambush

Early the next morning, Kaura was back at Lockwood House. A carriage owned by the Nelsons had brought her and what little luggage she had. She planned to stay in Oxford for two or three weeks at most and then return to London.

Joe still had business that kept him in the Scottish metropolis, but he had promised to visit her sometime and help with her research. He had several good contacts at the university from his student days.

Loren was waiting for her already. She had announced that she would be signing Kaura up for the 'transfer' as well.

Contrary to Kaura's expectations, however, the younger woman did not take her back to the street where a carriage would have picked them up, but instead led her down a wide marble staircase into the basement.

"The *Travel Hall* is down there, in the oldest part of the building," the young woman replied enigmatically when Kaura asked her about it.

As they walked through the colonnaded corridor lit by yellow witch lights, a familiar whirring sound reached Kaura's ears from the back left. She smiled.

"Heyo, sis!" Ariane chirped close to her ear as she alighted on Kaura's shoulder. "Our little apprentice here told me that you also belong to our humble guild. I can't tell just by looking at you. So you are probably not a magical unicorn. Still, it's nice to have you here. If you ever need anything, let me know. Three wishes and all that shit! But they better be interesting wishes. Otherwise I do nothing. Nothing at all! Mind you, if it promises some entertainment, I am always happy to be of assistance. For example, there was a guy who wanted to swim naked with a group of sirens in Hellas for a week. Well, it was not just about swimming, of course, hehe. That was fun. They hadn't caught a sailor in centuries, and they weren't about to let him go at the end of the week. I had to be very persuasive. He'll think more carefully about what he wishes for next time. By the way, I still owe you a joke..."

"Next time, Ariane, please," Loren interrupted. "The weekly portal opening is due to happen in five minutes."

With an almost shy sideways glance in Kaura's direction, she added, "Ariane's jokes are really good. She once told one to a one-eyed sailor in a port tavern over in Southwark. Tough guy, as tough as they come. The man turned as red as a tomato!"

She giggled, and Ariane let out a loud snort in her fine voice.

"You should have seen his face!" gasped the fairy. "Today's sailors aren't what they used to be! One subtle sexual allusion, and they're choking on their stout! What a shame!"

The Travel Hall was a circular room about thirty yards in diameter. The vaulted ceiling displayed a blue evening sky dotted with fluffy clouds. A column rose in the center, above it a golden glowing sphere, slowly rotating in midair. The orb was apparently made of solid gold and seemed to be illuminated from the outside, although there was no visible light source to account for it. It was covered with strange symbols that Kaura had never seen before.

Loren grabbed her hand and pulled her further into the northwest section of the hall.

Only now did Kaura realize that the outer wall of the chamber was formed by marble arches set into the wall. There had to be at least fifteen of them. Large, dull bronze statues shimmered between the vaulted arches. Kaura recognized the Goddesses of Love, Power, Beauty, and Wisdom, as well as half a dozen others she could not quite place. Each of the arches had an identifying mark carved into the tops of the vaults, which were supported by Greek-style columns.

Loren moved purposefully toward the gate marked OXF. It was the only one that was shimmering in a fluorescent blue. Beside it, five women in light white robes sat in a circle, holding hands. Their eyes were closed, showing great concentration. Another woman stood beside the gate.

Kaura felt a tingle of understanding in her stomach. This had to be a portal, probably the kind the Spaniards were looking for.

These people actually seemed to know things that might help her in her research.

All the other archways were dark and cordoned off with shimmering silky ropes. In the dim light, Kaura tried to decipher the names of the gates they passed. ORK, AVL, SNH, PRH, LHA, CAR, ART, she read, without being able to place the names. Since they had to be places, OXF had to be Oxford. Was PRH perhaps Pyrrha?

Her companion noticed her stare.

"The Travel Hall has not been fully operational since Merlin's escape. We don't even know where most of the portals used to lead. Only the Oxford one is manually activated once a week for practical reasons, to transport travelers and mail - and also so that we don't lose the knowledge associated with it. It requires a circle of five on each side. The portal holders need to recover from the exertion for several days. We suspect that it only still works because the distance between the connecting poles is so short. In the distant past, however, all of this seems to have been in constant operation. And it is said there were even portals leading to other planets."

She checked in with the gatekeeper, a white-haired woman of about seventy with a serious expression on her face. When she recognized Loren, though, she smiled.

"Hello Leah, good to see you!", the girl greeted her. "This is my friend, Kaura Leivenstein. We've registered for the Transfer."

"Hello Loren," the attendant said. "It's all right, you can go through. The field is stable."

Loren motioned for Kaura to follow, stepped into the bluish glow, and seemed to vanish into thin air. After a barely noticeable moment of hesitation, Kaura followed.

As soon as her body touched the shimmering surface, a cool tingling sensation coursed through her veins and organs.

With a determined step, she walked all the way through. A sharp pinch seemed to run through her nervous system, making her jump. Then it was over.

She realized she had involuntarily closed her eyes and quickly opened them again.

She was standing in a room that was much smaller than the one she had just left. It was also circular and lit only by a few candles on the walls. Five people dressed in heavy white winter cloaks were sitting next to the portal, but here it was three men and two women.

"Welcome to Oxford!" a voice came from below her waistline. Kaura looked down. Beside her stood a weathered, small-framed creature in a gray silk robe. It had pointed ears and its features distinctly reminded her of a mouse.

"Thank you, Master Oriel," Loren replied, stopping only three paces in front of her. "It's good to be home again. This is my friend,

Kaura Leivenstein." She made a gesture toward Kaura. "She is Gifted and would like to speak to the High Council."

The mouse-being looked at Kaura a little doubtfully, but with a friendly expression in his eyes.

"Hmm. Well, if you say so, Loren. So, let's get on with it. We still have to bring the mail sacks through."

Turning to Kaura, he added, "You'd better check in with Miss Callahan, the Headmaster's secretary. Loren will guide you."

Kaura followed the girl out into the stone corridor lit by natural light. She shivered involuntarily. It was noticeably cooler here than at Lockwood House in London. Through an open door she could see a snow-covered courtyard inside the circular enclosure of a cloister. It smelled like winter.

The Lockwood Society's Oxford headquarters was much busier than its quiet, stately Westminster counterpart. The cloister was teeming with mostly black-robed people of all ages and of every walk of life.

Kaura saw a small group of young Mongolians standing together and chatting.

An Arabic-looking teacher was talking to a red-haired girl about Loren's age. She was showing him something in a densely written notebook made out of yellowish parchment.

Further back, a dark-skinned young man rounded the corner. Over his black hair, he wore a headdress that resembled that of the Incas on an old engraving of the Spanish conquistadors that she had once seen in Inmarsund.

Somewhat above their heads, fairies buzzed back and forth, their facial expressions revealing that each one had extremely important news to deliver—or at least believed she did.

Occasionally, Kaura saw other non-human beings hurrying through the corridors. Some of them looked like Master Oriel. Then there were thick-skinned, furry gnomes with pointed ears that were almost as wide as they were tall, dog-like creatures that looked a bit like Atam, and two purple-skinned, very thin and tall beings with shiny black eyes and webbed feet.

Loren pulled her along, into a side corridor.

"Lunch break is almost over. Now everyone will go back to their lectures. In a few minutes it will be quiet around here again. A good time to catch Miss Callahan. She's always in heavy demand."

They passed through some huge anterooms with Gothic arches and intricate columns that seemed to be built of a multitude of twisted filaments. Still, everything here seemed much more conventional to Kaura. The corridors were drafty and cool, the stone slabs irregular, and the light in the darker rooms came from torches burning on the walls, as befitted medieval buildings. She asked Loren about it.

The girl laughed.

"Yes, London is luxury in every way. Everyone wishes they could do an internship there. The interior dates back to Merlin's time, while this building was newly constructed three hundred years ago. It's shameful. We couldn't possibly build Westminster now the way Merlin's people did two thousand years ago, even if we had the money and the architects. There are attempts to recreate something like the Mediterranean Garden here by magical means. So far it's only a pale imitation. And it consumes way too much energy. Someone has to sit there for a few hours every day to renew the charms."

Loren pulled her face into a thoughtful grimace and bit her lower lip. "I hate to think what will happen if the climate spell in the London facility ever fails. The poor plants! No one would know how to fix it. That's why I want to specialize in magobotany. It can't be that hard to make something like that and connect it to the integral field so that it works forever without someone sitting there feeding it energy all the time! I mean, Merlin's constructors were just witches and wizards after all, like us, right? Anyway, I think the

Atlanteans know a lot more. They just don't want to share it. That's why they're so secretive. I've thought about dying my hair white and sneaking in there. Like Mila Intan in her book *Unseen to Shamballa!*

She thought for a moment and then shook her head.

"Hmm, I guess that would be really dangerous... and I like to be cautious, so I probably won't do that. Well, we're here!"

In front of a wooden door, organically woven from glass and gold threads, she stopped so abruptly that Kaura almost collided with her.

Loren knocked.

A muffled "Enter!" came from inside the room and the girl pushed open the heavy door.

Upon entering, the first thing Kaura noticed was the familiar warmth of fire and the aromatic smell of burning wood.

Behind a massive desk of polished oak sat a woman of about fifty, with short gray hair and a cool expression. She was dressed entirely in white silk. The only splash of color was a red scarf bearing the emblem of the Lockwood Society, a black and gold owl.

An owl also sat on the perch that had been placed at the far corner of the desk.

Kaura couldn't tell at first if the animal was stuffed or real. Considering where she was, probably real.

As if in answer to her unspoken question, one of the bird's eyes winked lazily at her.

The Inmarsundian glanced at the figure behind the table. This woman looked as if she would still be calmly sitting at her desk even if the world was coming to an end.

A hint of curiosity crossed Miss Callahan's gray eyes as she pushed aside the document she had been reading, and looked at the newcomers.

"Hello, Loren!"

Her voice was deep and smoky. "I see you're back from your little field trip. And you brought someone with you."

Then she turned to Kaura. "Hello. Welcome to Lockwood. I don't think I've seen you here before. And I have a good memory. I'm Helen Callahan, assistant to the High Magister."

Kaura introduced herself and explained her problem.

Helen smiled vaguely.

"So, Inmarsund. And you want to speak to the High Council. You claim to be Gifted. And you have a Cloaking Amulet with you. Can you remove it for a moment?"

Kaura complied, but kept the pendant in her hand and immediately put it back on again.

The witch nodded in satisfaction.

"You have a lot of power. And you really do have no idea where your initiation took place?"

Kaura shook her head. Helen's doubtful tone irritated her.

"Believe me, I'd like to know that, too," she replied, slightly annoyed.

The Headmaster's assistant made no reply and stood up.

"Wait here. I will speak to Master Lumisworth."

She returned a few minutes later.

"You can go in now, Kaura, His Excellency will speak with you in a moment. Loren, thank you for your support. You did the right thing in bringing Kaura to Oxford. If you hurry, you can still make the second afternoon lecture. I expect we'll have your friend here as a visiting student for some time, and you'll have plenty of time to talk."

The girl touched Kaura's arm encouragingly, whispered a "The Headmaster is really nice!" and walked out.

Miss Callahan gestured imperiously to the open door behind her desk and returned to her reading. All of a sudden, Kaura seemed to no longer exist for her.

The room behind the door was in unbelievable chaos. At first, Kaura wondered if thieves or vandals had been through here. As her eyes adjusted to the gloomy semi-darkness, she concluded that the principal's office was probably just very full and that its occupant must have a rather unusual system of keeping things in order.

Behind some irregularly stacked towers of books, each almost six feet high, she noticed a movement. She winced involuntarily, expecting the crooked stacks of books to collapse at the slightest touch of air.

"Close the door and sit down, will you? Just make yourself comfortable! I'll be right there!", a disembodied voice mumbled.

She pulled the door closed and looked around the cramped hall trying to locate a place to sit. Finally, she spotted an armchair-like shape under a large pile of books. She stacked the books from the chair onto the floor and sat down.

Meanwhile, the figure behind the stacks of books continued to rummage through a bookcase somewhere below, visible only as a dark outline.

Kaura's eyes were slowly adapting to the dim light and she could see more. The shadow in front of the bookcase was now revealed to be the back of a shirtless man, tattooed all over with esoteric symbols. The tattoos were arranged in a circle around the area between the shoulder blades, where a concentric mandala of countless triangles was overlaid.

Wild, dark blonde dreadlocks swayed back and forth across a wiry, yet muscular back, adorned with a variety of tinkling bells attached to colored ribbons. Each movement of the man's head triggered a soft, melodious chime.

The figure continued to rummage, pulling out individual books, opening them, grunting in disappointment, and shoving them back in place.

Kaura's eyes wandered around the hall. Whoever lived here

obviously liked books, because that was the main content of this place - thousands, maybe even tens of thousands of them.

Hand-written pages pinned together with copper nails hung on the partially wood-covered walls, between old maps that, in Kaura's estimation, represented the state of geographical knowledge from several centuries ago and were long outdated.

Hundreds of amulets made of gold, copper, or even leather and bird feathers hung from pegs carelessly driven into the stone walls and shelves.

On the few tables not occupied by books were alchemical devices, crystal balls, vitrioles with liquids glowing in all colors, three-dimensional shapes, gemstones, and figures of the most incredible shapes and shades. A faint natural light poured in from above through a whitish, opaque skylight.

On two walls, there she also saw the outlines of tall windows set into the stone walls, vaguely reminiscent of those in an ancient church. They would probably have flooded the rooms with light had they not been covered with thick layers of cloths featuring cloudy rainbow patterns, Oriental-looking mandalas, and tree symbols.

"Ha!" the figure shouted loudly, and Kaura jumped. "There you go!"

Triumphantly, the man held up a thick book that appeared to be no different from the others.

He had half turned to face Kaura. She could see that the front of his torso was as extensively tattooed as his back. The Headmaster wore tightly cut brown leather pants and over them a wide belt with pockets of various sizes, decorated with colorful embroidery. His feet were bare.

Two kind eyes gleamed from a lean, bearded face.

" Hello. My name is Seneca Lumisworth. You may call me Sen."

Holding the huge book in his left hand, and extending his right, he came toward her, almost tripping over two different editions of the Encyclopedia Britannica scattered on the floor. The lean man, who looked to be in his fifties, caught himself at the last moment and danced the last few steps towards the young woman.

Politely, Kaura shook his hand.

"I am Kaura Leivenstein. At least, that's my adopted name. I suppose Miss Callahan has already told you why I'm here."

Sen grunted in agreement. He glanced around the room with a searching expression. Kaura understood that he was looking for a place to sit. She raised her hand and pointed to a second chair, which had also almost disappeared under the books and folios.

However, the headmaster was already wiping his hand over a low table set on the thick red carpet. As if moved by a ghostly hand, silverware containing the dried-up remains of a meal piled up and floated over to the door, where it landed on one of the somewhat smaller stacks of books, causing it to sway ominously.

Tensing, Kaura waited for the clattering sound produced by the inevitable collapse of the swaying stack, but the whole thing seemed more stable than she had thought and remained upright.

Meanwhile, the Chief Mage had settled down on the sofa table, breathing a sigh of relief and pulling his legs towards him so that he was sitting cross-legged on the creaking wooden table like a Buddha on his lotus leaf.

Invitingly, he held out the book to Kaura that he had not let go of during all this.

"Can you read this, girl?" he asked.

The book was so heavy that she almost dropped it when he handed it to her. Since he had carried it so lightly in one hand, she was not prepared for the weight. She placed the volume on her right thigh and turned it slightly so that she could read the title printed in small gold letters on the spine.

"*Aích Weitan Limarin,*" she murmured. "*Prophecies of the Final Days of Lemuria.*"

Even as she realized she had been speaking in a language she had never heard before, Kaura's vision went black.

She wobbled. Her muscles gave out and she lost consciousness.

A scene appeared in her mind. She was inside a large, dark temple hall. The hall was open to the outside, so it must be night. To the right, outside the temple ring, she saw individual stars twinkling between the pillars. No moon. A new moon night? The warm air smelled of the sea. Outside, plants rustled in the wind. Palm leaves?

She realized that she was kneeling on a small carpet, naked. Around her, in a wide semicircle, sat eighteen people, twelve women and six men, each on a silky white cushion, thin and rounded, about a yard in diameter.

The only item of clothing worn by those present was a large gold disc hung around each person's neck, all of which glowed warmly in the semi-darkness of the shimmering white marble temple.

"Sister," a melodious, ageless female voice rang out.

"We appreciate your sacrifice on behalf of our people. You know we would not have agreed for you to take this risk if we had seen any other way. It is our profound hope that you return to us healthy and well, and that our calculations for predicting the fluctuation of the death field around our continent prove correct. May your endeavor succeed. Do you have anything else to say?"

Kaura heard herself catch her breath and speak in a firm voice.

"I bless you, brothers and sisters. I will do everything I can to reopen the Portal and, with the help of the Aalids, free you and our people. If you measure my death in crossing the field, or if I am not back within five years, appoint someone else. Do not come looking for me. Let the ceremony begin. Peace be with you, loved ones!"

"Peace be with you, Supreme Sister," echoed the blurred outline in the semicircle. With a fluid movement, Kaura lowered herself to the ground and...

A finger on the spot between her eyebrows brought her back to the present.

When she opened her eyes, she looked directly into Sen's worried face.

The Headmaster smiled weakly.

"Well, that was an interesting experiment. I'm sorry, this is not how I imagined it would go. I'm glad you're back. Here, have a drink."

He held out a moderately clean glass filled with a pungent smelling liquid. "Vodka," he said. "Imported directly from the Siberian witches. I've got water somewhere, too, if you would prefer."

Kaura took the glass and downed it all in one gulp. It was a good thing she had spent a fair amount of time among sailors the last few years, she thought.

The drink actually made her feel a little better. She sat up straighter.

"Thank you. What kind of book is this?"

He blushed slightly.

"My only real book from Lemuria, in Lemurian. Since Helen told me you have an aura like an Atlantean, although you definitely don't look like one, I thought I'd try the second option. And that really did drop a penny on you, didn't it? I just didn't think it would blow you away like that. I'm really sorry."

He looked slightly contrite, but immediately regained his scientific inquisitiveness.

"So, what is it? Do you remember anything now?"

Kaura shook her head uncertainly.

"Yes, there was a memory. Of a ceremony. And there was talk of me accepting a task. And of a portal to be opened. Somehow, I still can't make sense of it. It felt like the memory of another person, unknown to me. But I've never heard of any place called Lemuria.

Meanwhile, the Principal had returned to his meditation seat on the couch table. He leaned forward a little and looked at Kaura with interest.

"Hm, yes. At least you know how to read Lemurian. So, Lemuria. You must know Atlantis. Hard to get to, very reclusive people. Still, we have Atlantean magicians visiting us from time to time. Occasionally, they even allow outside visitors into the interior of their island, though conveniently, they completely forget the details of their journey when they return. So, Atlantis is something of a mystery. But there is virtually no concrete information about Lemuria. We don't even know exactly where this legendary land is located. It is only thanks to old reports from Merlin's diplomats and circumstantial evidence like this," he pointed to the book still closed in Kaura's lap, "that we can be sure that Lemuria is not a figment of the imagination of crazy esoterics and witch hunters.

He shook his head with a hint of annoyance. This man was not used to being faced with a riddle that defied his brilliant mind. "There are all sorts of ideas about where the Lemurians might be found, from the middle of the Gobi Desert in Mongolian territory, to the high mountains of the Asian subcontinent, or the middle of the Pacific Ocean, which the expeditions of the Spanish and more recently our own Sir Francis Drake have only begun to explore. Others suggest that Lemuria may be in the interior of the Earth - or even on the Moon, or on a more distant planet."

Slowly, the headmaster was getting into his speech, and his enthusiasm for science and research was becoming so obvious that Kaura involuntarily grinned and nodded silently to herself. This was the right kind of person to go to if she wanted to solve the riddle of her origins.

"From the reports in the Avalon archives, it seems that the Lemurians are, or at least were at that time, magically gifted in quite different spheres. Many of the highest achievements of early

British magic were probably owed to Merlin's good relations with this people."

A smile appeared on Sen's face, containing both genuine affection and a touch of greed.

"Anyway, I think I have a real Lemurian sitting here before me. And I would very, very much like to help you remember. Your contribution to the restoration of wizardry in Scotland could be irreplaceable. Perhaps you will even be able to connect us with your friends in Lemuria. Just imagine! A second flowering of British magic!"

His face lit up dreamily.

"We're not there yet, unfortunately," Kaura slowed him down. "Right now, I'd be happy if I could just master the most basic applications of sorcery. Probably any first grader here at your school could still teach me."

She made a face.

"At the very least, I should find out what kind of mission I came here to accomplish. And I still don't know if my memory loss has the same cause as my magic block or if it has nothing to do with it."

Sen nodded.

"Very well, my dear. Tell me everything now, and please try not to leave out any details. Then I will talk to my lovely colleagues on the High Council and see what we can do for you."

* * *

Five days later, Kaura was sitting in a comfortable chair surrounded by twenty-one gifted individuals who specialized in magical psychology.

In order to have enough privacy, the rector had had one of the private salons normally used for receptions of external dignitaries cleared out, so that the ritual could take place undisturbed.

Kaura had spent the last few days attending various basic classes in Applied Magic. As a result, she was able to see auric fields and distinguish between the different energy flows more and more clearly.

With her own power, however, she could not even levitate a goose down or light a candle. She accepted this with almost supernatural composure, which impressed the magisters of the academy almost more than her supposedly highly "mature" energy field.

The adopted Inmarsundian–or, was she really a Lemurian, could that be true?–knew herself that she should have been frustrated about failing again and again. With other things she sometimes was, but this particular issue, which seemed so important, seemed to leave her emotionally completely cold.

With a shrug of her shoulders, she had always let go of that thought, too, and patiently kept trying.

The lecturers did everything to stimulate Kaura's memory. They were fascinated by their fellow witch, who, according to rumors already known to all after only a few days, despite Kaura's request for discretion, was supposed to come from mythical Lemuria.

Ylkeitha, the lecturer in magical travel methods, had been thrilled

"With this intensity of your aura you should be able to walk through walls, at the very least. Maybe even *shift*, dissolve in one place and reappear somewhere in the world! No one here has been able to do that since Merlin's time!" she had raved.

Even she, however, could not elicit any more concrete results from Kaura than all the other mages, who were all highly interested in Kaura's buried talent.

The High Council had then decided to scan Kaura energetically to find out more about her condition. Consequently, now she sat here, in this hall brightly lit by a multitude of floating balls of light, and waited for a procedure to begin, which, she had been told, was performed only very rarely, but was supposed to be completely safe.

The magister of psychomagic turned to her. He was a taciturn, gray-haired man with a serious face who went by the name of Doug.

"All right, we are ready. As you already know, we're going to use a method that we normally use here in a slightly less elaborate form for magically detecting and healing physical ailments. A very simple spell sequence in principle. You may get a little cold during this, and perhaps visions may appear. I will tell you what I see during the ceremony, and you can share your perceptions with us as well. Ready?"

Kaura said yes, leaned back in the chair, and closed her eyes. For a fleeting moment, she missed Oscar, the massage chair in the guest quarters of Lockwood House in London.

A change in the room immediately brought her back to the present. In her inner space, she felt the twenty-one light silhouettes around her expand and combine. The combined energy flows converged at the place where the magister must be sitting.

The glow—or perhaps she could also have called it a *density* or *vastness*, she thought to herself—intensified. Then she felt something *reaching for* her. The feeling was only slightly unpleasant, like groping, searching fingers in her body and mind.

The magister began to speak.

"I am now in your third outermost envelope layer. As expected, your extremely high energy potential results in an almost impenetrable envelope, so we will need the full circle of twenty-one to penetrate all the way through."

He emitted a satisfied growl. "Ah, now I'm through and one level deeper. Now I can also see your talent, and the shell of energy that keeps it from becoming effective. To me, that shell around the center of your heart looks like a blue and white ball of wool. I have never seen anything like it. That energy structure almost seems alive."

A longer break followed.

"Now I am even deeper. I can now also see several dark places in your inner head that seemed to be connected to structures floating outside in your field. Perhaps the shock catapulted parts of your personality out of your embodied, experiential reality. Some of these outside fragments are also surrounded by these blue-white elastic armors. Others are more accessible. I might even be able to peek inside there. For now, I'll just try to move the unsheathed pieces back to you. Is that all right?"

Kaura tried to nod, noticing that she couldn't move her head at the moment.

"Yes, you can go on. I don't feel anything like what you describe, but I can't move my body and everything seems to vibrate or wobble in a certain way. In the area around my eyes I feel great sadness, as if tears are about to come."

Her voice was impassive, enraptured.

The magister nodded.

"Just let everything flow through you as much as you can, and try to relax. Breathe in and out deeply. I'm going to start on the first fragment now."

At first, Kaura felt nothing. Then her whole body began to move slowly, to bend without her doing anything.

Then an undulating vibration jolted through her spine, almost forcibly raising her up and then causing her to slump back down.

Her counterpart exhaled deeply.

"That would be the first of three unarmored fragments. Has anything changed?"

Kaura took a deep breath.

"No... Yes, I do... hm, hard to describe. I just feel a little more present. Can you keep going?"

The psychomage grunted his agreement.

This time the twitching of her body almost tore the young woman out of the chair. Tears ran from her closed eyes. She sobbed.

"Yes, now something is coming. I have to open a portal to... to...

protect the Earth? Or for someone else to protect the Earth? It's all so foggy..."

Tears now ran freely down Kaura's cheeks. At the same time, her mouth took on the determined drawl that her friends knew so well. She would not give up now.

"Go on!" she demanded.

When her closed eyes blinked for a moment, she glimpsed the face of the magister sitting across from her. It was red, sweaty, and wore an expression of extreme concentration.

"Next," he groaned.

This time it felt to Kaura as if her whole body was being screwed into itself and torn apart. She drew in her breath abruptly.

"Yes, it's becoming clearer now," she whimpered between the spasms of crying that shook her body.

"Great Mother, help me!", she moaned. "Can we take a break?"

The magister thoughtfully cradled his head, dripping with sweat.

"If I retreat now, we'll have to wait at least a week for the helpers here to recover enough to penetrate the outer layers again. I suggest that I at least try to unravel one of the blue and white structures."

Kaura agreed.

"It's getting better already, just a moment of weakness. I'm afraid it won't be quite that easy, though. Even though so much has gone wrong with my order now, it might just help me get access to the rest."

She closed her eyes, took a deep breath, and tried to relax again.

Suddenly, a buzzing sound filled the room. Movement arose around Kaura.

She opened her eyes and saw that the psychology magister had lost consciousness and was slumped in his chair. Some of the bystanders were tending to him. The bluish glow around the group of magicians had disappeared.

She held on to the back of her chair and tried to stand, but found that her muscles still did not fully obey her. Her strength seemed to return only very slowly. All her limbs felt heavy as lead, as if she had spent a day lugging bags of grain weighing dozens of pounds in the Leivenstein's warehouse.

"How is he?" she turned to one of the magister's aides.

"He is still in shock from the backlash of the connection and is exhausted, but appears to be unharmed," the blonde middle-aged woman replied. "These blue and white entities also seem to be able to develop active defenses. Well, now we know at least that. And you seem to have recovered some of your memory. That should be of burning interest to the principal. There he is already," she nodded toward the door, where the muscular chief magister was talking anxiously to one of the aides.

After Kaura's health had also been checked by one of the med-imagicians and declared unobjectionable, she rose with difficulty and walked over to Sen.

Heavens, she felt like an old woman, she thought to herself, gathering her thoughts.

The principal immediately interrupted his conversation as she approached and turned to Kaura. He had covered his tattooed torso with a black gown, the same that all members of the faculty here seemed to wear.

"Glad to see you are well!"

He eyed her with a hint of relief. "Malcolm here told me that some of your memory fragments have been recovered. Or at least it seemed that way from the outside."

Kaura nodded seriously.

"That's right. And I do understand a few things again now. At least as much as I was supposed to know when I was given my mission a little more than five years ago, I think," she said.

She looked at Malcolm, who had stood in the second row of those who had lent their energy to the Psychology Magister.

"Did you tell the Headmaster about the blue and white tangles?"
He nodded, and she continued.

"The blue and white protection devices were placed by my sisters to prevent me from telling anyone where my home is and how to get there, should I get caught. Clearly Lemuria. I don't remember anything more about it, except for the fragment of memory that came up when I read the title of your book. Neither can I remember anything about my past."

Sen took her by the arm gently.

"Let's continue this conversation in my office. You can relax there. I have a Cube Stone. It should bring your energy level back up in no time."

With a slight tinkling of the small bells in his hair, he was on his way. When they had reached his office, walking past Miss Callahan, who as always was engrossed in reading some kind of files, Sen handed Kaura the black stone. Contrary to its name, it was egg-shaped. She immediately felt a surge of power flow through her. She nodded in gratitude.

Sen helped her into the upholstered chair. Miraculously, it had been kept free of new piles of books since their last meeting.

"Well then, tell me. If you want to. And if your mission allows it."

With an expectant look on his face, the Headmaster drew up his legs - sitting cross-legged on the small wooden table seemed to be his preferred position when talking to someone in his office.

"I think so," Kaura replied. "It seems that I was deliberately left with only the memories related to my mission. And I believe that we may share the same interests."

Enjoying the warmth emanating from the stone in her hand, she sank back in her chair. Then she began to speak.

"There is a group of beings who call themselves the 'Gods'. Their home is not here on Gaia, but elsewhere, but they have been here on and off for several millennia. I don't know much about them—no idea if that's because of my buried memory, or if my Sisters haven't found out more either. In any case, the human talent for magic seems to be something extremely rare among these beings. So rare, in fact, that in the past, some three thousand years ago, they undertook regular "harvesting expeditions" to Gaia in which they abducted magically gifted beings - preferably of the human variety. Lemurian records do not say what they did with the kidnapped sorcerers and witches, whether they enslaved them or put them to a worse fate. They simply disappeared from the face of the earth, carried away in great airships. At that time, the ancestors of my guild, with the help of an outside race, erected a so-called Banning Field to keep the gods' ships away from Gaia. But the centuries of peace have made us all lazy. For over a thousand years, no one in Lemuria has had any contact with the beings whose knowledge formed the basis of this protective field. They call themselves Aalids and are closely related to us humans. I do not understand the reason for why this contact broke off. What is certain is that the people of Earth have become more and more isolated from each other and from the outside.

Sen leaned forward and fixed Kaura with alert eyes.

"*Was* based? Does that mean that this protective field no longer exists?"

Kaura nodded.

"Not for about seventy years, we think. Because Lemuria is so isolated from the rest of civilization, and since no one from our ranks disappeared at first, we didn't even notice it for decades. It was only when the universal magical field itself began to weaken, and our techno-magic devices and the abilities of human magicians began to fail, that Lemuria became aware of the problem. I was sent to try to restore the central portal system and to seek help from the Aalids. Once the portals are working again, it will most likely also be possible to reach Lemuria directly, and end the captivity of my people.

She shrugged at Sen's questioning look. "Before you ask, I have no recollection of why or how my people were imprisoned on their continent, nor how they managed to get me out. But it seems to have something to do with why it was deemed necessary to shield my magical abilities in order to complete my mission. The main purpose of the shield, however, was to break through a boundary that our psychics thought the "gods" had placed around the portal facility. Apparently, that was more important than preserving my ability to defend myself. I carried a programmed key in the form of an amulet to remove this block myself once I had overcome the shield. Shortly before the sinking of the galleon on which I was traveling, I tried to use it, prematurely, to save my life. It failed. Why, whether it was treachery or an error in the creation of the object, I don't know."

Frustrated, Kaura made a face.

Sen watched her intently and listened motionlessly as she continued.

"I disembarked on the soil of the Aztec Empire, crossed the Isthmus between the Pacific and Atlantic Oceans, and found passage to Hellas. During a stopover in Ireland, I was told that the Spanish had sealed off the entire Mediterranean and were searching for a person of my appearance. I had to change my plans, but while still on the peninsula I ran afoul of Spanish agents who seemed to be openly cooperating with the Irish authorities - and who were also equipped with Atlantean technology and modern weapons. I managed to escape and reach the Atlantean border on foot. There, despite my travel documents, I was captured by Atlantis soldiers and handed over to the Irish. An official in Dublin, who disagreed with the government's collaboration with the Spanish ruler, helped me escape once more, before the inquisitors arrived. Trying to be as unpredictable as possible, I made my way across the Irish Sea to Holyhead with the help of a local fisherman, and from there overland to London. There I finally bought passage on a Swedish merchant ship and slipped aboard undetected–or so I thought. From Gothenburg, I planned to travel overland to the Nordic Witches and ask for help in getting to Pyrrha–"over the back road", so to speak, across the Black Sea, which is not yet under the control of the Spanish-Ottoman Sultan and his Inquisition."

Kaura breathed deeply as the memories of her ordeal rose. "Then the ship got caught in a storm and was badly damaged. Still, it probably wouldn't have sunk if an Atlantean airship hadn't appeared and ended it all. I don't think they saw me, or they probably would have killed me on the spot. I'm convinced that they sank the ship because of me. Why else?"

Cold anger now showed on Kaura's delicate features. "The plan would have almost succeeded if I hadn't been found and taken aboard by a Baltic merchantman the very same day. And since my memory was still unstable from the hiding process, the shock must have catapulted my short-term memory into an inaccessible area. That is why I have now lost five years, while the 'gods' have had lots of time to further consolidate their power."

They were both silent for several minutes, lost in thought.

Then the Scottish Chief Mage cleared his throat.

"I think I can help you reach Pyrrha, Kaura. What you've just told me puts some of the news of recent years in a different light. I think we at Lockwood Society have a vested interest in seeing this portal opened."

Seriously, he leaned forward.

"The question is, do you still have the means? You've lost the key to unlocking your Gift. The outcome I saw down there in the chamber is not encouraging either."

She shrugged.

"When my energy was really needed, it was there twice so far. Maybe the blockage will weaken on its own in time. Then I might be able to speed it up just by practicing for a while."

Sen agreed. "All right. You can attend the lectures here for as long as you like. Meanwhile, we'll figure out together how to get you through the Spanish front and into Pyrrha."

* * *

Just two weeks later, however, Kaura was in for a surprise that would force her to abruptly change her plans. She was having lunch with Loren and two other students when one of the guard fairies fluttered up and alighted on Kaura's shoulder.

"Happy munch time, ladyboss," she chirped, "you got a visitor. Complicated name, George something-or-other. Sounds Hellenic. Guy says he knows you. Some dude called Joe sent him. Waitin' for ya in the public lobby."

Stunned, Kaura exchanged glances with Loren.

"George Papoutsis! This is Mikhail's manservant from Inmarsund. I'll be down in a moment."

Loren looked longingly at the rice pudding in front of her, then back at Kaura.

"Would you like me to come with you?"

She waved her hand with a smile.

"No need. You'd better enjoy your dessert! I'll see you in class. I can't wait to hear what news George has. And what happened in Inmarsund after I left town."

In a hurry, Kaura walked down the large, curved staircase into the public area of the college and turned to the left into the ornate entrance hall. She came to a stop at the rear entrance.

It was a quiet Wednesday afternoon. A few guard fairies hovered in a corner, chatting as their buzzing, multicolored dragonfly wings cast glittering reflections of light on the walls behind them. A small group of docents walked purposefully toward the main exit.

And sure enough, there was George! He was standing in front of a shelf displaying various trophies and goblets. He was studying the inscriptions engraved on them, his hands buried deep in the pockets of his doublet.

"George!" she called, waving as she dashed toward the man she had last seen slumped unconscious in a hallway in Inmarsund. "I'm so happy to see you well again!"

The older man looked up and a smile came to his face.

"Kaura! It's good to see you! I have news for you from Joe."

He stepped forward to embrace her.

With a smile, Kaura's eyes met his, and it was at that moment that alarm bells began to ring in her head. There was something strangely intense in George's eyes. She flinched back.

It was all happening in a split second. Even as the old man used his left arm to pull her toward him with astonishing strength, Kaura turned away.

At the same time, she noticed that his right hand was still in his coat pocket. Intuitively, she knew that he was going to pull it out now. Something hard scraped the side of her stomach.

Reflexively, Kaura thrust her elbow to the side and hit the arm that held her. Her shoulder struck George's breastbone with a dull thud, sending him tumbling backward into the row of shiny goblets.

Metal crashed and clanked as she completed her turn and continued to plummet.

As if in a trance, she saw a large, curved scimitar fly from George's right hand and bite into the cushion of an armchair next to the shelf. Then her body hit the rough stone floor of the hall with a hard thump.

For a moment, the impact took her breath away. Then she rolled up over her shoulder and came to a standing position, ready to fight. Barely two seconds had passed.

The six winged sentries from the corner were still closing in and had reached her and George a moment later.

Held by invisible bonds and circled by three of the fairies, the servant floated in the air. His face was contorted with hatred, and he struggled with almost superhuman strength against the currents of solidified air that held him.

"Don't hurt him," Kaura gasped. "I don't think he's himself."

One of the now grim-faced guardian fairies glared at the knife.

"Whoever he is right now, he probably didn't mean to give you a tattoo with that thing, sweetheart. We'll turn the killer over to the Oxford City Guard. Let them pull him up by the rope. Shouldn't take long. Sure thing."

"No, wait!" Kaura still struggled to keep her composure. "This is... was... *is* a friend. I think he's under some kind of spell. We should question him here. The matter concerns the Headmaster!"

The spokeswoman of the guard fairies - she had pink eyes and wings of the same color - looked at her questioningly.

"Well then. We can check out the murderous toad for ourselves. Take him to the detention cell," she instructed the three fairies who held the air shackles.

And to another, "Hey, Maria! Call the Superboss and the Psychomagic Chief Guy and tell them what happened here. Let them decide whether we will interrogate the criminal ourselves or call in the Guard.

The flying creature whizzed away while the head fairy turned to the onlookers. Despite the few passersby in the lobby, a dozen people had stopped. All of them looked over curiously.

"'Nothin' left to see!" the pink-winged fairy yelled at the top of her lungs. Her voice boomed through the room like that of a circus announcer—she had probably magically amplified it.

"Keep movin', keep movin'. And don't you dare even think of yapping about this to anyone, you nosy buggers! Or you'll have me to deal with! This is a private matter of Lockwood College. Keep on the move!"

She motioned for Kaura to follow her. In an adjoining room near the servants' quarters, George had already been tied to a chair, now with physical ropes made of hemp. He seemed to have calmed down a bit. When Kaura entered the room, however, he immediately began to struggle against his bonds with all his might.

"Kill, kill," he gasped, sounding like a madman. This impression was reinforced by the vacant look in his eyes.

Breathing heavily, the Headmaster and the Professor of Magopsychology entered the room together a short time later. They both seemed to have been running.

Sen's gaze fell on Kaura.

"Thank Goddess, you are unharmed! The guard fairies told me about the attack. You seem to have good reflexes. They say you know this man?"

He pointed to George, who was slumped in his chair with a crazed look on his face and had foam dripping from his mouth.

"George. He's a friend from Inmarsund. When we had to flee, we left him behind."

Kaura's eyes clouded over.

"We hoped that his position as a servant would keep him out of trouble. It seems that we were wrong. I don't know what the Spaniards did to him to turn him into this. If it was the Spaniards."

Sen growled grimly.

"We'll know in a minute. Most people think we wizards do nothing but straighten bones and talk to trees. But there are other things we can do as well! Doug, get to work and tell us what's going on with him!"

The gray-haired Psychomagician stepped forward and placed a hand on George's forehead. The man writhed like a wild animal.

"Hold him a little tighter, please," the professor asked the guard fairies buzzing about behind him. Suddenly the manservant's head movements stopped, now only allowing his eyes to roll wildly and aggressively in their sockets.

Doug grumbled and nodded.

"Ah, like that," he murmured. "Hmm, not that hard at all. Great mother, they really have no idea how to do this. Ah, now... Well, my dear, now you are free."

He removed his hand from George's forehead and the older man collapsed. It seemed as if all his energy had left him in one fell swoop.

"He'll be his old self soon, and then be able to tell us what happened himself."

Doug turned to the onlookers and waved his thanks to the guardian fairies.

"You may release him now. Stay here for a while until we have cleared up the situation, just to be on the safe side"

Then he turned to the others. "He had a very simple, but quite effective mental weave placed over his will. It probably contained various inner compulsions. One of them was the order to kill Kaura. The prisoner himself will be able to tell us what else was involved. I simply removed the whole complex. He will be himself again."

Fifteen minutes later, George opened his eyes. Unable to understand at first, he looked around at the small group of humans and fairies that surrounded him. Then, memory seemed to flood back into him.

"Oh great Buddha, what have I done!" he groaned.

Desperately, he looked around. When he recognized Kaura, he breathed a sigh of relief.

"At least you survived! I wasn't sure for a moment..."

He fell silent.

Quietly, Sen addressed him.

"You are among friends here. We know that you were subject to a compulsion that was magically implanted in you. Now, will you tell us what happened?"

George's face was filled with disgust and shame, as he began to share his story.

When he had opened the door in Inmarsund that evening, expecting to greet Kaura, his senses had gone blank. He only remembered two shadowy figures outside in the driving snow.

He had woken up in the dungeon of Inmarsund's Spanish residence. Or so he thought, since the guards spoke Spanish and Arabic to each other. Then he had been taken for questioning to the office of an elegantly dressed Spaniard who had introduced himself as Don Alonso. He had been asked a variety of questions about the events at the mansion, most of which he had answered willingly, as they did not seem incriminating to him. However, he had refused to provide information about visitors and contacts of Joe and Mikhail, not knowing if they were also prisoners and what the Spaniards were wanting from them.

His refusal, however, had elicited only a dry laugh from Don Alonso, as had his demand for immediate release, since he had broken no laws.

The Sultan's representative had rung a bell on his desk, and a small man in a ruby red robe had entered the room. He had sat down next to George and told the Spaniard everything the servant from Hellas had tried to keep from him, including Kaura's identity.

In the end, the Inquisitor had whispered in a curt tone that this was all that the stout servant knew, and left.

George's hope to be released from the dungeon after that had been bitterly disappointed. They took him back to his cell and chained him up again.

A little more than a week later, he was blindfolded, taken to a ship, and once again locked up. Upon arrival, he was met by four more of the sinister figures in ruby robes and 'turned' in a brief procedure. That's what they had called the process when talking to each other.

Afterwards, George had no longer been the master of his own will and carried out the orders given to him without the slightest resistance, although he could still remember everything.

"A nightmare!" whispered the old servant. "And yet I am sure it happened. A carriage took me to a place near the Nelson house. Only then I realized they had taken me to London. In the street I was to meet Joe Nelson, who was evidently on his way home, and lure him into a side street without arousing his suspicions. And so it happened. He was suspicious, all right. But he followed me anyway when I told him it was very important and I couldn't talk right there. In the alley, the inquisitors overpowered him with their magical powers, put a sack over his head, and immediately took him away. I just stood there and waited for my next orders. I didn't even feel the desire to help him! I won't ever forget the way he looked at me when he realized I'd betrayed him!"

The manservant writhed in pain as the memory threatened to overwhelm him.

Sen laid a sympathetic hand on his shoulder.

"Don't blame yourself, man! Even experienced magicians have fallen victim to compulsors. The history books are full of it. There was nothing you could have done."

Kaura had gone pale as death in the meantime.

"They took Joe," she said tonelessly. "When was that, George?"

"It must have been early evening the day before yesterday, if my sense of time is not deceiving me," her friend replied. "Then I was sent to the doorman at Nelson House. I had to give my name and deliver a message purporting to be from Joe, saying that he had an urgent matter to attend to which would keep him away for several days. Then I was returned to my prison. The next day one of the inquisitors and a female assistant in a nun's veil took me in a carriage to Oxford, where we spent the night in a house of which I did not see much. Then, shortly before noon, I was brought here. You know the rest."

Exhausted, he fell silent and closed his eyes for a moment. Sen leaned forward a little, along with the wooden chair on which he sat astride.

"Do you think you can give us a clue as to the location of this house where you spent the night? It may be that the Inquisitor and the woman are still there."

George thought for a moment.

"Not exactly. The carriage windows were covered, so I couldn't see anything of the streets. There were only a few turns and a fairly long, straight stretch of road in the middle of the trip. Ah, and as I got into the carriage, I saw part of the house. It was four stories and pitch black, with large angular columns in front, I think they were made of black marble. The carriage was parked in a courtyard separated from the street."

Sen and the Magister of Psychology exchanged glances.

"That sounds like the building of the Legation of the First Day Saints, a private clerical society from Madrid. The Inquisitors must feel very secure to choose such an obvious place to hide," Sen opined.

He rose with a grim smile. "There, that's enough. With this, we know enough to inform the local representative of the Royal Guard. They will do their utmost to catch the assassins. I fear, however, that the Spaniards have already given us the slip. They probably have the college under surveillance and so have known for an hour already that their attack has failed."

"I'm not so sure about that," the second mage objected. "Maybe they care enough about Kaura's death to stay in town and stage a second attempt. And maybe they don't know that we have the means to neutralize their hypnotic spell and thus know their where-abouts. Because there's one more thing I haven't told you yet: The compulsive tissue had a part that was probably designed to kill the bearer if it were touched from the outside. We know such structures from black magic research. It was just extremely sloppily made, and very easy to disarm."

He gave George an apologetic look. "I did not want to frighten you, my friend, and so I kept quiet until now. You have my assurance that all foreign parts have been removed from your mind. You will feel no after-effects. Except for the memories of the time under duress, they will remain with you".

The Headmaster thanked the Magister and gave him leave to return to his lecture. Then he motioned for two of the guarding fairies to follow him.

"I will now go to see the Prefect of the Royal Guard."

On his way out, he turned to the head guard fairy.

"Diana, please see to it that this man is given one of the guest rooms to clean up and rest. Have the kitchen send him something to eat. And both he and Kaura will each be assigned a fairy as a personal guard. In case our Iberian pals try something again. All visitors to the college are to be screened and escorted to their destinations."

The pink-winged fairy saluted with a dashing, only slightly ironic-sounding, "Aye aye, Superboss, sir!"

Sen took a last look at Kaura.

"As soon as I return, we will see what we can do for your friend who is in the hands of the Spaniards. Until then, I ask you to be patient, Kaura, and not to act on your own."

Not even two hours later, Kaura sat across from Sen, who filled her in on what had happened in the meantime. It was not much. The Royal Guard had been very interested in the information that Gifted members of the Holy Inquisition were present on Scottish soil and had immediately sealed all the gates leading in and out of the city. Anyone attempting to leave was now subject to strict scrutiny.

Lockwood and Oxford's second magical society, Easing, had provided specialists to search for the Spanish magician, at the request of the Guard. At the same time, messengers on horseback had been sent to London to inform the Queen and to initiate the search for Joe Nelson.

Kaura listened in silence and nodded.

Then she spoke, slowly and firmly.

"I've been thinking about what we can do to save Joe. I could offer myself as bait to draw out the Spanish spies in Oxford, arrest them and question them about Joe's whereabouts. But we don't even know if they're still here. So we'd be wasting too much time."

Sen nodded in agreement.

" Then what do you suggest? You look like you have a better idea."

Kaura's gaze became hard.

"We do not even know if Joe is still alive. They may have already learned what they wanted to know from him. Either way, time is short. I like to think that the Royal Guards in London are doing everything they can, but they can't beat four magicians. How could they? Against people who can do to most of us what they did to George? So I ask you to give me three or four people who know how to fight with magical means and open the portal to London ahead of time. I know enough about energy magic now to know that we can locate three or four strong sorcerers if they're together and if we're within a few miles from them, and the Inquisitors must be powerful. They will stand out, especially in London, which, unlike Oxford, is not crawling with mages."

Sen glanced at her thoughtfully. There was a fire in his eyes that Kaura had never noticed before.

"Your thoughts are going in the same direction as mine, Kaura. I have already contacted London telepathically. They are preparing the counterpole for the Portal. I myself will be going with you. I haven't been able to get out of my office here for far too long. They can manage without me for a while. This will be fun. Actually, I used to work as an experimental magician for high-risk projects when I was younger. Did I ever tell you that?"

Kaura shook her head and let the wiry High Mage pull her to her feet.

"Gather your things," he growled. "We leave in half an hour. Doug is unfortunately unavailable due to his teaching duties. But Simon Beauville is almost as good at psychomagic, I'm sure he'll be willing to come along. I will also be asking Irene Middlesworth and Eagle Gunnarsdottar to join us. They are two of the best counter-black magicians we have here. And of course Diana with a detachment of guard fairies."

Without looking back, he stormed out the door, calling loudly for Helen, his assistant.

Despite the seriousness of the situation, Kaura found herself grinning. The aging principal seemed to blossom under this challenge.

Almost guiltily, she suppressed a pang of desire that began to spread through her stomach. Yes, she was attracted to Sen. But this was neither the time nor the place to indulge in such thoughts. Especially not now, with her friend and lover Joe missing and possibly dead.

She composed herself and went to her room to pack her few belongings.

In the hallway she met Loren. The girl was beside herself with worry.

"Hey, I heard what happened! They were going to kill you! What now? Did the assassin talk?"

Kaura grabbed her upper arms.

"Calm down, my dear. I am fine. But I must hurry back to London. Joe is in danger. Sen is having the Portal opened."

The brown-haired Scottish woman listened with an open mouth.

"The Portal? Right now? Then it must be important. I would love to go with you and help. That would be more exciting than sitting here and studying. If only I had already finished my degree! I really like you, you know."

Kaura nodded and gave her friend a hug. She felt the calmness of her body transfer to the girl and her breathing sank deeper into her belly.

"I have to go now and get ready. I'll see you again, maybe soon. Good luck with your studies!"

She kissed Loren on the forehead and hurried down the hall.

For the second time in two months, she hurriedly stuffed her few belongings into a linen bag and rushed out the door.

This was starting to become a bit of a habit, she thought to herself absently as she made her way through the crowds of unsuspecting students who were once again on their break.

7

The Hunt Begins

In the anteroom to Oxford's Travel Hall, Kaura found the assembled group ready to go. Only Sen was still missing. George had also come. He had recovered somewhat by now and wore a determined expression on his face. "I must tell Joe's mother personally what has happened," the gray-haired man said simply. "I could never forgive myself otherwise. And maybe Mikhail is still in town, too."

A few minutes later, the Headmaster arrived. He was accompanied by five young men in black robes.

A fleeting smile crossed his lips as he surveyed the assembled group.

"I'm not one for long speeches," he said. "Just this: what we do here is for the sake of magic and the Gifted all over Gaia. You have all volunteered, knowing that we face a dangerous enemy who will stop at nothing. For that, I thank you!"

The five men who apparently were responsible for activating the Portal had already preceded them into the Travel Hall.

A faint blue glow flickered out of the Gothic archway through which Kaura had arrived in Oxford barely three weeks ago.

Led by Sen and two fairies fluttering beside him, the group entered the room where the Portal was already glowing steadily, blue-silver like the sea just after sunset.

The dark-blonde leader of the group, seated in a semicircle next to the portal, turned to Sen.

"The portal is stabilized and we have received the signal feedback, sir. You may pass."

The High Magister of Lockwood nodded his thanks and quickly followed the two guards into the blue mirrored area. Kaura and the other four humans walked right behind. Four more fairies, armed to the teeth, brought up the rear.

In the great Great Travelling Hall of Lockwood House in London, the travelers arrived, single file and flanked by the guards with their multicolored, flickering wings.

Leaning against the column with the golden sphere above it was an old woman of dignified appearance. Her gray hair was tied in a large bun above her head. Her brown-green eyes flashed them a curious glance from beneath bushy eyebrows.

"Hello, Sen!" she greeted the Headmaster. "To what do we owe the unexpected honor of having you visit under such mysterious circumstances?"

With a smile, the man walked up to her and hugged her.

" Straight to the point, as always, Moira! That's what I like about you."

He turned to the small group that had stopped behind him.

"This is Moira Marsfeld, head of our London office. Most of you already know her."

He pointed at Kaura and George.

"These two are friends. They're part of the reason I came."

Moira shook hands with both of them and welcomed each of the remaining members of the group by name. Then she invited them all upstairs to her office, which was generously furnished and had floor-to-ceiling windows that offered a sweeping view of Whitehall Palace and the Thames far below them, and which, Kaura noted with little surprise, seemed to be located on a much higher floor than the building could possibly have.

When Sen had briefly summarized the previous events and explained why they were here, her face became more serious.

"That doesn't sound good, Sen. You have my full support, of course. Four hostile mages here in the city! Great Mother!"

Sen growled, agreeing.

"This is why it is so important for us to start our tasks immediately. Irene and Eagle are going to set up their crystal balls and calibrate them for this area. Is there a room up here on the top floor where they can do their work without being disturbed?"

Moira nodded and rose.

"I will see that all the necessary arrangements are made at once. I will also provide you with some additional guards for courier services and protection."

When she had left the room, Kaura turned to Sen.

"I will accompany George to Nelson House and talk to Jane Nelson. She may have more information for us. And she needs to know what is going on."

"Take Simon with you, and one of the guard fairies waiting downstairs. Simon will be able to warn you in time if you are attacked by psychic means. We must be prepared for anything. Also, Nelson House may be under surveillance or even infiltrated."

That settled the matter for Sen. He turned to the two counter-magicians, who were animatedly discussing the proper placement of the location pentacles so as to cover all of London.

A little later, Kaura came down the stairs, accompanied by George and Simon. The young psychomage had short, reddish-blond hair and seemed rather shy. He did not speak much, but Kaura noticed that he observed his surroundings very carefully.

Every now and then, Kaura caught a sideways glance from him. Maybe he found her attractive, she thought, amused. Well, as long as it didn't distract him from his duties... After all, and despite his young years, he was supposed to be one of Lockwood's most capable mages.

At the bottom of the stairs, a familiar buzz suddenly reached Kaura's ears. So, she was not surprised when a gruff fairy voice chimed up just behind her ear.

"Heyo, boss. Didn't take you long to show up again. Missed London, didn't you? Not much going on in Oxford. All bores down there! And you brought the Superboss with you. He was probably bored too. Have you slept with him yet? And now he can't live without you anymore, can he? Follows you everywhere? Nice muscles he has. And those tattoos. Very sexy."

Ariane clucked her tongue and giggled.

"Not my size, unfortunately. I mean literally. Otherwise nothing could hold me back! Unfortunately, there aren't that many tattooed fairy boys out there. They are all way too well-behaved. They don't even know how to swear properly. So, anyway, I am supposed to look after you wimps to make sure you don't get hurt in the big bad city! Where are we going?"

Kaura decided to ignore the more salacious part of Ariane's speculation and smiled at the miniature woman who was now hovering about a yard in front of her face with buzzing wings.

"Hello Ariane, yes, I'm happy to see you too. We're on our way to the Strand. Nelson House. And there might be some magically endowed Inquisitors trying to get at us while we're there."

"Inquisitors, huh?" the fairy squeaked in surprise. "Since when do those types hang around here? This isn't Spain, where they can frolic around with their thumbscrews and iron maidens! Just a bunch of idiots and phonies! As long as they have their soldiers by their side, they have the courage to do their thing. But there is zero substance behind it! I tell you, as soon as a real woman starts showing them the ropes, they tuck their tails in and bury their shitheads in the sand, these olive-eaters!"

Kaura made a face.

"Still, they kidnapped my friend Joe and may well have killed him. And they tried to have me assassinated in Oxford by George here. They implanted him with a magical psychic compulsion. It would be a mistake to underestimate them."

The guard fairy was silent and gave George a suspicious look.

"Well, since our little pal here is still on the loose, I guess the problem has been resolved. So, let's be careful. Even though Daring and Heroism are my middle names. Ariane D.H. Tinkerbell! Does that ring a bell? Famous family. My great-great-grandmother saved Merlin's life three times. And then there's the whole Peter Pan story! That one was a cool fella, too. Parallel dimension. My great cousin got into him. Unfortunately, they didn't have any kids together. The size difference... Okay, you want to go to Nelson House. Let's go. I'll send for a carriage. In-co-gnito! In case the big bad Spanish Red Riding Hoods are lurking outside wanting to grill you poor little wolf cubbies. And put your hoods on! We wouldn't want anyone to recognize you."

The journey along the Thames was uneventful. The coachman announced them at the gate of Nelson House, and the carriage headed straight for the front door of the large mansion.

Simon had spent the entire journey focusing upon detecting possible magical fields around them, and had noticed no interferences, and neither had there been any attempts at contacting or attacking them.

Quickly and with their hoods pulled low over their faces, the three companions got out of the carriage and hurried into the house.

Ariane had temporarily hidden herself in Kaura's satchel.

"'Cause of my conspicuously radiant personality," she had explained with a grin.

Jane greeted them with a troubled face. When she recognized George, a glimmer of hope flashed through her eyes.

"George! Was that you, the day before yesterday, with the message at the gate? Do you know anything more about what happened to Joe, where he went? It's not like him to disappear like that. And so soon after that ugly business in Inmarsund!"

George flushed and lowered his eyes. He left it to Kaura to briefly explain what had happened.

Simon introduced himself and explained that there was no way for magically untalented people to resist a hypno-weave anchored by four mages.

Jane lowered her head and placed a hand on the servant's arm.

"I don't blame you, George. In fact, I think Mikhail and Joe shouldn't have left you in the mansion like that. Well, what's done is done."

Everyone fell into an anxious silence as Jane led them upstairs to a parlor facing the street and invited them to sit down.

Joe's mother rang a small bell on the table beside her and ordered tea and biscuits. Then she turned back to the others.

The normally resolute woman in the green and gray silk dress seemed to be struggling to keep her composure.

"Well, at least there is a chance that my son is still alive. I blame myself for not insisting on more precautions. After all, we suspected there were more Spanish agents in Scotland. We just felt too safe here in the kingdom."

Kaura nodded sadly. It was completely against this woman's nature to blame herself or others. It showed how shaken she was. They had to turn their focus back to the possibilities of taking some constructive action to save Joe.

Simon seemed to feel the same way.

"We will do everything we can to find out where your son is being held, Mylady. The possibilities of our society are not to be underestimated. And the Royal Guard has already been notified."

Jane nodded gratefully.

"I am worried that the Spaniards may try to take him to Granada. A conflict between Queen Elizabeth and the Spanish-Ottoman Empire has been looming on the horizon for some time. Joe is an important man at court, and he is close to the Queen. He could be useful to the Sultan as a hostage if a declaration of war is indeed made."

Kaura put down her teacup and leaned forward.

"Do you have any way of having all the ships leaving London inspected? After all, the Nelsons are one of the most influential families in the kingdom."

The Scottish woman seemed a little calmer now. She sat up straighter and took a sip of her tea.

"Yes, of course. I will unofficially ask all ship operators if they have observed anything, including for the ships that cast off within the last two days. That should cover most of the possibilities. Over-all, though, there are a lot of independent captains calling into London. And let's not forget that they could have taken him away over land."

She rang twice with the brightly chiming bell, the handle of which showed a filigree figure of the Goddess of Wisdom carved from ivory.

"In addition, I will ask the Guard to search all ships still at anchor. Please excuse me for a moment. I will prepare the appropriate messages immediately. My private secretary Trevor will deliver them to the court himself. I will also apply for an audience with the Queen. I am sure she will receive me promptly when she learns of Joe's disappearance."

With energetic steps she left the room. There was a muffled conversation with someone in the antechamber to be heard, and then they were left alone.

Kaura, Simon and George sat in their chairs in a brooding silence. Even Ariane, who had made herself comfortable on a bookshelf, said nothing for once. Her iridescent violet eyes gazed pensively into empty space.

Simon took a deep breath and stood up. He walked over to one of the large windows that looked out over the courtyard wall to the alley below. He gazed out thoughtfully.

Although it was only the end of February, and the winter officially still lasted until the twenty-first of March, this day definitely felt like spring.

The first yellow flowers had appeared on the bushes, and the oaks in the courtyard of the mansion were covered with small shoots that already hinted at the light green of the sprouting leaves that would soon cover the trees.

Suddenly, he gave a start. He had noticed something that did not belong among the colorful hustle and bustle of passersby, draft horses, street dogs, and brightly colored vegetation.

Unobtrusively, he stepped away from the opening.

"Don't come near the window!" he warned the others. "There's something down there in the street. The light field of a mage. Unmistakable. He or she is leaning against a wall diagonally across from the gate, watching the mansion."

Fluttering like a dragonfly, Ariane appeared behind him, poking her small, blonde head over his shoulder.

"Tell me where, and don't make any fancy moves!"

He described it to her.

An expectant grin slid across the features of the guardian fairy.

"We'll go get him, Simon. Won't we? He's going to wish he'd never heard of Ariane D. H. Tinkerbell!"

The psychomage seemed much less enthusiastic than the winged being, yet nodded.

"I think we should be able to deal with him. Unless he's got someone to back him up."

Ariane laughed.

"Backup? That one? These inquisi-diots, they all believe that the world lies at their feet. "Holy" and all that shit, my ass! And they're probably even more arrogant if they can do magic. All we have to do is to get out of this place without attracting his attention. Then we're going to sneak up behind the holey shoe! And BOOM!" she crowed. "Once we get him to Westminster, he'll talk like a grave! Uh, I mean like a waterfall! They're not the only ones who know about torture, those holy cockroaches! We fairies can do that, too. Only we are a lot nicer. And prettier!"

With a raised eyebrow, Kaura looked over at Simon.

"Are fairies all that, um, articulate?"

The young man grinned wryly.

"More or less. They're louder in groups. But Ariane here is something of a celebrity, I would say."

He winked at the fairy, who was fluttering like an impatient parrot at the exit door.

"You betcha, psychoball! Come on, let's go!"

Then she blinked at Kaura and George. "We'll be right back. Don't have a care in the world. Success is two hundred percent guaranteed!"

The door slammed shut behind them before anyone could respond.

A short time later, Jane was back.

"Where did your companions go?"

Kaura told her.

With enough distance to the window they both looked out. But they could not see anything out of the ordinary at first. Then Kaura blinked.

"It must be that man over there in the brown woollen coat and the green harem pants. Now he's not leaning against the wall any-more, he's pacing back and forth," Kaura said.

"Let's go down to the entrance hall," Jane suggested. "Maybe we can distract the spy so your friends can approach unseen. George, I was going to ask you anyway to ride down to the harbor and give this message to Abigail, the steward of our harbor facilities."

She handed him a roll of parchment.

"This is the order for the survey of the other shipowners. Abigail will know what to do. You can tell her everything. She's practically family."

Downstairs, Jane beckoned to the servant who had brought the tea earlier, then turned to Kaura and explained her plan.

"You and I are going to take George outside and talk for a while. That should give the fairy and your friend a chance to sneak up on the spy without being noticed, especially since George's presence is likely to surprise him. James here will quietly inform the sentry at the gate to let your friends in as soon as they have the stranger in hand.

Kaura nodded. She estimated that enough time had passed for the fairy and the mage to get out into the street unseen. James, the servant, had shown them a side door a few minutes ago without knowing exactly what it was about.

Jane opened the door to the front yard of the mansion and waved to the stablehand.

Kaura and George followed her, trying not to stare through the open gate at where they knew the Inquisitor was. The boy headed for the low stables to the side of the property to saddle a horse for George and bring it out. Then Jane turned back to them.

"George, I suppose you want to rejoin Mikhail? Abigail can tell you where to find him. I would advise you both to leave London for some time until the area is safe for you again. Abigail can arrange a carriage for you to our seat in Somerset. The caretaker there is elderly and will appreciate your assistance. You'll be safe there for the time being. You..."

A deafening bang drowned out her words. At the same time, a bright flash flooded the immediate area. For a moment, Kaura thought she had gone blind. More subconsciously than with her senses, she felt a beam of bright light shoot toward her from outside the courtyard, bouncing off a shimmering purple bubble around her like a stream of water off an upturned bowl.

The world spun around her. As if through a dark veil, she saw Jane sink to the ground beside her. George was standing there, frozen in place, obviously not understanding what had just happened.

"Neither do I," Kaura's mind flashed.

There was a scuffle going on outside the gate, the nature of which she could not quite make out. Jane was kneeling beside her, holding her ears. Her silk dress was singed and gave off an acrid smell.

"Oh heavens, what was that?" Kaura heard as if through a giant cotton ball.

Jane, apparently quickly regaining her senses, got to her feet and motioned to the approaching gatekeeper to rather go deal with the commotion outside the gate.

"He must not escape! The man in the brown coat!" Kaura croaked, not knowing if the guard could even hear her. The man seemed to have understood what they wanted from him, for he drew his sword and ran back to the gate.

By the time he got there, it was all over. Seven fairies fluttered around an unconscious figure whose cowl had slipped back to reveal a bluish, bald head. Beside him, Simon wiped blood from his eyes with the back of his hand, smearing the red liquid all over his face, making it look as if he had been massacred. He seemed to mutter something. Or maybe Kaura just couldn't hear it because her ears were still deafened.

Sen jumped out of an approaching carriage, followed by the two counter-magicians. Softly, as if from afar, Kaura heard his voice.

"Everything is under control, folks. The danger is over. Keep moving. We'll take care of the assassin. In the name of the Queen, keep moving!"

The Headmaster recognized Kaura, who had walked up to the gate in the meantime, waved and said something, probably at a normal volume, but she only saw his moving lips.

She shook her head, uncomprehending and still dazed. He took her arm and pointed to the carriage. Without resistance, she let him lead her to the still open door of the carriage and climbed in.

Beside her, like a flash of purple and gold, Ariane fluttered into the carriage and waved cheerfully. Sitting down, Kaura looked back out. Through the open window of the carriage door, she saw the lifeless form of the Inquisitor float up between the two sorceresses and be maneuvered into the interior of a second carriage that had now also arrived.

At the gate in the outer wall, Jane gestured to the gatekeeper and seemed to give him instructions. Then the entrance darkened, and first Simon and then Sen pushed their way in to join her.

With a wooden crash, still muffled as if by absorbent cotton, the door slammed shut and the carriage jerked violently as the coachman released the horses' reins.

Sen touched Kaura's forehead with the index and middle fingers of his right hand, and a cool, trickling shiver ran through her entire body.

Suddenly, she could hear again. Beside her, the gaunt Scot repeated the motion for Simon, and it seemed to stop the bleeding immediately.

"You were a little ahead of us," Sen called over the rumble and creak of the carriage. He made a quick circular motion with his index finger, and the interior of the carriage fell abruptly silent. Only the bumping and swaying of the wooden vehicle was as violent as before.

"There, that's better," he continued at a normal volume. "We'll be back at Lockwood House in a few minutes anyway. What were you thinking, standing around outside, practically under the nose of an assassin sent by the Inquisition?"

Kaura and Simon tried to answer at the same time and fell silent.

Simon gave way to the dark-skinned woman with a gesture.

"We assumed it was just an observer," she said. "We wanted to distract him to give Ariane and Simon a chance to get to him unseen." Kaura felt herself blush. She really could have been more careful, especially in view of the last attempted assassination that had happened just some hours ago.

Simon nodded in agreement and turned to his superior.

"That wasn't needed, but I also had no idea that the guy would start conjuring Witch Fire when he saw Kaura. Luckily, I saw the spell while he was still setting it up and was able to put a protective shield around the three of them. We're lucky no one else was in the way. No one would have survived that... Why did you turn up so soon? Had we known, we would have waited for you, of course."

Sen laughed grimly.

"When Eagle and Irene set up their Tracking Pentacle, we were in for a surprise. They found only two places in the city with high concentrations of magical energy: Lockwood House and the Nelson Mansion, where we knew you would be. That's pretty unusual for a city this size, although as we all know, mages don't like to travel much these days. Anyway, at first we thought the birds had already flown the coop. Then Eagle realized that the signature at the Nelsons' was too strong for Simon alone. And Kaura still has her pendant. She could have taken it off, of course, but we wanted to check it out anyway. Looks like we got there just in time."

"" We had already stopped him, Boss, Simon and I!" chirped Ariane between them. "Only we couldn't foresee the witch fire. That damned wicked spatula! Son of a whoring cockroach! One-legged amoeba! Cold planet bed-bug! Does he even know what he's unleashing here, this bloody crucifix-headed cannonball?"

"I'm afraid he did," Sen replied calmly. "And I also fear that his associates are no longer in London. That makes me fear the worst for Kaura's friend. At best, they've just dragged him off somewhere. At worst..."

He shrugged.

At high speed, the carriage whipped around a corner and through a gate. Only then did the horses slow down.

Behind them, the rapid clatter of more hooves could be heard, as the teams of two other carriages were approaching and slowing as well. Then there was the squeaking of metal hinges as the gate closed and was locked behind them.

Kaura was the first to climb out of the carriage. Her knees almost buckled as her feet hit the gravel of the courtyard. She held on to a spoke of the wagon wheel until she could stand on her own.

"Quick recovery spells take the energy for healing from your body's reserves," Sen remarked, noticing her swaying. "You weren't badly hurt, so you should feel better soon. Once you regain access to your own power, you'll be able to draw on field energy for something like this, so you won't be weakened by the process."

Followed by the two witches, with the air-cuffed prisoner hovering between them, the small group entered the back of the house. Glancing behind them, Kaura saw that Jane had also arrived, probably in the last coach. The grey-haired woman gave her a tired but encouraging wave.

In the hallway, Sen spoke to one of the black-clad maids. Then he followed the group into an adjoining room. There, the fairies had already placed the still unconscious Inquisitor on an armchair and tied him up.

"Much too nice for that musty cockroach! He'd deserve a bed of nails!" Ariane whispered angrily. The guard fairy had made herself comfortable on Kaura's shoulder and watched critically as her colleagues tied the ropes. In a large semicircle behind the prisoner, all the magicians Lockwood House could muster had been hastily gathered.

Kaura could see the field they had placed around the Spanish agent. It glowed green and would prevent him from accessing his magical abilities while he was being interrogated.

Sen beckoned Simon to join him as he faced the bound being.

"While I'm questioning him, you read his mind. Even if he lies, he'll think of the right thing. Try to find out who he is, where he's from, anything else you can. And don't be squeamish! If you have any more questions, connect with me telepathically."

He turned to Eagle, who was standing at one end of the semicircle next to the prisoner.

"We can begin. Wake him up!"

Grimly, the Headmaster leaned forward, causing the tiny bells woven in his dreadlocks to jingle.

One of the guard fairies - this one with greenish iridescent wings - brought an instrument that looked like a Mongolian metal chopstick twisted inside itself. Almost tenderly, the fair-haired, brightly glowing creature ran her fingertips along the stick several times until the tip began to glow. She touched the wand to the bound man's forehead, drawing a symbol that Kaura couldn't quite make out. Then she fluttered back into the circle of six fairies that hovered just below the massive beams holding up the ceiling, and who were observing the proceedings from above.

The Inquisitor's eyelids flickered. Again, Kaura marveled at the man's bluish complexion. His skull was more elongated than she had ever seen. Was this some sort of strange human being, a magician like themselves? Or a magical being from another world? A demon? Did Sen know what kind of creature they were dealing with here? She would have to ask him about that later.

Then the creature opened its eyes, and most of those present—except the Headmaster—took an involuntary step back. The Inquisitor's eyes, deep black and shining like obsidian, showed no emotion. His mouth opened to reveal a row of sharp, pointed teeth. This was most assuredly not a human being, Kaura decided.

"I see I am in good company," the Inquisitor breathed. "I will allow you to submit to me and to untie me. No harm will come to you."

The corners of his mouth lifted in a kind of smile. His sharklike teeth gleamed in the light of the small artificial sun that hovered in the center of the ceiling.

A cold, black gaze fixed on Sen, who returned it calmly, without blinking. Ariane clawed her hand into Kaura's shoulder and muttered incomprehensible words, too low for the young woman to hear. From the sound of it, they seemed to be curses and insults.

Sen's voice was sober and hard.

"You are in no position to make demands here, I'm afraid. If you are reasonable, if you speak, perhaps we'll let you live. Maybe we'll even exchange you for the man you kidnapped."

The creature made a hissing sound that was probably meant to be a laugh.

"The barbarian is long dead. We have cut the key out of him."

Simon, standing at one side of the room, shook his head slightly as Sen continued to speak, seemingly unperturbed.

"Why were you outside of Nelson House? And why did you try to kill the women?" he continued.

The creature hesitated for a moment.

"I'm not going to tell you anything. Why should I? You will soon be slaves of the Great Masters anyway. If you release me now, you will live long enough to experience this honor."

Sen grimaced.

"Where are your accomplices? Where is Joe Nelson, and what are you going to do with him? What key are you talking about? What kind of creature are you, and where do you come from? How many of you are present within the Inquisition, and what is your role there? Who are the Great Lords, and what is their plan? Speak, or we shall use other means."

The Inquisitor pursed his lips and spat. A poison-green flash shot in the direction of Sen's face. Almost simultaneously, one of the fairies hovering near the ceiling waved her hand, and the green spittle vanished in a small orange-yellow explosion. There was a smell of burnt vinegar and acid.

The tattooed principal seemed completely unmoved. He had not even flinched.

"For the last time. What is your mission? How many Spanish spies are there in Scotland, who are they and where are they, what are they here for? Where was Joe Nelson taken? What are you doing with the kidnapped magicians? Who are your masters? You are not really working for the Spanish Crown, are you? More likely, you're using the Sultan for something. For what?" Sen's voice grew more and more harsh.

He glanced sideways at Simon. The psychomage nodded and shrugged at the same time.

"You think you can get something out of me like this? You are all slaves already, you just don't know it yet," the bound man whispered.

"This girl will yet wish my *Cleansing Fire* had caught her."

The Headmaster's gaze turned icy.

"Well, you asked for it. Simon, do your thing!"

He took a step back. An expression of intense concentration entered the face of the young mage standing beside him. His eyes seemed to be staring into space with a fixed gaze.

The bound creature on the chair let out another hissing laugh. Then the sound suddenly broke off. The blue color of its face took on a slight greenish tint.

"No, it can't be," it whispered.

The Inquisitor began to scream in agony as if he were being tortured. The screen field around him changed color slightly, and the noise became quieter—probably either the mages or the fairies had changed something about it to let less of the noise through.

Sweat ran down Simon's face.

"I'm getting there," he panted. "Masters... Rignar! Who or what is Rignar?" he shouted at the Inquisitor.

At the same moment, a bright explosion flashed inside the bubble, reflecting off the inner walls of the magical field.

Kaura reflexively turned away, expecting to be hit by a searingly hot shock wave. But nothing happened. The air in the room remained as cool and still as before.

Sen gestured imperiously to Eagle, who was commanding the shield mages.

"Keep the field up until we see what happened in there. We can't help him anyway."

The woman nodded. The field, now intensely blue, billowed like a soap bubble. Nothing could be seen inside except black-gray steam and smoke that gradually thinned. Soon it became clear that the Inquisitor had disappeared. The chair and ropes were now nothing more than smoldering debris. In a circular area around the chair, the oak floor was charred black and littered with embers. Scorched pieces of green and brown wool lay scattered about—remnants of the prisoner's clothing.

Sen nodded to Eagle.

"He is gone. You may remove the shield now."

A gush of hot, smoky air poured out into the room with a slight hiss as the blue bubble disappeared without a trace. Someone coughed.

Kaura noticed that the warm air immediately began to move, a suction being created in the direction of one corner of the room. Once again, she marveled at the perfection of the magical air conditioning in this ancient building.

"Well." Sen seemed in no way rattled by the unexpected event. "At least it saves us the question of whether or not to turn that son of a bitch over to the Royal Guard. He probably deserved to have his head impaled on one of the bars of the South Bastion at London Bridge. But capital punishment is not really my thing."

He turned to Simon.

"Do you have what we need?"

The red-haired man smiled.

"The essentials, at least. The most sensitive information was protected by densely woven energy screens, likely put there by someone else. Much more professional work than what they'd done to George. In the end, though, I almost got to the identity of the 'masters'. Then I must have triggered the suicide circuit."

Sen nodded.

"No risk, no fun. Frankly, I don't think we've seen the last of our friend yet. That looked more like an evasive spell than a self-destruction one to me. I read about something like that once. It seems that Merlin's dark adversaries also used such energy weaves."

He turned away from the burnt spot on the floor.

"Let's go to the large drawing room. It will be less smelly there while we listen to Simon's report. Besides, it's time for afternoon tea. My stomach is already rumbling."

Soon everyone was holding large porcelain cups of fragrant, bergamot-flavored black tea.

Cakes, scones with clotted cream and jam, as well as heaps of small triangular sandwiches were carried up by two servants on multi-tiered silver trays.

Carefully, Kaura poured a little milk into her cup, watching the white liquid spread in an expanding cloud across the shimmering golden-brown liquid of the tea.

Yet another explosion, she thought. She wished against all reason that her life would be limited from now on, at least for a time, to bringing her explosions that smelled of bergamot and tea-leaf.

As she added some honey and stirred with an ornate silver spoon, Simon began his report.

He gave a nod of appreciation to Sen.

"Your questioning technique was spot on, Sen. With so many questions, he had no time to even think, and I was able to pluck the right answers from his mind like ripe plums. These Inquisitor-Mages are really strange. On the one hand, they can use witchfire and embed curses in the minds of people, but on the other, they don't even seem to know how to effectively shield their thoughts. I even wondered if it was all a trick. But I don't think it was. Maybe they just don't have any experience with mind readers. After all, there aren't many of us."

While he collected his thoughts, he took a sip of his tea and hastily stuffed a small, triangular sandwich into his mouth.

Still chewing, he continued.

"Sorry. I'm starving. Well, Joe Nelson isn't really dead, and these Inquisitors don't even know exactly what this key they're looking for is. By now they seem to suspect that it is Joe himself. In any case, they have received orders that once he is captured, he is to be immediately taken to Ireland, from where a Spanish ship is to carry him to the Mediterranean. Our friend did not know exactly where the ship was waiting. Two of the Inquisitors are with him. The ship is called the Empress of Cork, and it left London yesterday. The port of destination they gave in their papers was Cork. Our prisoner and the one who was assigned to carry out the assassination attempt on Kaura are–were, in his case–now the only remaining Spanish mages in Britain. Or so he believed. He had had no contacts with any other Spanish spies."

"Did you find out anything about their hideout in London?" Ariane interjected with her squeaky voice.

"Yes. Apparently they were officially listed as guests at the Sanctuary of the Martyrs of Rome. Another one of those private ecclesiastical societies. The Queen should have all these institutions placed under unobtrusive surveillance."

"We will suggest it to her. Go on," Sen urged him.

"I couldn't quite put my finger on the place where those fellows come from," Simon went on. "He had memories of great cities full of similar-looking blue-skinned beings. So it seems to be a large civilization. There are relatively few of them in the Inquisition, a few dozen perhaps. And as you suspected, Sen, they feel vastly superior to their human compatriots and the entire Spanish-Ottoman nobility. Although the latter do seem to be under the impression that the beings do their bidding. How the whole thing is supposed to be compatible with the dual religion of the Sultanate, I don't understand at all. Oh, well... As we all know, the end justifies the means, according to Mr. Macchiavelli. So the Spaniards probably won't ask too many questions as long as they think they'll gain an advantage. That's about it. The fact that we are all supposed to end up as slaves has something to do with all the magicians they kidnapped in the last few decades. He really believed that, by the way; it wasn't meant to be a bluff. And it was the plans of their 'masters' that were connected to the mental mechanism that made our friend take his leave so suddenly. I almost had the impression that I was penetrating the armor. Then came this name–Rignar–and when I asked him about it... BAM!"

Simon clapped his hands, making everyone jump and nearly causing Kaura to spill her tea. Then the young psychomage fell silent.

A short time later, Moira knocked on the door frame and entered the room.

"Am I interrupting? No? I thought you would be interested to know that in Oxford an Inquisitor was found out when he was trying to leave the city. The news just came in through the telepathy department. He was killed in a skirmish with the King's Guard and some warlocks from Easing College. The battle has apparently caused quite a stir among the general populace, and the Wizards' Colleges are doing their best to limit the damage to our reputation. It does help that the other mage was a Spaniard. And that the whole thing was done in collaboration with the Royal Guard."

Sen thanked her and she withdrew immediately to attend to her duties.

Now Jane spoke. Despite the seriousness of the situation, she seemed somewhat more relaxed, now that she had learned that Joe was still alive.

"We don't have a second to lose," she said, looking around challengingly. "I would send a ship after them myself. But with my son being guarded by two of those *things*"–she looked like she was about to vomit–"that would probably not be of much help."

She looked over to Sen.

"High Magister, if Lockwood can help our family in this situation, I shall not forget. I will have a new school built for you if you wish."

Sen gave her a friendly smile.

"I don't think that will be necessary, the old one is still quite serviceable. However, no one in our society ever had any objection to accepting a generous donation."

He sighed. "We would try to help Joe anyway, from what we

know so far. I have little interest in ending up a slave to these mysterious 'masters'."

Jane placed her hand gratefully on his arm.

"Then we are agreed. I will put the Pride of Edinburgh, the fastest and best-armed of our ships currently moored in London, at your disposal. Can I use one of your messenger fairies to inform the captain?"

Sen agreed, waving to Diana.

Five minutes later, one of the guards shot out of an open window like an arrow. She carried a message writtenby Jane in miniature script in front of her chest.

A short time after the fairy had left, the wizards set off as well. They had decided to take three large rowboats down the Thames directly to Nelson Harbor in Southwark. Jane would leave them at her house, which was about halfway down the river.

Kaura took a seat on one of the sturdy benches of the dinghy she'd been assigned to. Ariane, whom she hadn't seen for a while, also fluttered up.

"Hello, fairy!" Kaura tiredly greeted her friend, "I thought you'd let me go without saying farewell.

"Goodbye, my ass!" the fairy replied in her thin but raspy little voice. "I'm going with you, of course, boss! Without me, those Inquisidiots would have you squished in a fluff! I don't want that for you wimps. It would be a downer! Not to mention the Superboss! Be a real bummer to lose him! Those tattoos, there ain't no second coming!"

She lowered her voice. "But actually, I'm supposed to be your bodyguard. Because he's worried about you, the Superboss. I told you, he likes you... you just wait, soon there will be tattooed kiddos running all over the place!"

Kaura blushed at the fairy's vivid imagination and tried to imagine tattooed toddlers. She giggled.

"You're good at lifting my spirits anyway," she grinned at the fairy, holding on to the gunwale as the rowers pushed the dinghy away from the dock. The boat rocked violently.

The current carried the small convoy swiftly down the Theme, the Watermen skillfully maneuvering between the heavy river traffic. Soon, they had Whitehall Palace looming up on their left.

"One thousand five hundred rooms," muttered Ariane, who by now had settled comfortably on Kaura's shoulder. "Largest palace in Europe! One heck of a dig. Bigger than the Vatican. Well, those guys haven't had much to say anymore since the Spanish-Ottoman reformed the Church and merged it with the Musulmans. Anyway, that palace! I am telling you, you wouldn't believe what goes on in there. You always have this idea that these kings and nobles are somehow respectable. Don't you? But let me tell you, they party! That's where it's at! That's where the blue pigs are gallivanting. Lots of fun. Being a fairy, you can get in anywhere. The bouncers are lickin' my feet, I tell ya!"

Tired, Kaura turned away, hoping the fairy would take the hint.

The little creature did, and fell silent. Presently, they were both lost in their own thoughts.

Fifteen minutes later, they reached the landing jutting out into the river from the big backyard of Nelson House.

Kaura bid Jane a heartfelt goodbye and asked her to take good care of Atam, who would have to stay without her for longer than originally planned. The dog had suffered greatly in the rough North Sea weather on their journey from Inmarsund, and Kaura did not want to put him through another long sea passage if she could avoid it. Jane had no objection to the idea, as the dog would hardly want to be away from the Nelson cats anyway. The three of them obviously still got along well.

When they were almost ready for casting off again, Kaura had a thought.

"Can I get something from Joe's room?" she asked Jane. "He had a book with him. It contains some notes that might be important to us. Maybe it's still there."

The Scotswoman nodded, and Kaura joined her on the jetty. Jane led her inside and up the stairs.

Joe's suite of rooms was in complete chaos, and she involuntarily drew a comparison with Sen's study. Still, she didn't have to search for very long. The Atlantic edition of *Mila Intan's Travels* stood on a half-empty bookshelf, in full view, leaning against a carelessly stacked pile of other volumes.

Kaura flipped through the pages quickly until she found the passage containing the reference to the portals. Meanwhile, Jane had fetched her a quill with ink and a piece of blank parchment from Joe's overloaded desk.

Concentrating, she dipped the quill into the inkwell and carefully copied the note, including the strange symbols next to it. She dried the page, waving it back and forth a few times at the end to dry any remaining wet patches.

Then she carefully folded it and placed it in her shoulder bag.

Hugging Jane goodbye one last time, she hurried down the stairs and ran back to the boats, where her friends were waiting impatiently.

Soon, London Bridge towered over the boats like a wall of stone and wood. Since there was no high-water at the moment, the massive wooden dinghies crossed the eddies and waves under the span without any of the occupants getting wet.

Shortly after clearing the bridge, the rowers turned right and approached the Nelsons' extensive dock facilities.

The large four-masted hull of the Pride still lay where Kaura had last seen it.

There was a great bustle around the ship at this early evening hour. Sacks and barrels of all kinds were being carried aboard, stacked and loaded.

Wooden crates filled with cannonballs were swung from outriggers into the ship's hold. Chickens clucked in their cages, and sailors and dockworkers communicated with one another in loud shouts.

Ignoring the helpfully extended hand of an oarsman, Kaura grabbed the rungs of the metal ladder attached to the dock and pulled herself up with a few powerful heaves.

A small group of people were already waiting for her. Next to Sen, she recognized the harbormaster, Abigail, as well as captain McGregor. She went over to greet them.

Abigail immediately threw her arms around Kauras neck and pressed herself against her, trembling with emotion.

"Good heavens, I heard what happened. Poor Joe! And you were going to be killed!"

Gently, Kaura pulled away from her and nodded.

"Luckily, I got away. And we'll find Joe, too. They don't have much of a head start."

Elias McGregor growled in agreement and held out his hand to Kaura.

"Welcome back, Miss Leivenstein. Kaura, I mean. We'll be ready to cast off in half an hour, leaving the Thames with the remnants of the outgoing tide."

He nodded over to the Nelsons' administrator. "Abigail here has decided to join us as well. She cares deeply about Joe's fate."

Surprised, Kaura looked at the other woman, but then smiled. Despite her emotionality, the blonde Scotswoman seemed to know how to fight when she had to.

Soon they were all aboard. Kaura was greeted enthusiastically by the members of the crew, almost as if she were a long-lost family member.

She was assigned to sleep in the owner's quarters, where she and

Joe had stayed on the voyage from Inmarsund. She was surprised that Sen or Abigail had not been given this honor, but gladly accepted.

It was only a few days later that she learned that Sen, the designated leader of the rescue operation, had stepped aside in her favor. Supposedly, he had pointed out that there was a strict hierarchy among mages based on their energy levels. And in that respect, she outranked him by a considerable margin.

Sen and Abigail had each taken an empty chamber on the aft deck, while the others occupied shared accommodations on the mid deck.

Like most of Nelson's galleons, the Pride was not just a merchantman, but was also designed to carry passengers. This now proved to be useful.

On the large table in the passengers' mess, Eagle and Irene had already installed a small version of their tracking pentacle. The crystal balls had been magically affixed to the tabletop. The two witches assured that the installation would not shift even on the open sea and would indicate strong magical potentials up to about ten nautical miles away.

Shortly before nightfall, the mooring lines were let go and the sails set. The great wooden ship began to move leisurely downriver towards the Thames estuary, carried by the ebbing tide.

For a long time, Kaura stood on the balustrade of the quarterdeck behind the helmsman and watched as the great city behind the Galleon fell away into the evening mist.

It was out of the corner of her eye that Kaura saw a figure step up next to her. It was Abigail. The other woman nodded a greeting and leaned against the stern balustrade beside her. A faint scent of jasmine wafted over from her hair, which was fluttering in the brisk evening breeze.

The women sighed almost simultaneously. They both stared for a moment into the ship's wake, which spread out behind the stern like a curving fan of shimmering foam.

"You like him too, don't you?" the Scottish woman broke the silence.

Kaura just nodded.

"I don't mind," Abigail said thoughtfully. "And I know you Baltic people believe you can't own someone. So do I."

Kaura nodded again and smiled.

"I'm glad you feel that way."

Abigail swallowed.

"I like you a lot, too. Would you... would you share the bed with me tonight? No strings attached? I'd rather not sleep alone right now."

Kaura gave the freckled woman a sideways glance. Then she smiled and leaned in closer.

"May I kiss you?" she asked.

Abigail nodded shyly, and their lips met.

8

Into the Lion's Den

The next morning, the *Pride* was pounding through the choppy waters of the English Channel. The Breton coast had to be hiding somewhere off to port in the mist. To starboard, some of the chalk cliffs the Scottish South was famous for shone white in the distance. Sir Elias lowered the spyglass he had just been using to scan the horizon.

"I can't see us catching up with them before they reach Ireland," he said. "Their lead is just too big. Our old girl here may be a speedy one, but not quite that speedy." Full of affection, the captain patted the big sailing ship's bulwark.

Sen calmly stood at his side.

"Then we'll have to try something else. I see two possible courses: Either we cruise near Cork and check all departing ships with our location pentacle, or we head straight for the harbor and try to find out if the Spaniards are still there, and if not, what ship they took."

Sir Elias grunted in agreement. Above him, the wind, blowing steadily from the northeast, sang its song in the bulging sails.

"I favor the second option. If they changed ship fast enough and are already on their way to Gibraltar, we'll lose them otherwise."

"I don't think they did, but you're right," agreed the Headmaster, who by now had swapped his black robe for a waxed, dark beige canvas jacket. The bells in his thick hair jingled constantly, but so softly that they were easily drowned out by the sound of the wind. He looked thoughtfully down at the main deck.

There, four members of the fairy contingent were fluttering around the stays of the main mast, buffeted by the wind and bantering with some of the crew, who were just working on trimming the sails.

It seemed they were comparing curses. Just at that moment, one of the sailors blushed furiously and began to stammer.

Sen laughed in amusement and turned back to the captain.

"Your men could learn a lot from my fairies. At least when it concerns creative profanities."

Sir Elias grinned.

"I haven't seen any of those for far too long. They used to hang out in the bars in most ports, getting drunk on one mug of beer that lasted the whole group for hours, and annoying everyone with their stories about the other worlds. Everyone liked them anyhow. Shame, this anti-magic sentiment the Spanish have been spreading everywhere for decades now.

He pointed to the chiming bells in Sen's hair.

"And what is that on your head, my friend? You're tingling like a small herd of mountain goats. Or is that too personal a question?"

Sen grinned mischievously.

"Continuous cleansing of the energy field," he replied. "It makes it almost impossible for black magicians to read my mind or even dominate me."

His grin deepened. "Of course, I could do this without the bells if I had to. But they tend to confuse people. I like to look unusual.

And they make me more attractive for women. Mysterious, if you know what I mean."

Sir Elias cocked his head hesitantly but didn't reply. It was obvious that the connection between a jingling hairstyle and success with the female sex was not entirely clear to the old sailor.

He understood tattoos, even though he himself wore only an anchor on his upper arm. But chiming dreadlocks? Those wizards really were a crazy bunch!

And to think that this man was not just any wizard, but the leader of what was supposed to be the most respectable sorcerer's society in all of Britain! Well, at least he was likeable enough. And he gave the impression of knowing what he was about, which to McGregor was the most important thing in view of the nature of their opponents.

The captain turned his thoughts to other, more pressing matters and passed some new instructions to the navigator.

Below him, Sen had now spotted Kaura and Abigail, who had come out onto the main deck together, their faces slightly flushed.

He waved cheerfully to the two women and, hands still in his jacket pockets, balanced down the companionway from the quarterdeck.

The continuous movement of the ship did not seem to bother him at all. The wizard moved across the deck as confidently as if he were walking on the brushed marble floor of his Oxford college.

"Anything on the Pentacle?" he asked Kaura. "No? I thought not. But as of tonight, someone should always be there to keep watch. Soon we'll be leaving the Channel and approaching the Irish peninsula. We may be coming across the ship with those we're looking for at any time, if they've already left Cork."

The Irish Peninsula was connected to the miniature continent of North Atlantis by a mountainous land bridge and was inhabited by people of distant kinship to the Atlanteans.

The Irish cities formed only loose alliances, which had led to both Spain and the Scots squabbling for influence on the island.

Kaura did not know the current political position of the trading city of Cork, located in the southeast of the peninsula. Cork was one of the so-called *Middle Ports*. Probably they were still rather neutral, since the Inquisitors intended to transfer to a Spanish ship there, and at the same time Sir Elias assumed to be able to call the port without any problems.

Her gaze was lost in the distance behind the waves, topped with small white foam caps.

She thought of Joe. And of Abigail, who was leaning against the bulwark between her and Sen, the older woman's body nestling softly against her now and then as the ship rolled. Of how she felt about Sen. And if she would ever be able to use her magical talent again. If she did, that would make her one of the most powerful women in the hierarchy of Scottish witches. Assuming she would choose to stay on the Island.

Kaura shuddered. First, she had a mission to fulfill. For human-kind and a people she couldn't even remember. Why had she been left alone in this way?

Who were those Lemurians? And she was one of them, had agreed to lose all her memories for years, only to be sure to reveal them to no one. Why were her people so reclusive? And were they really still her people?

The inhabitants of the Baltic coastlines had won her heart and she felt at home there. And now there were these Scots, who had helped her with all their abilities, without caring that she wasn't one of them, and without asking first what she could offer them in exchange.

But her mission was not only important for the Lemurians, she reminded herself. Those 'gods' obviously did not mean well, and their plans seemed to include the entire world. So, she had to open this portal and ask the Aalids for help. And to achieve that goal, she had found the best companions a woman could ask for.

Smiling, she looked over to Sen, who winked at her confidentially.

"It'll be fine," the old mage said, licking a few drops of spray from his lips as they splashed over the bulwark and right into his face. "Everything."

* * *

A day later, the *Pride of Edinburgh* was moored in the docks of Crosshaven Harbor, a few miles downriver from Cork. Eagle and Irene had split into shifts, with at least one of them keeping an eye on the tracking pentacle at all times.

The Scottish galleon had not, it seemed, even come close to any other ships carrying mages along the way. Their best hope was that their missing friend was still in prison somewhere in Ireland, waiting to be transported to Spain.

The *Empress of Cork* had also been spotted on their arrival, anchored in the largest natural harbor on the peninsula. However, the Pentacle had not responded here either. So at least the two Inquisitors must have already left.

Kaura, Abigail, Sen, and Diana, who spoke for the guardian fairies, met with Sir Elias in the captain's chamber to discuss strategy.

"Our only clear lead is the *Empress*," the captain said. "True, I have already sent some men ashore to ask around a bit. But I'm not getting my hopes up too high. We don't seem to be very welcome here at the moment, even though Scottish ships are still officially tolerated in Cork. Have you noticed the hostile looks from the workers and passers-by on the quay? I think the Spaniards get a lot more sympathy from the people here than we do."

Kaura couldn't help but make a comment.

"If your queen wasn't trying to expand her influence by bringing her settlers here, too, I think relations between her and the Irish would be a little better."

She snorted contemptuously. "Of course, the Spanish are no better. Right now, all anyone seems to think about is expanding their empire as far as possible and subjugating as many other defenseless people as possible."

Diana fluttered forward and plopped down on the table. Her considerable bosom almost slipped out of the narrow strip of cloth that covered it. The fairy's eyes glowed an intense pink and she grinned adventurously.

"Instead of beating around the bush, let's do something! Here's a plan: tonight, we'll grab the captain of the Empress and grill him. I mean, make him sing. Make him talk. Whatever!", she said. "We fairies should be able to approach the ship unseen if we're fast enough and stay just above the surface. They'll think we're just extremely good-looking bats if they see us. We can't get Simon there unseen, and we can't influence people's wills with our magic. So, he'll have to brew us a truth serum we can pour down the Irish captain's throat. A welcome drink, I say! And a second one to erase us from his memory afterwards. Then at least we'll know where we stand. How's that?"

She blinked and thought for a moment.

"That was the harmless version," the fairy then added, a hopeful look entering her eyes. "'Cause I know that Sen always gets nervous when the subject of thumbscrews and whatnot comes up. Why are you all staring at me like that? Oh well, one can always dream... So, you really don't want to hear the second version? For a mature audience only! There are not only thumbs that can be put into thumbscrews!"

Kaura cleared her throat and turned to the others.

"Diana's first alternative does sound like a viable plan, doesn't it?"

She glanced at Sen. "Provided Simon can actually pull something like that off."

The Headmaster nodded in agreement.

"We have brought everything we need for making potions. The essential components are already premixed in vials."

He turned to the captain.

"Elias, we need access to the galley as soon as possible, a fire, and about an hour to work undisturbed. Can you give us that?"

The captain agreed.

"The cook will not be happy to have to interrupt his preparations for dinner. I will break it to him gently. Follow me. Let's talk to Simon and then head over to the galley together.

* * *

Colin O'Donegal, captain of the Irish merchant galleon Empress of Cork, had every reason to be celebrating that night.

The burly man sporting a red beard and tangled hair that no man-made comb had ever been able to tame had draped his green velvet coat over a chair in the captain's quarters, downing one glass of cheap whiskey after another and talking to himself.

"Oh Great Mother Mary," he sighed, still half aware that his speech had become somewhat sluggish. He rarely drank this much alcohol. But today he really needed a good swig.

"Finally, those crazy folks are gone. They say they belong to the Church. But they look like they're in league with the devil! I hope I never have to carry such passengers again! It makes me want to retire to the country somewhere and start growing carrots!" he muttered to himself.

With a touch of unease, he remembered the prisoner they had brought aboard. The man was still waiting to be picked up in a well-locked and guarded compartment on the mid-deck. He had not seen him himself, except when he had been brought aboard at night in Southwark with a burlap sack over his head. O'Donegal had asked no dangerous questions. One did not poke one's nose into the affairs of the Holy Inquisition.

But whoever this man was, he felt sorry for him. Who knew what they were going to do to him in Spain. He would be lucky if he ended up as a galley convict on board one of those horrible oar-studded man-of-wars that the Spaniards used to patrol their harbors.

The captain shrugged. Tomorrow it would cease to be his concern. The Inquisitors would hopefully send some soldiers to fetch the prisoner from the ship. He fervently hoped that he would never have to see these strange men again.

Dazed from the alcohol, O'Donegal lay down in his bunk, fully dressed, and immediately fell asleep.

Sometime during the night he was awakened by a soft clanging. The captain was about to reach for his dagger, which always lay on a shelf beside his bed, when he realized he could not move.

"Don't even think about it, Irish snoozebag," a small voice sounded next to his left ear.

"And you ain't calling for help either. Your guards up on deck are all out there snoring. We didn't have to do all that much to be of assistance, I tell you. Limp dicks, my ass! Don't wet yourself. We just want you to yodel some information for us. Nothing bad is going to happen to you. We got no beef with you. We just want to know where the two chestnut-heads and their prisoner went. You know who I'm talking about?"

O'Donegal groaned.

He had the feeling that there was a ghost in his head. He tried to look around. But he couldn't move. And in any case, there was not enough room for a human being to stand behind him. Who was talking to him? Had he gone mad? Was he hearing voices? Was he possessed by demons?

Every now and then, a fleeting shadow flitted across the chamber wall in the light of the moon that had risen outside his window, and soft giggles echoed through the room. He felt hot and cold all at once.

Demons indeed? Or Satan himself? But since when did the Devil speak in a female falsetto?

At that moment, a red light flickered up behind him, its shadow revealing a distorted figure with two huge wings and a gnarled staff with a glowing tip.

"Spare me, demon!" the captain croaked breathlessly. "O Holy Mother Mary, save me!"

"Demon, my ass," the voice behind him chuckled. "Thanks for the compliment! Your Mother Mary can't help you now. She is on vacation. Well, actually we do have a Mary right up here with us. But the most she can do is smack your ears."

There was a pause, then something seemed to occur to his diabolical tormentor. "Or throw you into the deepest pits of hell, you miserable sinner!" she snarled. "Have you ever heard of the Last Judgment, does that ring a bell? Well, here you have it. Hey, Mary! You're wanted! Swing your demonic ar... er, your demonic leather wings over here and show the man what it looks like down there!"

The fine voice lowered to a dangerous growl and suddenly seemed to echo from all sides. "Now, are you willing to talk, or do we have to pull some other strings? *Demonic* strings? Mary is already on her way."

O'Donegal was confused, and panic started to rise in his guts.

The only thing that he knew was that he did not want to end up in hell. The captain began to speak with a trembling voice.

* * *

Meanwhile, the small group huddled on the main deck of the Scottish galleon moored at Crosshaven Quay waited anxiously to see how the fairy mission had gone.

The seaport's dark stone buildings rose like a jet-black wall behind the ship. The last lights behind the curtains of the townhouses had already faded by the time the small group of fairies had left, their limbs and faces blackened with charcoal, no more than dark shadows in the cloudy night sky.

Somewhere in the dark alleys a dog howled, and another answered it from afar. A faint glimmer of pale moonlight reflected off the surface of the water, where somewhere, out of sight in the darkness, lay the Irish ship whose captain they hoped to learn Joe's whereabouts from.

Simon stared intently into the darkness and blinked his eyes.

"If only things go well over there," he whispered. "All it would take is for them to miss one of the guards. Then all hell will break loose here in no time."

Kaura put a hand on his arm, reassuring him.

"The Pride is prepared for battle and ready to sail. The wind is at its best. Besides, Diana and her companions will know how to defend their hides."

The dark brown face of the Lemurian, who was more than a head shorter than the gaunt Scottish psychomage, was barely visible, only dimly lit by the moon and the stars that sparkled between the clouds.

"I think she's right, Simon," added Irene, the older of the two Lockwood witches. "As long as the Inquisitors are not in the on the ship, there shouldn't be any significant threat to the fairies. They can handle any non-mage with ease. And most mages as well," she added. In the darkness, her smile could not be seen, but it resounded in her voice.

Sen agreed.

"Once we know where they took Joe, we can work out a plan to get him back. Once that's done, we'll help Kaura get into Pyrrha, open the Portal and call in those Aalids. They'll rebuild the shield, kick the 'gods' out, and then we can get back to the really important things in life.

Sen made it sound like he was talking about a pleasant stroll in Oxford's University Gardens on a Sunday afternoon.

Kaura nearly choked as she suppressed a loud giggle.

"Well, if it's that easy, then we have nothing to worry about! Apart from the fact that we don't yet know where to find Joe, I don't know how to open that portal, and even if I did, both shores of the Mediterranean between us and Pyrrha are crawling with Spaniards and those terrible Inquisitors who want to enslave us all. I admire your optimism, Sen!"

"You'll see, this will all be much easier than it seems."

The Principal's smug grin was easily discernible in his voice. "After all, you're not here with some nobodies. Look. My girls are coming back."

Everyone peered across the dark water. But it took a long moment for anyone else to see them.

"That dark spot over there? You must have the eyes of an eagle, Sen. I can hardly see anything moving there," Sir Elias said.

Now Kaura mumbled her agreement as well. She had also noticed the somewhat darker shadow against the background of a cloud.

"Hmm, it's not just the fairies. They're hauling something. Something big. A sack of some type! Do you think they raided the Irish ship?"

"I doubt it," answered Sen. "If they were carrying a cask of rum, I wouldn't be surprised. No fairy is averse to a good sip of spirit, and they can be quite proactive about it. But this is something else. I think a human figure. In a fishing net!" He opened his eyes even wider, trying his best to see more.

"Did they capture the captain of the Empress? That was not part of the plan," Sir Elias said.

"A few more minutes and we'll know," Kaura replied.

A short time later, in the faint light of the crescent moon hanging low in the sky, the fairies were getting close enough for everyone to see the glitter of their translucent wings. Their whirring sounded much more strained than usual.

Two of the fairies held onto each of the weighted corners of the net. It looked like a small, ordinary piece of fishing equipment. The seventh—Ariane had also accompanied her peers from Oxford—seemed to jump in whenever one of her companions got tired.

The unwieldy flying object maneuvered awkwardly between the port shrouds and across the main deck.

A muffled fairy voice sounded.

"Attention, unloading now. Mind your heads down there!"

Something crashed to the planks with a loud thud, followed by a low cry of pain.

Simon advanced quickly, ready to cast a spell that would stop the person in the net if they resisted or tried to flee. The others followed more hesitantly.

"Don't worry, Simon-Baby!"

Diana fluttered up in front of the psychomage's face and saluted casually in Sen's direction. The black paint on her face was streaked with thin threads of silver fairy sweat, giving her a genuinely demonic appearance.

"Fairy contingent at your service, Sen, head honcho, sir! That Irish snorebag was quivering, I tell you! There was no need for Simon's tea, no need at all. Except for a little sip at the end, to make the fearless warrior forget that he almost wet his bed. The Inquisitors are in for a jaw-dropper, they are!"

The fairy laughed wryly. "Oh, and since the Nelson boy was in the vicinity, we decided to bring him along. He's fine."

She paused, seeming to think. "Well, he was fine when we packed him. Now he might have a scratch or two. But you mages can patch him up real quick, I'm sure! Report finished! Over and Out!"

This time, even Sen stared in surprise at the shadow that had collapsed in the middle of the deck and now started to move with a pained groan.

"Well, that was one hell of a ride," Joe croaked, scrambling to his feet and, still half wrapped in the net, taking a few quick steps over to the bulwark, where he vomited with a heavy gurgling sound.

"Joe!"

Kaura ran to him and put a hand on his shoulder. "You're alive!"

" Barely," the young man replied, still choking. "Flying with these fairies is worse than any North Sea storm. Not that I'm ungrateful," he added, then threw up again.

"Airsickness," Ariane said seriously. She had settled back on Kaura's shoulder. "Can be a thing. The boy will be fine. You will be able to drag him to your bunk soon enough. But then you'll probably have to share him with the Scottish girl. Or you'll all just go together. The two little witches are probably keen on him, too." She cast a cool sideways glance to where Eagle and Irene were standing, looking over at them.

"I don't know why you all fancy him," the fairy sniffed. "Way too under-tattooed for my taste. Sorry, kid, I didn't mean it that way! You're pretty okay. And certainly anatomically well-endowed and all. Throw up all you like. Do you need an anti-airsickness wish? I can grant you one. Because my sweet girlfriend here likes you."

Joe shook his head.

"I'm fine, thanks. Just a little woozy. Are you all here for me?"

He looked around, trying to make out the people standing around him in the darkness.

Sen took a step forward and held out his hand.

"That's about right. I'm Seneca Lumisworth of the Lockwood

Society at Oxford. My friends call me Sen. I'm here for Kaura. I'm glad to see you survived the company of the Inquisitors."

Joe shook the Headmaster's hand with a friendly smile.

"Lockwood Society, huh? Are they all mages too?" He glanced at the bystanders, whose faces he could not make out in the moonlight.

"For the most part," replied Sen. "We can introduce ourselves more fully in a moment."

Sir Elias pushed past him and patted Joe warmly on the shoulder.

"Joe, old buddy, glad to see you alive and well!"

Then he turned to address the others. "I suggest we leave immediately, with as little fuss as possible. We have done our job here in Ireland, and they will soon be able to put the pieces together when they learn that a Nelson ship has been here. We should get as much of a head start as possible. Though they will probably assume that we are trying to escape to London instead of heading into the lion's den."

Joe raised his eyebrows.

"So, we're not heading home, we're going into the lion's den... Guys, this is going too fast, you'll have to explain this to me. Besides, don't forget this is my ship. We're not sailing anywhere without my permission, and we're certainly not going to see any lions."

Kaura put a hand on his arm.

"We'll explain everything, Joe."

The captain tipped his head.

"I'll take care of the casting off maneuver now. We'll do everything with as little light and noise as possible."

He grinned. "Until they wake up in a few hours, the people of Crosshaven won't even know we're gone."

"'Sleepyheads, all of them!" muttered Ariane on Kaura's shoulder as they made their way together to the mess.

At that moment, Abigail came up on deck; instead of waiting for the fairies to return, she had retired to her bunk to rest for a few hours. The faint rumbling in the hull as the crew prepared the galleon for departure had awakened her.

Puzzled for a moment, she looked at the group coming toward her out of the darkness. Then she recognized Joe. She ran to him and threw herself around his neck.

"Honey, they found you! I wasn't expecting it this soon. Uh, you smell like vomit. What happened?"

"We'll all find out in a minute," Kaura interjected, still holding Joe's hand. "Let's go inside. Then we can light the lamps and talk over a cup of wine. There's some sausage, cheese and bread left over from dinner. The cook has used the afternoon to restock with some local specialties."

They made themselves comfortable.

Everyone except the ship's officers and crew were there.

Joe sat in the middle, surrounded by Sen, Kaura, Abigail, Simon, and the two defense witches, Eagle and Irene. Ariane sat on Kaura's shoulder, her violet eyes wide with interest.

Diana and her guardian fairies had settled on a bookshelf.

As the ship was pushed away from the quay, swaying to the side, Joe began to tell his story.

In fact, there wasn't all that much to tell. After he had been drugged by the Inquisitors in the back alley in London that George had lured him to, he had been left alone for a couple of hours in a dark. From there he had been taken to the port in a carriage that same night and locked away on the Empress of Cork.

"From the accent of the crew, I could assume it was an Irish ship," he added. "That was all I knew, as apparently the crew had been instructed not to speak to me. During the voyage, the Inquisitors themselves brought me food. Creepy fellows they are." He shuddered.

The ship had cast off right away and sailed down the Thames

on the ebb tide. The Inquisitors had only talked to Joe once the whole time.

"They asked me a few questions about what had happened in Inmarsund. When I refused to answer, they just laughed. They said that Kaura was worthless to them and that it was certain that she would not live long. I was very concerned about this. They also revealed to me that I myself was to be a key to that portal Don Alonso had been talking about in Inmarsund, in the service of their 'master'. And that I was probably not going to like the rite that went along with it very much."

During his captivity, Joe had plenty of time to ponder the meaning of these words.

"I wondered if it might have something to do with my blood relationship to the Atlanteans. After all, there is some Atlantean blood in my family. And I have been to Atlantia myself. But I certainly didn't receive a key or instructions that had anything to do with a portal."

He shrugged.

"I haven't seen the Inquisitors since we dropped anchor yesterday morning. And then these charming beings"–he smiled at the fairies affectionately–"woke me up with some no less charming, loving words, threw a net over me like over a fish, and flew me here. For which I am very grateful. That's all."

He grinned weakly. "Now I am most interested in how you found me, what has happened in Scotland in the meantime - and why you want to sail into the lion's den, wherever that may be," he concluded his report.

He pondered for a moment, then something else occurred to him.

"And most importantly, do you know anything about George's fate? I just can't believe he would have gone over to them, no matter what they promised him."

Kaura took over to describe what had happened. When she finished, Joe nodded, lost in thought.

"Yes, that fits. And yes, I also think we must go to Pyrrha. Kaura is right. I don't want to end up as a slave to those blue-skinned creatures. Or to their masters."

All nodded silently. Only Ariane couldn't help but curse again, but she spoke so quietly that only Kaura could hear. The young Lemurian blushed slightly.

Sen pointed to the pentagram of crystal balls on the table.

"It's best to leave it there. That way we'll know in time if another mage is approaching. Although it doesn't seem that our friends have found ways to send messages over long distances that could overtake us. They'd have given us even more trouble if they had, I expect. But you never know. Or we could run into a routine Spanish patrol carrying Inquisitors, that could happen too."

Joe let out a bitter laugh and shook his head.

"I don't think the Spanish are still looking for magicians in their territory. They have been doing it long enough, and with enough success. You're probably safer from the henchmen of the Inquisition inside the Empire than anywhere else. But we're sailing on a Scottish ship, that will get us in trouble at Gibraltar at the latest. That is a very tight spot. And easy to block. We might have to fight our way through. But then we would probably be hunted down mercilessly. And there's no neutral territory between there and Malta. No, we must find a way to slip through undetected."

The tattooed principal grinned mischievously over his wine at that and stroked his stubbled beard.

"I think we can help. Can't we, Simon?"

* * *

Three days later, the temperature began to rise. The galleon was already sailing in the midst of the Gulf of Atlantis, off the Portuguese coast by a margin that was judged safe. Portugal was another country that had lately been added to the realm of His Most Ecclesiastical Highness, Sultan Philip II.

Instead of the Scottish Red Ensign, a perfectly imitated Spanish flag of yellow, red, and white fluttered cheerfully from the stern of the former *Pride of Edinburgh*. Her name had also been changed to *Santa Isadora de Agadir*.

Joe had recovered from the rigors of his captivity and now shared the aft deck owner's quarters with Kaura, though she had relinquished her place to Abigail a couple of times, sleeping in the administrator's bunk to give the other two some privacy.

Twice during those days, triangular sails had been sighted on the western horizon, probably belonging to Ottoman patrols. Otherwise, the sea in this sector had seemed deserted, which struck everyone of the crew who had sailed here before as highly unusual.

"We should at least be seeing a Portuguese merchantman or a fishing boat now and then," Sir Elias wondered. "What in the Great Mother's name is going on here? Are the Spaniards gathering for a major attack on Atlantis, and everyone knows about it but us?"

"I don't think the Sultanate would attack the Atlanteans head-on," Aran, the first officer, pointed out. "Enslaving badly armed natives, that is what they can do. Atlantis is another ball game entirely. Even if no one knows exactly what they're doing on their island continent, they're most certainly not defenseless."

Joe grumbled in agreement. He was standing next to them on the quarterdeck, scanning the horizon with his scope. The Londoner had adjusted to the warmer temperatures, now wearing only a beige linen shirt and brown canvas breeches.

The heavy signet ring with the Nelson emblem dangled from his neck on a leather cord. He did not like to have anything on his fingers and usually preferred to wear the ring like that.

Kaura and Abigail appeared on either side of him.

"Seeing anything?" the tall Scotswoman asked. Under the southern sun, the freckles above her nose were already beginning to multiply, and her straight blond hair was blowing in the warm sea breeze.

Joe shook his head.

"Just the ocean. Once we get to Gibraltar, though, there'll be more to see than we'd like. I hope Sen's Spell of Disguise will work. It takes a lot of confidence to stand here as a fair-haired man speaking Scottish and just believe that my counterpart will hear a dark-haired Spaniard talking to him in Spanish or Arabic."

His face scrunched into a grimace.

Kaura nodded.

"Maybe we should test it amongst ourselves. That might make it easier for us to build up the necessary confidence. I'm going to talk to Sen and suggest that we do that."

Abigail grinned mischievously.

"Oh yes. Maybe he can make you a Siberian witch princess and me a Nubian queen. Really black-skinned. That would be different."

Joe gave her a sideways glance with half-lidded eyes.

"And then all three of us disappear into the bunk together, is that what you had in mind? What would you like our two top spellcasters to turn me into then?"

"I've always wanted to get into bed with an Indian *maharajah*," Kaura said. "It would be interesting to see how accurately this disguise spell works. For example, if I could really unfurl a turban or if you'd just reach into the void at close range."

"As I understand it, it works in the brain of the recipient," Abigail replied. "So, you'll experience exactly what you expect to experience when you enjoy the Maharaja's turban. But just how it works in the details is what I'm really curious to see."

On March 12, 1869 after Buddha's Awakening, the newly named

Isadora rounded Cabo de São Vicente, the southwesternmost point of continental Europe, of course well out of sight of the granite cliffs and of the Portuguese fort they had built a few years earlier at nearby Sagres.

Lisbon had also been bypassed, though this had elicited some wistful sighs from both Sen and Elias McGregor.

"We're not on a pleasure cruise here, Mr. Headmaster, as you well know," Kaura had joked.

Sen had just sighed again.

"Yes, of course. Ah, Lisbon... I knew a girl there once, you know. Algarvian sea witch. Directly related to the mermaids. Only without the fish tail. And Belinha was even distant kin to the Hellenic sirens." His gaze had wandered dreamily off into the distance beyond the eastern horizon, where he imagined the Portuguese city to lie. "She made a breakfast that was beyond divine..."

Kaura had only laughed, wondering at the pleasant tickle in her stomach, this almost imperceptible desire to share her breakfast with this wizard who must have been at least twenty years her senior.

She had turned away brusquely, ignoring the thought while she felt his amused gaze at her back. Did he suspect what she had been thinking?

Now she found herself standing at the bulwark with Eagle and Irene. Ariane rocked next to her in the shrouds, enjoying the warm wind that blew her long blonde hair in all directions like a billowing flag. She looked over at Kaura with an innocent expression in her big violet eyes.

"You're thinking about tattoos again, aren't you? I can tell just by looking at you," the fairy said cheekily. A leering grin lit up her face. "While you're here having fun with London Sonnyboy, you're missing out on the best this lame dinghy has to offer!"

With an exuberant gesture, she encircled the deck of the great four-masted galleon.

"Great Mother, you are from the Baltic! I thought you would be a little more uncomplicated. Everybody being with everybody and all!"

Kaura laughed good-naturedly.

"Just because we don't believe in monogamy as the only form of relationship doesn't mean we do it with everyone, dear Ariane. Although I must admit that I like Sen quite a bit."

She blushed, realizing that she had actually said what she thought. And done so in the presence of the other women and Ariane. It was likely that the fairy would have nothing better to do than to flutter over to Sen and tell him about it. The sorcerer was currently below deck with Simon, making the final adjustments to the cloaking shield that had been placed around the galleon.

"Ha!" the fairy crowed. "I knew it! You've got it all figured out, my little Lemurian witch! Don't worry, I won't tell the Superboss. Let him find out on his own. Too bad I'm so small. Otherwise, the three of us could... Oh, my Goodness, those tattoos!"

She almost choked on her hair, which had just been blown into her mouth by a gust of wind, coughed and tried to push it back with both hands, losing her balance in the process and falling overboard.

Kaura and the two witches immediately reached out to help, but the fairy had already caught herself and fluttered back to them in the gusty northwest wind.

"Oops," she muttered, a little quieter than before. "You saved yourself a nice *fairy overboard* maneuver there. But well, a little bit of practice wouldn't hurt the boys around here. They have an idle life. Back at the Guardian Fairy School, things were quite different. It was badass, I tell you! I was known as *Dirty Harryane*. You wouldn't understand. Another dimension... Well, I'm off to tell Sen that you're in love with him. See you later!"

With her purple glittering wings and her light blonde hair blowing in the wind, she fluttered across the deck in an irregular trajectory. At that moment, the fairy did indeed resemble a large, colorful butterfly. The sailors she passed all greeted her deferentially.

Kaura and the other two women looked after her with raised eyebrows.

"What a personality. But you can't really be cross with her," Eagle muttered. Her dark brown eyes flashed with amusement under perfectly curved lashes.

A black-haired witch with roots in the northeast of what the Spanish called the New World, she had come to Scotland via Atlantis. She had spent several years living on the double continent between Britain and Africa.

Like Joe, however, she never spoke of this mysterious land and how the Atlanteans lived there. Even about the infamous Battle of Tenochtitlán, in which she had fought on the side of the Atlanteans and Aztecs, she spoke only rarely and in vague references.

Eagle's associate, Irene, had originally emigrated from Germania and sought asylum in Scotland when the Elector of Brandenburg, under pressure from the Spanish, had outlawed magic. Pale and grizzled, though only about forty years old, she was the calmest and most level-headed of the generally rather flamboyant group of mages.

Kaura sometimes thought that Irene would have done well to lead them all. But with the mages—at least with the Lockwood mages—everything seemed to be based on pure magical strength. And since Irene, despite her other qualities, was the weakest member of the group, she was considered subordinate even to Eagle, who was more than ten years younger. That was, if you could speak of subordination at all, given Lockwood's rather loose understanding of hierarchy.

Kaura liked the unassuming woman and sometimes turned to

her when she needed an unbiased ear to talk to. The others were just too wound up sometimes. It was almost as if they were constantly on some kind of stimulant.

Well, Kaura thought, maybe that was just a side effect of great magical powers. Almost unlimited energy, always available, from the universal field. It could make one feel cocky. She wondered if she would be the same once she had access to her full powers again.

She detached herself from the bulwark and excused herself from the two witches to go back aft.

As Kaura was about to leave, Eagle touched her arm confidentially. "I'm sure you've noticed. Sen really likes you."

Kaura thanked her for her frankness and turned away, lost in thought. She decided to have a closer talk with the mage sometime.

* * *

Less than one full day's sailing later, the galleon reached the Strait of Gibraltar. Sen and Simon had placed a scaled-down version of the field they had created for the entire galleon on the captain and boatswain that morning, to demonstrate its effect.

The entire crew had watched in amazement as the two men turned into real Iberians before their eyes, even giving their orders in Spanish, although they later swore they hadn't noticed and had been speaking their native tongue.

That had calmed everyone's nerves a bit, even if the few most hardened skeptics among the crew still couldn't quite imagine that anyone looking at the galleon through a telescope from, say, a mile away would see Spanish sailors scurrying all over it.

But everyone understood that this was their only chance to sail through Gibraltar Strait unnoticed by the Spaniards, who surely had heavily armed patrol fleets stationed at the entrance to the

Mediterranean, which they basically considered their Sultan's private property.

Sen had also pointed out that creating a cloaking field for the entire ship and its crew had exhausted him, Simon, and Eagle to the point that they would have very limited access to their magical abilities for several days.

"If anything goes wrong now, you will have to fight yourselves. But the fairies can still help you. They have a slightly different kind of magic, but they are fearless fighters if necessary," the chief mage had added.

The renamed, former *Pride* had sailed a long detour in the afternoon, in order to pass through the Strait with the last light, coming in from the Southwest instead of North. Sir Elias hoped to avoid too much scrutiny with this, since everyone would understand that a Spanish merchantman would want to reach the safety of the waters off their homelands at night. Although the Spanish-Ottoman Empire had massively cracked down on piracy in recent years, raids were still known to occur, even near the well-guarded ports of Algeciras and Tangier.

So now the big ship trudged through the Gulf of Atlantis, driven by the northwest wind, towards the entrance of the Mediterranean Sea. So far, everything had gone exceptionally well.

Three times during the day, the sails of larger ships had been sighted. They could have been patrols of the Spanish Armada. None of them had come close to the speeding *Pride*. Still, the mood on board was tense.

This was the time when it would become clear what the tricks of the two mages were really worth. If everything went according to plan, their way to the Hellenic archipelago would be open. The Spaniards would not even know that a wolf in sheep's clothing had crossed into their home waters. The neutral Hellenes would probably be able to provide information on how to get past the Imperial troops and on to Pyrrha, which was supposed to be somewhere in the area of Spanish-occupied Alexandria, upriver on the Nile. So far, so good. If all went well.

In the worst case, though, they would have to fight their way through, everyone on board knew that. And if that happened, the Sultan's troops would certainly start hunting the Scottish ship mercilessly.

Ed, the *Pride's* gunner, had checked the guns several times for readiness. The crew, with the exception of the watch, were hanging around on deck, seemingly bored. Those who knew what to look for, however, immediately noticed that everyone was constantly casting suspicious glances out over the sea.

Then, at last, from the lookout in the main mast, came the relieving call, announcing that all was about to be decided.

"Mastheads to starboard. Looks like multiple ships."

Sir Elias' face took on a grim expression.

"Now we'll see what our camouflage is worth," he growled, glancing over the deck. Then, he noticed something.

"What will any Spanish inspectors see in these?"

He pointed to the six fairies practicing aerobatics on the main deck, deftly dodging the crewmen adjusting the lines. "Colored little birds? Not even a Caribbean pirate ship has that many parrots on board!"

"Probably seagulls," grinned Sen, who was standing right beside him. "Or they don't see them at all. Every brain reacts differently to the Disguising Spell. The field only conveys that this is a harmless Spanish merchantman and that our friends shouldn't trouble themselves with it. The brains of the onlookers do the rest on their own, constructing their reality so it all fits into that idea."

He glanced down at the fairies once more.

"I will tell them to stay below deck in case we are stopped, though. The fewer unusual things the veil has to cover, the better and longer lasting its effect will be."

As the sun moved down, the sails on the horizon grew larger. The lookout had reported that they were three caravels, bearing the characteristic red crucifixes of the Spanish fleet on their hoisted sails.

As the other ships approached, it became more difficult for everyone to continue working as if nothing were wrong.

Now it was clear to all that the speedy warships were well armed for their size.

Seven guns protruded menacingly from each side's open gunports, and two rotary cannons each were mounted on the forecastle and quarterdeck. These could be quickly reloaded from the rear by their operators, scattering deadly volleys of shrapnel across enemy decks.

Sir Elias stood on the quarterdeck with his first mate, Aran, and waved to the Spaniards.

"Those are fourteen-pounders. Pretty big for such small ships," the first remarked quietly.

Meanwhile, the three caravels had spread out, ready to attack the larger ship from upwind if necessary. This was an invaluable advantage in a battle that Sir Elias would normally never have conceded and countered with a maneuver of his own. But the camouflaged *Pride* held its course.

"If it comes to a fight, we'll have a whole other set of problems anyway. So, let's play sheep," grumbled the captain, half to himself.

"Baaa," Aran agreed, grinning broadly.

Behind him stood Sen, Eagle and Kaura, who would pose as the ship's aristocratic passengers in case the Spanish inspectors came aboard.

Joe had retreated below deck with Abigail because of his conspicuous blond hair.

"The less inconsistency there is, the fewer things can go wrong," he had muttered, and his fair-skinned lover had agreed.

Because of her dark skin, Kaura could have been mistaken for a North African noblewoman even without a camouflage spell, and Sen had hidden his striking but still almost brown hair under what Kaura found to be an extremely ridiculous cap of green velvet, the lower edge of which was decorated all over with gold brocade embroidery.

The Headmaster smiled at her.

"Do you still think my headdress is, ahem, *jester-worthy*?" he asked her as the flagship caravel approached within shouting distance. "I can assure you that Spanish nobles do wear such things. Too bad I don't have a ruff. It would make me look even more authentic."

Kaura's face twisted into an ironic grimace that looked very unusual in her finely cut features.

"Puke bag, that's what Ariane called your thing, and I haven't found a better word for it yet. The Inquisitors should hunt down people who think such things are pretty instead of harassing harmless magicians! It would make the world a better place to live in. Why did you even bring that with you?"

He grinned.

"This 'puke bag'–apart from the fact that it looks so pretty–is the millennia-old symbol of dignity of the Principals of Lockwood, handed down from one holder to the next of this revered office. Almost no one knows this, as even most of my predecessors had developed a slightly different fashion sense, pointy hats and all. But I figured, hey, now you can finally put this thing on without anyone making stupid comments."

Eagle laughed.

"Guess you thought wrong, Your Serene Highness! Well, at least your hair doesn't jingle as wildly now as it usually does."

The Spanish caravel closed in and signaled to the disguised *Pride of Edinburgh* to pull alongside.

Leaning against the quarterdeck railing, among the helmeted Spanish officers, stood a younger man with a black goatee. He actually wore a headdress similar to Sen's.

The mage nudged Kaura with his elbow, grinning.

"I told you so. With a ruff, even," he whispered. "You Philistines just don't know how to dress smart!"

"Don Vilonso de Guadalajara y Vilareal," the dark-haired, brightly powdered man bellowed over to the galleon. "Fleet Commander of Her Majesty's Coast Guard. Ship, destination port and cargo!"

Sir Elias raised his voice.

"Greetings, Don Vilonso! Captain Alfredo García, *Santa Isadora*! We come from Agadir with a cargo of cloth and wood, bound for Palma de Mallorca! Long live His Most Ecclesiastical Majesty!"

The nobleman on the other ship seemed to grow a few inches taller and saluted dashingly.

"'Eternal life to the Sultan!" he bellowed. "Pass! May God bless your journey!"

The caravel bore away and continued its course south. Its two escort ships trailed behind like obedient puppies.

A collective sigh of relief went through the *Pride's* crew. The men who had been crouched behind the guns, ready to fire even through the closed ports, stood up and stretched their limbs. The tubs of glowing charcoal used to light the fuses were returned to the galley.

McGregor exhaled slowly, then grinned.

"That went exceptionally well."

He patted Sen firmly on the shoulder. "Well done, my friend. We're on course for Pyrrha now."

"We passed the first test, at least," his ever-cautious first officer added beside him. "Let's hope it'll stay that way."

The galleon sailed on, passing between the first lights of Tangier and Algeciras, which slowly flickered into existence across the water.

The great shadow of the Rock of Gibraltar, indistinct against the sky in the rapidly deepening twilight, lay ahead on the port side. The first stars had already begun to appear, and they seemed to be winking confidentially at the ship and its crew far below.

9

Dangerous Dreams

On the morning of March 16, the weather started to change. Initially, everything seemed fine. It was getting warmer, and some of the deckhands were working shirtless. The climate seemed to lift everyone's spirits a little.

Kaura, for her part, was admiring the various tattoos on the men's muscular upper arms. On one of the Baltic ships sailed mainly by women, she would have taken off her own shirt now, too. It was warm enough for that. But here, she thought, that might have been misinterpreted. After all, this was a Scottish ship. Half-naked women were not usually seen on deck here.

Nimbly, she clambered up the companionway to the quarter deck.

There, Sir Elias was engrossed in talking to Aran. They both seemed to be worried and kept pointing at a low bank of clouds on the southwestern horizon.

"There'll be bad weather, if I'm not mistaken," he said.

The First nodded.

"Yes, the discoloration is typical. We may just be able to evade it."

"I wish. But I don't think so. The front is moving in fast. To be on the safe side, have the storm sails ready and the bulkheads secured," Sir Elias ordered.

Then his eyes fell on Kaura. "Is this your first time sailing the Mediterranean?" he asked her.

The green-eyed woman nodded.

"But I can easily imagine that the storms here are just as nasty as they are in the Baltic. Both bodies of water look like no more than a large puddle of pee on the map, as my Aunt Resa would say. But there's more to them than that."

Her face darkened involuntarily. It had been a long time since she had thought about her aunt. She hadn't heard from her in months, even before leaving Inmarsund. She hoped that Resa was well and had managed to return home by now.

The Shipmaster interrupted her thoughts.

"All too true. We'd better get ready. Can you inform the other passengers?"

Kaura nodded and went to tell Joe, the magicians and Abigail to make their chambers storm-ready. The fairies would probably be happy to know that something was finally going on around here. They had been complaining about boredom for quite some time.

"We couldn't even kick the Spanish Armada's fat ass!" Diana had complained at dinner the day before.

"So far, my dear, so far," had been Joe's reply. "I hope I'm wrong. But I think you'll have lots to do before we get to Pyrrha."

Three hours later, the storm was upon them.

The sky had turned yellow. The wind was now blowing full force from the southwest, driving the great galleon like a projectile through the foam-tipped waves. Sir Elias had already ordered a few sails to be taken down, which reduced the speed only imperceptibly, though.

Everywhere the gales whistled and howled in the shrouds and

bracings. The lookout had already been called down to the deck, as moving in the shrouds would soon become too dangerous for anyone. The cloud front was now very close and loomed menacingly over the galleons stern. Lightning flickered in the black wall like Witchfire.

It was not long after the sails had been taken down and replaced with the storm sails that the wind died completely for a moment.

The whistling and howling vanished from one moment to the next, giving way to an oppressive silence in which only the creaking of the rigging and the murmur of the water could be heard.

Then the first gust of wind hit the galleon like a hammer blow. The ship heeled sharply to port, almost plunging its bulwark into the waves. Sluggishly, it regained its balance.

Then the storm began in earnest.

Soon everyone who didn't have to be out on deck had retreated inside. The captain and Paddy, the helmsman, had tied themselves fast on the quarterdeck. Safety lines had been stretched across the ship for the crew to hold on to as the breakers passed over. The storm drove the *Pride* to the east without mercy.

"At least this way we'll get where we're going faster!" the captain yelled to the helmsman, who could barely hold on to the helm even with his huge hands. "Do you need help with the rudder?"

Paddy shook his head, dripping wet from rain and overcoming seas.

"I'm all right, sir!" he yelled back. "But maybe we should have the drag lines out by now. It's getting worse!"

A few orders rang out, and dripping wet men shimmied across the deck. The heavy hawser lines had already been laid out and were now put around the mainmast. They were lowered into the water on both sides of the ship, and their purpose was to hold the galleon in the waves and prevent it from being swayed by the huge breakers.

Belowdeck, it was pitch dark, as no lights were allowed due to the risk of fire. It was uncomfortable, to put it mildly, thought Kaura, who had retreated to her chamber. Last night, they had decided that Abigail would live with Joe for some time, and they had exchanged accommodations. Both of them were now out in the mess with the others.

Kaura settled back in her bunk and continued to try to fight off the nausea she was feeling. She was thankful that no one could see her pale face. The breakers thundered against the side of the ship like the blows of a hammer.

The only ones having a good time were the fairies.

"Finally, something's happening on the snoozer," Kaura heard one of the guard fairies crow as she flew at high speed past her door through the swaying and creaking interior of the ship, apparently playing tag with some of her fellow guardians.

The storm lasted from afternoon into the night.

At one point, Kaura heard a loud crash. She listened.

Screams rang out on deck, barely audible over the deafening howling and whistling of the wind. The ship was lurching heavily to starboard and seemed to be having trouble leveling itself. This was not good.

With determination, she sat up, pulled on her canvas jacket, and groped her way forward through the groaning hull to the nearest bulkhead. She kept bumping her head and shoulders against the walls of the passageway as the Pride was buffeted by the waves, tumbling from one trough to the next.

As she pushed open the bulkhead, a gush of seawater nearly took her breath away. In front of her, three sailors were frantically trying to sever the rigging of the foremast. The mast had broken and was hanging over the starboard bulwark like a kind of drift anchor, held in place only by its shrouds and braces.

The mast had to be removed from the ship as soon as possible, for it was putting it in serious danger of broaching and capsizing in the crashing waves.

Pulling herself forward along one of the taut safety lines, Kaura drew her own cutlass and, like the others, began to hack wildly at one of the lines that still tethered the mast to the ship.

One of the men looked over at her in the dim half-light of the stormy night only occasionally lit up by stroboscopic lightning, and nodded gratefully. Time and again, the breakers would come crashing over the gunwale and they would have to stop what they were doing and hold fast with all their strength to avoid being washed overboard.

Twice Kaura almost lost the knife when she had to grip the line with all her strength to keep from going overboard. But then 'her' piece of the rigging was finally cut through and disappeared into the darkness with a whip-like crack.

Stubbornly, she turned to the next one. A few minutes later they were done. Exhausted, Kaura and the others watched the broken mast drift away astern. The young woman smiled at the drenched sailors and scrambled back to the bulkhead.

The men exchanged confused looks.

"Now, that's what I call a woman," one of them shouted over the wind.

"Haven't you ever been to the Baltic?" a second shouted back. "'Tis a different custom yonder. It's mostly the women who go out to be sailors down there!"

Back in her chamber, Kaura peeled off her dripping wet clothes and donned dry underwear, no easy task with the ship moving so violently.

When she was almost done, the galleon lurched hard to starboard. She banged her head against the wall of the chamber so hard that for a moment she could only see stars, and her vision nearly went black.

Simultaneously, something moved in her subconscious. For a moment, she believed she was back in the North Sea, on that fateful stormy day the Galileo sank. And beyond that... there was something else.

It was as if all she had to do was reach out and everything she was, where she came from, what she knew, would come back to her.

Another image flashed through her mind. She was alone in a small boat, struggling against the waves. The boat was narrow, a canoe, and it had an outrigger attached to it with sturdy cross-braces. Then, the image was gone and everything was back to normal.

Kaura closed her eyes and punched her pillow hard with her right fist. Damn it! She had been so close to unlocking what was in her mind. Sighing, she let herself sink into the bunk and tried to sleep. It wasn't easy, because the vessel was dancing and lurching wildly in the waves, which broke like thunderous hammer blows on the exterior of the hull and across the decks. As she always did when she couldn't sleep, Kaura started counting her exhalations backwards, starting from one hundred and counting down. She didn't remember where she had learned this way of calming her mind. It must have been a remnant of her earlier, forgotten life.

Even in the weeks after the Galileo's accident, when she lay awake at night and woke up drenched in sweat, counting had always brought her relief. It was the same now.

After a seemingly endless stretch of time, she slowly drifted into a fitful sleep inside the storm-tossed ship.

Just as she was about to fall into the soft weightlessness of sleep, she thought she heard a voice from far away.

"The answer lies in the dream world," the voice seemed to whisper. "Dream world, dream world, dream world..." the words echoed softly in Kaura's consciousness.

* * *

By the next morning, it was all over. The sea was still choppy. Gray clouds passed over Kaura and Eagle at high speed as they came up the companionway to the quarterdeck.

The galleon looked badly battered.

The foremast was gone. Parts of the bulwark were shattered, and there seemed to be something wrong with the rudder.

The men on board all looked like walking corpses, deeply exhausted and drenched in salt water.

Sir Elias looked at Kaura through red-rimmed eyes.

"The men have informed me of what you did last night." He gestured tiredly with his calloused hand to where the foremast had been.

"Thank you. I don't think I need to tell you that you're actually too valuable to our mission to risk your life like that."

She shrugged.

"It's not good for my health, either, if the ship broaches and sinks. If in doubt, I'd rather die out here fighting than in my bunk."

Out of the corner of her eye, she saw Eagle smile at her approvingly. The Algonquin witch had a sense for the value of courage.

"That doesn't look good," Kaura sidestepped as she pointed down to the deck. "Can you fix it with the resources on board?"

The captain shook his head.

"The rudder is a mess, and we need a new foremast. We'll get by for a while with the jury rudder the ship's carpenter is rigging now, but I wouldn't want to risk a second storm like the one we just had with it."

He spat overboard to the leeward side.

"As soon as the sky clears, we can establish our position. I suspect we are at least as far as Algiers by now. We could get what we need there. Algiers is officially part of the Spanish-Ottoman Empire, but it's considered a pirate hotbed where the Dons don't exercise much actual control."

"So no Spaniards, instead we go mess with the pirates," grumbled Joe, who by now had appeared on the quarterdeck, hand in hand with Abigail, and had heard the captain's last words.

Sir Elias nodded in agreement.

"I'm afraid we have no choice. We won't get far with the jury rudder. In Oran, the Spaniards are strong. And on the other side, in the Balearic Islands, sit the Catalonians. We'd definitely run into some of your Inquisition pals there."

He grinned wryly. "Besides, we still have the wizards. And the guardian fairies. I think they would be happy to have a go at some real Algerian pirates for a change."

Joe had kept a thoughtful silence while the captain's was speaking. Seeing Sen down on the main deck, with Diana fluttering beside him, glittering like a pink star, the London merchant's son waved to them.

"Can you come join us up here for a moment?"

A purple flash shot down from the top of the main mast. Ariane had apparently recovered the courage to return to one of her favorite haunts on the ship, the top of the mast. She saluted briskly in the direction of Sir Elias as she sat on Kaura's shoulder.

"Lookout reports: no enemy ships in sight," the fairy crooned in her squeaky voice and giggled immediately. "Well, that was quite a ride last night. Rarely have I had so much fun. Only our little float doesn't look quite so good now. On a fairy ship, such a lukewarm breeze wouldn't cause this kind of damage, I tell you! Nobody builds better ships than the fairies of Sirius Q. Besides, ours can fly. If it gets rough, wham, we'll just warp over the clouds. Or underwater."

Kaura smiled at the small creature.

"Would you like to take a tour of Algiers, Ariane? Algerian pirates. Could get exciting."

The guard fairy's face lit up.

"Algiers? Whoa! I've always dreamed of visiting Algiers. They have genies! They are distant relatives of us fairies, you know. They also grant wishes. These bottles they live in are supposed to have the coolest interior design, I've heard about it! Oriental carpets, fountains, hanging gardens and so on!"

Sen and Diana had meanwhile arrived on the quarterdeck. The mage tilted his head uneasily as the captain explained what he was planning to do.

"Well, I don't know if our cloaking spell will hold up against something like this. It should be able to affect the perception of a few hundred spectators, but when we're on the quay in a city like Algiers and there are thousands..."

Sir Elias shrugged it off.

"Africa is a long way from Northern Europe. We simply pass ourselves off as Irish, allies of the Spanish. They won't know the difference here. That should be enough to avoid any awkward questions. And the fairies, please keep a low profile. Even though it is said that the Algerians are more liberal than other parts of the Spanish-Ottoman Empire.

Sen nodded.

"Agreed. Let's have the necessary repairs done at the earliest opportunity. We should leave as few traces as possible. In a city like this, the walls will have eyes and ears. If someone recognizes us, sooner or later the Inquisitors will learn that there is a Scottish ship in the Mediterranean.

"Pah!" Ariane was not impressed. "By the time those morons in their pithole in Granada figure it out, we'll already be in Pyrrha and then back again!"

Sen looked at her thoughtfully. The fairy was probably right, he thought, but he had made it a habit never to underestimate an opponent.

"May the Great Mother see to it that you're right, Ariane," he muttered.

The *Pride* neared the Algiers harbor fortifications toward evening. Like an organically woven carpet, now shimmering orange in the light of the setting sun, the cluster of whitewashed houses stretched out in all directions, cradling the bay.

The damaged galleon luffed up and headed for the eastern side of the harbor, where the sounds of hammering and some unfinished ship frames in the typical low-slung Oriental design indicated that at least some shipyards would be located here.

Aran pointed to a large area where work was still in progress despite the late hour.

"This looks quite promising. I'm sure we'll get a new mast there. And new fittings for the rudder."

A small harbor sloop briskly approached the arriving ship.

As in every port in the world, customs and port authorities were not long in appearing. At first they were hailed in Arabic and Spanish, and then it turned out that the town clerk even spoke Scottish, albeit with a heavy accent.

Sir Elias explained that the galleon, under the name of Santa Isadora, was an Irish ship that had already unloaded its cargo in Alicante and had been driven off course by the storm.

No further questions were asked, the dues seemed reasonable, and the official referred them to one of the shipyards that, he said, handled somewhat higher quality wood at fair prices than most.

The crew moved the ship directly to the pier of the shipyard named by the official. While the captain and the ship's carpenter negotiated with the shipyard's manager in a small, shabby wooden shed, many of the men looked longingly across towards the bustle of the big city, where the lights were now slowly flickering on.

The air smelled of thousands of small cooking fires, oriental spices, roasted lamb, and the inimitable sweet-tart aroma of Arabic coffee.

Sen, Kaura and Ariane had decided to spend the night on board due to the lateness of the hour, and not head out into the city until the next morning.

The crew, on the other hand, was impatiently awaiting the return of the captain, who would decide whether there would be shore leave.

Aran smiled.

"You won't get any booze from the Muslims anyway, boys. But there may be other pleasures ashore. We'll see what the master decides."

That night, Kaura tossed and turned in her bunk. In the adjacent chamber, Abigail and Joe were making love to each other raucously. Normally, this would not have disrupted the young woman's sleep. Today, however, she found no peace. And not just because she was sharing her lover with someone else.

The image of the sneering High Inquisitor during his interrogation had settled in her mind. "You are all slaves already, you just don't know it yet," the being had whispered.

"This is what awaits us if they win," the thought ran endlessly through her mind. The prospect of ending up in the hands of one of those creepy, blue-skinned creatures sent cold shivers of dread down her spine.

Memories pressed against her mind like water against a dam, and yet they remained out of reach. Almost, she thought, almost she could grasp them. Her brain was trying to tell her something.

She tried to recall the image from the night before, the canoe with the outrigger cutting through the high waves, but it was incomplete. And there had been something else, just before she fell asleep. A voice...

She racked her brain in vain. Next door, the mixture of moaning, yelping, and soft humming was reaching a crescendo. Kaura rolled over to the other side and promptly hit her head on the raised side of the bunk that was designed to prevent her from rolling out in heavy seas. Even though she slept naked, covered only with a light linen sheet in the balmy Mediterranean night, she was sweating.

Eventually she fell asleep. In her dreams, she ran down endless corridors and staircases, pursued by an invisible enemy.

After what seemed like an eternity of running, she could go on no more. Panting, she stumbled over one of the steps and fell, her face grazing the rough cobblestone floor.

She tried to gather herself, afraid she wasn't fast enough, that she would be caught. Why did she only think of running and not of fighting? The thought flashed through her mind and immediately gave way to panic. Something was getting closer and closer.

With the last of her strength, Kaura struggled to her feet and frantically pushed open a door that appeared beside her. Inside, bed-sheets were hung out to dry, huge, billowing pieces of white linen.

Panicking, she fought her way through the fluttering fabric, which seemed to try to restrain her with a vicious hiss. Finally through, she opened another door and dashed into the next room.

It was cool and quiet in here. Water was babbling somewhere. There was a fire burning in the fireplace, but it did not give off any heat. Across from the hearth, she noticed a wall. It seemed to be made almost entirely of glass.

Beyond it was a landscape unlike anything Kaura had ever seen before. Huge red, black and gray rocks formed bizarre, rounded patterns. This was the Dreamworld, she suddenly knew. Had the shock of last night's storm awakened some new, buried ability in her?

A part of her was aware that she had immense powers in this world. But at the same time, she didn't know what she was supposed to be doing here and how to access those powers.

She turned her attention back to her surroundings. Down in the valley, towering trees rose above gurgling streams, rivers and lakes. A waterfall, surely several hundred yards high, seemed to tumble from nowhere between two large round mountain peaks. In the meadows grazed large, brown animals with wide-spreading antlers. They reminded her vaguely of moose, the big animals that could be found in the far North and whose images she remembered seeing on the copper engravings for sale at the market in Inmarsund.

A volcano loomed on the horizon. It must have been more than two miles high. From its flattened top, a dark plume of smoke, shimmering opal-like in all colors, rose into the light pink sky.

"Hm. A visitor. Unannounced. Not very polite," a cold female voice sounded behind her.

With a startled intake of breath, Kaura turned around.

Now, her instincts as a fighter took over and calmed her. All of a sudden, the young woman was as cold and deliberate as the voice that had just spoken.

"Who are you and where am I?" she demanded.

"I could ask you the same thing," the stranger replied, approaching with measured steps. "After all, you have intruded into my realm. You must be somewhere in the Mediterranean, I can feel your physical presence."

The other woman was at least two heads taller than Kaura. Her skin shimmered like mother of pearl, and her eyes were deep blue, while her softly parted lips had a sensual and at the same time somewhat imperious drawl.

Her hair fell with a white-golden sheen over the blue silk dress that revealed rather than concealed her feminine form.

Human, but only almost, Kaura thought to herself. There was something surreal about her counterpart, something deeply alien.

The woman sat down on a rounded structure of fabric that Kaura recognized as a seat only at second glance. She made an inviting gesture with her hand.

"Sit down and have a drink!"

A large golden goblet appeared in Kaura's hand without her consciously lifting it. Suddenly, she felt a thirst that had not been there before. The impulse to drink became almost overwhelming within a second.

Uncertain, she looked down at the reddish, shimmering brew in her hand. Small bubbles rose from it from time to time. The woman with the golden hair watched her expectantly.

With a decisive gesture, Kaura placed the cup on the small table next to her chair.

"First, please answer my questions. Who are you?"

The other woman sighed.

"Aha. A rebellious one you are, to boot. This doesn't sit well here, little Earthwoman. You shouldn't be proud of being able to enter the Dream Plane. It happens from time to time. But that doesn't mean you're even close to being my equal."

Her eyes narrowed to small slits and with a small movement of her right hand she drew a simple symbol in the air.

Suddenly, Kaura was kneeling on the carpet in front of her, aware that she was naked.

The woman nodded in satisfaction.

"That's better. You've never faced a Goddess before, I suppose. So, I will forgive you. When I'm done with you and you wake up, you will be loyal to me. Where could you be? Maybe you are further away, in the Northlands. Most of the Dreamers that we don't own yet are with the witches in Siberia," she said.

She suddenly fell silent as her eyes moved to Kaura's breasts. To the point between her breasts, to be exact.

The stranger reached forward and with a jerk ripped the fish-hook pendant from Kaura's neck. It glowed with a soft, warm light. Almost simultaneously, she let out a scream of pain and dropped the small amulet as if it were a white-hot piece of metal. Her eyes widened in horror as she stared at Kaura.

Within a second, however, fear gave way to anger, and she slowly raised her hands.

"Did you think you would trap me so easily, Lemurian? In that pathetic disguise? Me, a Goddess! Your reign on Gaia is over! Without your precious Aalids and their machines, without the Halminite, you have nothing left to stand against us! Your sisters will kneel before me, as you do! And you shall hand their allegiance over to me!"

The woman's hands had now reached shoulder height and began to glow.

Kaura felt something cold and metallic begin to solidify around her neck.

An image flashed through her mind. She saw the wrinkled face of an old Arab she didn't recognize, who shouted, "No one has ever found a way to remove one of these bands from a slave's neck!"

Then the Arab changed into Don Alonso, in Joe's study in Inmarsund, yanking the Nordic energy witch by her glittering leash.

"Kill her, Sheka!" the Spaniard roared, his face contorted with hate, and drew his scimitar.

In the same second, a tremendous wave of glowing energy shot through Kaura's body. She seemed to dissolve into fire, become fire herself, billowing and surging like a huge, blazing inferno.

For a moment she saw the surprised face of the Goddess, saw the glow of the other woman's hands turn into a white ball of fire that shot toward her in slow motion. Then the space around her dissolved into a black fog, and she found herself on a deserted beach in the middle of the night.

Gasping, Kaura tried to process the abrupt change from a fight to the death to this scene of absolute peace.

She felt her body start to shake and allowed it to continue until the violent stirring in her muscles eventually subsided.

Only then did she realize that her arms were resting on her thighs, and she slowly straightened up, steadying her breathing with an iron will.

A warm, sea-scented summer breeze blew around her, moving her long hair, which fell wide and soft on either side of her face, over her white silk dress, which lay on her otherwise naked body with a touch as light as a feather.

Kaura noticed the intense scent of flowers. She involuntarily reached for her head and found something soft. A wreath of blossoms, velvety, fragrant, nestled against her touch. Plumeria, she thought.

Palm fronds rustled in the wind behind her. She heard crickets chirping, night birds calling, and the shrill *ko-qui* sound of tropical frogs emerging from the adjacent jungle.

The surf in front of her rose up to form a series of high, dark walls against the star-filled night sky, breaking into white, faintly reflective foam with a thunderous roar.

Kaura became aware that something inside her had changed. She was breathing more easily, more freely.

The area around her heart felt like an infinite space, holding the potential of all being.

Her feet were kissed by the soft sand, yet she did not feel separate from it. She knew she was one with the Earth. She looked at the stars and knew deep inside that they were the play of the same consciousness as herself.

"Enlightened from the beginning. Without birth or death," she murmured softly to herself, and everything around her seemed to glow from within, becoming even clearer and more vibrant.

Waves of joy and bliss flowed through her, and she knelt to caress and kiss the small stones at her feet. Her body vibrated with a familiar power.

As a test, she turned her left palm upward and, with a focused thought, produced a small flame that obediently flickered to life. She smiled. Then she turned her attention inward.

Effortlessly, she found the places in her consciousness that were wrapped as if with glowing thread, and patiently, but without hesitation, unraveled them.

"Oh, I see!" she breathed.

The First of the High Priestesses of Lemuria lay on her back in the sand and laughed until she could no more.

She lay like that for a long time.

Sometimes she opened her eyes and watched the Southern Cross glittering far above her in the velvet-black night sky, the Milky Way forming a shining arc far above her. Then she sensed someone approaching.

"Lorenia," she murmured.

"Dearest sister," the dark figure behind her replied, bending down to kiss her on the mouth.

As their tongues met and she tasted the other Lemurian, a shiver of pleasure ran through Kaura's body. Slowly, she sat up. The moon was rising as a round, pale yellow disk over the ocean, and she could see the relief on her old friend's face.

"We thought we had lost you," Lorenia whispered. "A year ago, Irigenak left to try as well. He didn't want to wait any longer. You know how he is. The magic source continues to weaken, and the fluctuations in the killing field around our continent that have allowed us to send you out alive have become even more sparse. We had to act, even though we promised you five years."

"I ran into trouble. And I lost the Key," Kaura replied. "It turns out that we have enemies in Atlantis as well. Now I'm finally on my way to Pyrrha. It should only take a few more weeks. But our plans had a flaw. The Spaniards have been aided by the Kai'ala. They were able to find me despite the cloaking spells."

Lorenia sucked in the air.

"Then Irigenak may already be captured, or dead."

"I can't help him now. But he is a cunning one. If anyone gets through, he will," Kaura replied. "Soon I will be in Pyrrha, and there I will have to find another way to overcome the barrier. I have received help from Scottish wizards, an island kingdom here in the North, where Merlin's Avalon used to be. If I fail, turn to the Oxford-based Lockwood Society and, possibly, to the Siberian witches."

She stared at her toes, which played as if on their own in the black sand glistening in the moonlight.

"It was a mistake to do this alone. We became too solitary, too arrogant, too disconnected. Seek contact with the outside world again. Only together with the other magical peoples can we save Gaia."

The other Priestess bowed her head.

"Let it be as you say, beloved sister. I am so glad you are alive! The others will be overflowing with relief. Our side of the Pyrrha Portal will once again be guarded day and night. I hope we'll be able to hold you in our arms again soon!"

She cuddled up to Kaura, who gently stroked her hair.

"How are things in the Rainbow Valleys?"

Lorenia shook her head.

"All has been quiet for the past few years. It's impossible to leave the continent, and the source of our powers and our technomagic devices is getting weaker and weaker, that's all. For most of us, life goes on as before. So far. But many now regularly practice the old magic. Combat and defense. And others have begun to study the old sciences once again." Her gentle face took on a sad expression, and tears glistened in the corners of her eyes.

"Fighting. It hasn't been necessary for thousands of years. Why can we creatures not all just live together in harmony, Kaura?"

Kaura cradled her head.

"I still believe we can, sister. The A'kaala just haven't figured it out yet. They're still too stuck in their pain of separation from Source. Now they even permit their minions to call them 'gods'.

She smiled indulgently.

"And there is also something deep inside us that makes us experience this conflict now in our world. We will fight, and we will win. But above all, we must see this as an opportunity for healing and forgiveness. It is about nothing less than the transformation and healing of ourselves and our world.

Lorenia met her gaze with her deep, iridescent brown eyes.

"Well said, beloved. Come back soon. We miss you here. I will wake up now and tell the others the good news. Iso and Selena will be so happy to learn of your survival! They never believed you were dead, said they would have felt it if that had happened. "

Kaura was still smiling when the other woman became transparent and disappeared. Then she opened a Dream Portal and stepped through. Before allowing herself to fall into a restful deep sleep, she placed a shield around her inner space that would protect her dreams from uninvited visitors for the rest of the night.

* * *

When Kaura awoke the next morning, she immediately looked inside herself and then smiled contentedly. Everything there was as it was supposed to be.

Then the events of the night before caught up with her. Tears of relief welled up in her eyes. She had her memory back! At the same time she felt the responsibility weighing on her shoulders again, without which she had felt so ignorant and carefree for the last five years.

Responsibility for her people, for Gaia, for all living beings in the universe.

Nearly ten thousand years of accumulated life experience hit her in one big burst, like an explosion in her consciousness.

At the same time, she realized that this had been what she had wanted for so long - to forget everything and just be one human being among many, with limited horizons, small goals, partners and friends who wouldn't grow old and die, while she would always be the same woman of about twenty-five.

She inhaled and exhaled deeply, reminding herself of the knowledge that had been imparted to her - of the Oneness of all being.

Everything had its reason. And her re-awakening, in spite of everything, was a reason for celebration, not for melancholy! She had her abilities back! And with them, she would be incomparably more helpful to her companions than in her identity as Kaura from Inmarsund, the girl without a past!

She let the joy of meeting her old companion Lorenia, the memories of the warm waters of the Pacific and the knowledge of being embedded in the Lemurian community sink deep into her and let out a small, joyful whoop. Then she collected herself.

Glancing at the lamp, by means of a focused thought, Kaura lit a small light in which she could see herself.

The chamber had a small metal mirror, but instead of walking over to it, she simply pulled a small reflective field up in the air in front of her face while sitting on the edge of her bunk.

Carefully, she touched the scratch on her left cheek with her fingertips. So, she *had* already been physically in the Dream during the chase. And during the encounter with the unknown woman who called herself a Goddess and whose name she did not know.

She sent a little more light into the tips of her right index and middle fingers and ran them gently over the scratch.

Satisfied, she watched the small wound disappear and transform back into healthy brown skin.

Expanding her consciousness, she searched the city for other wizards. She found a few, but none had the characteristic signature of a Kai'ala.

"None of those so-called Inquisitors around," she muttered. That was something to be grateful for, at least.

Then she began rummaging through her sheets. After a few seconds, she found what she was looking for. The *Ta'elekai's* sturdy leather strap had been ripped neatly apart.

She picked up the fishhook-shaped amulet, spoke a few words, and watched as the leather grew back into one piece. Then she hung it around her neck.

Of course, she did not need the amulet. For a priestess with her abilities, it was little more than a child's toy. But it reminded her of home. And of Aalyjah, the matriarch of the Leivenstein family, who had taken her in so generously and lovingly when she had nowhere else to go. She stroked the pearly piece of bone thoughtfully, and the spiral engravings shone for a moment like the sun.

By the time Kaura stepped on deck half an hour later, the sun had already risen over the bay, sending its fiery rays down upon the North African 'White City' and its bustling harbor.

The Algerian craftsmen of the shipyard were discussing the necessary repairs with the ship's carpenter, through the help of an interpreter.

Almost without thinking, the Lemurian cast a protective spell that kept the heat down to a comfortable level.

Great mother, she thought with amusement, when she realized what she had done, but all this comfort really was a bit decadent. Had she ever missed being able to control her environment's temperature at will in the last five years? She didn't think so. But it *was* nice.

She decided to show Sen the spell. It would be interesting to see if he could do it with his, by Lemurian standards, rather limited powers. Comforts were certainly something he appreciated.

Just as she had thought of him, the Headmaster of Lockwood College climbed up the companionway with Simon. Both men smiled as they recognized her.

"Sleep well?" Sen grinned, blinking his eyes in a confidential manner. "That wasn't you in Joe's chamber last night, was it? It took me two spells to finally fall asleep. And half a bottle of whiskey."

She laughed, his light manner matching well with her relief to be herself again.

"Are you envious, Headmaster? But no, I wasn't. And I had trouble falling asleep, too."

His grin widened.

"Then perhaps I should have come over and shared the bottle with you. We might have been able to raise the noise level a notch."

Kaura winked at him cheerfully before answering.

"Maybe you should really do that next time. Or maybe I'll knock on your door now that I know you keep a stash of whiskey there."

He raised his eyebrows.

"Since when do you like whiskey? Usually you tend to hold back on the spirits, as I noticed."

She leaned closer to him.

"I've been around a lot of sailors these last few years. But maybe the alcohol is just an excuse. You don't usually seem to drink much either, although you did try to get me drunk back at Oxford. Do you always do that with your students? I'm not complaining, though. I like whisky. Now and then. In reasonable quantities."

Sen's face took on a slightly guilty expression, then he seemed to decide it was better to change the subject.

"You've always been a visitor to me. But what I really wanted to say was: you look good this morning, Kaura! What's up?"

She smirked.

"Not much. Except for the fact that I finally got my memories back last night."

Sen stared at her in surprise.

"Back? Just like that? How did that happen?"

Simon and everyone else on the quarterdeck who had heard

Kaura's announcement surrounded the young woman, offering congratulations and clamoring to know more.

The principal calmed them all down and suggested they go down to the officers' mess so they wouldn't be so conspicuous.

"Only one more thing. May I?"

Without waiting for an answer, he placed a finger on the center of her chest.

When Kaura felt the touch of the magical current, her first impulse was to interrupt the flow and push it back. But it was only a fine probing spell. So, she allowed it. She did trust Sen, after all.

Three seconds later, the mage nodded and removed his finger.

"Thank you. I just had to be sure. No traces of black magic. You never know. Last night someone tried to penetrate my mental barrier. Pretty dark energy. That wasn't you, was it?"

Kaura shook her head.

"Actually, I did have an encounter which could very well have gone wrong. Instead, I got my memories back. Maybe the one I met in the Dream came looking for me and knocked on your door, too."

The Scottish wizard just nodded and didn't ask any more questions for the time being. They went down to the mess together, informing the two Scottish witches and the other fairies along the way.

At that early hour, it was still pleasantly cool, inside the ship. In a few hours, one would literally be cooked if one stayed below deck too long.

Sir Elias had already arranged for some canvas sunshades to be stretched over the main deck, so that those who were off duty could relax in the shade during the hot hours.

After everyone had settled, Kaura told them about her experience the night before. All listened intently. Especially when she told them about the 'Goddess'.

"Do you mean that you now know who these enigmatic lords of the Kai'ala are? And who Rignar is?", Simon asked.

Kaura nodded.

"We don't know much either. Rignar is not a 'who' but a 'where'–the mysterious home planet where the A'kaala sect, whose members like to call themselves 'gods'–settled many millennia ago. No one knows where to find them, although legend has it that the ancient Lemurians themselves banished the sect there. They stripped the exiled of all their magical and technological abilities and left them to fend for themselves".

Kaura went on while all of them listened closely without interrupting her.

"About the same time the Atlanteans came to Earth, they suddenly returned, along with the Kai'ala who acted as their henchmen. This was a little over nine thousand years ago. The magical abilities of the "gods" at that time were still extremely modest compared to ours, although they were technically quite advanced, similar to the Atlanteans. In any case, a lot must have happened since then - the woman I met in the dream world had extraordinary magical powers."

Kaura raised her shoulders.

"At that time, the Kai'ala and their masters were defeated and it was assumed–*we* assumed–that the problem was finally solved. Obviously that's not the case. I suspect that they are behind all the problems, and they are also manipulating the Spaniards to serve their purposes. And they have, in fact, effectively checkmated the entire power of the Lemurian magicians.

Kaura refused to say what exactly had happened to the Lemurians.

"Later. It's a long story," she told the others.

Then they all went their separate ways.

Sen, Simon and Eagle went into the city in search of rare oriental ingredients for their potions, while Kaura joined Abigail and

Joe for a stroll through the parks of the African port city, seeking the comparative coolness of the shade cast by the large cedars that grew there.

In the evening, Sen had promised to lead the Lemurian and Ariane, who was burning with interest, to *Mira'aleitha*, the ancient Djinn district at the other end of the city.

Kaura seemed distracted and deep in thought. Although her two companions tried again and again to include her in their conversations, she only found her way back to the carefree lightheartedness she had radiated as the girl from Inmarsund in rare moments.

Too heavy was the weight of responsibility that she felt rested on her shoulders. Whenever the pressure threatened to become unbearable, she would stand by one of the larger trees and hug it.

It was only in these moments that a sigh of momentary relief would pass through the petite body of the High Priestess. For a while, she would be merry again before falling back into her dark brooding.

10

Epilogue

Resa Leivenstein was seething. The brawny commander of the Baltic cog *Stralsund* had been kept waiting for her audience with the police minister's Chief of Staff for three hours straight. And still nothing had happened. The Chief of Staff! Not even the Minister himself would see her, although she had letters of recommendation from the highest levels of Atlantean society. And even though she had been campaigning for this opportunity for almost three months.

Kaura's foster aunt, her blunt face reddened under her straw-colored hair, snorted angrily. Three months, almost four, had passed since she had been detained by the Atlantean border troops in the port of Moraníu, along with every other foreign ship in the country. Shortly thereafter, they had been brought here to Atlantia under the supervision of one of those strange flying pieces of cake those white-haired idiots used to get around their shithole of a continent.

Resa clenched her fists. Well, maybe they weren't idiots. It would have been a mistake to underestimate the islanders. They would have a reason for what they were doing. And dangerous they certainly were, even if the people in the streets of the capital seemed harmless enough, only attending their strange, introverted entertainment events.

The Inmarsundian shuddered involuntarily at the thought that people here considered it art when someone created pills that made their users experience strange stories and feelings. Tapping her foot impatiently, she looked out from the waiting room on the forty-third floor of one of those crazy glass crystals they called buildings here.

From up here, she could see the glittering expanse of the Atlantic Ocean in the distance. Freedom, seemingly so close and yet so unattainable.

What it meant that the Atlanteans had allowed her and her crew into the city at all, she didn't even want to think about. Would they ever be allowed to leave the island after all they had seen and heard?

Well, she would do everything in her power to free the "Stralsund" and return it safely to its home port on the Baltic Sea. Even if she had to feed that staff idiot so much honey that the sticky liquid would drip down the stairs of his daft ministry.

Resa forced a mask-like smile onto her face when the Chief of Staff's secretary, dressed in a brown silk robe, informed her that the "High Lord" would now receive her.

She had promised Irma, her first officer, under oath that she wouldn't make things worse by alienating any Atlantean government officials. Well, she would do her best to try. She gave a nod to the woman who, with the push of a button, opened the sliding door to the adjoining room, and stepped inside.

From a throne-like seat that seemed to have been carved entirely out of solid crystal, a pale man, dressed in a blue robe embroidered with gold, looked down at her. He wore an impatient expression that told Resa he probably thought he had much better things to do than deal with the concerns of an annoying foreign merchant ship commander. And with a woman, no less!

The Atlanteans already had a hard time understanding that a woman could work at all. The fact that Resa was even in command of a large ship went far beyond the understanding of the officials she had dealt with so far. They had always been asking her where the 'real captain' was. She had hoped that the higher social classes would think a little more openly. But so far it didn't seem that way.

The man on the throne-thing was glancing down boredly at a small metal plate in his hand and seemed to be reading something on it.

"You have a recommendation from the Secretary General of the Intercontinental Chamber of Commerce, asking us to grant you access to Minister Ixkarel," the man murmured without looking up. "What do you want?"

Resa took a deep breath to keep from exploding.

"It should be clear from my request that we—myself and my crew —have been held against our will in Atlantis for over fourteen weeks now. We pose no threat to your country. I therefore request that the Minister allow us to leave. I..."

The Chief of Staff waved his hand carelessly.

"Request denied. We will let the Secretary General know that we have heard you. You may leave now."

The Inmarsund skipper took a deep breath to tell the man in no uncertain terms what she thought of him and his 'hearing'.

Then she paused. A look of disproportionate terror crossed the government official's face. Did she look that angry? Would he back down now?

Then a low voice sounded behind her, resembling the hiss of a snake.

"You have failed, Exikel," said the hate-filled voice of a man who had appeared right behind Resa, apparently without using the door at the entrance.

Surprised, she looked around.

The newcomer had the long, white hair of most Atlanteans. But he was almost a head taller than any of his countrymen Resa had seen so far.

And his intense blue eyes had no pupils–or rather, they were so large that the white beside them was invisible. Like a seal, she thought, shuddering–a monstrous, raging, blue-eyed seal.

The stranger did not acknowledge her at all. He just stared at the Chief of Staff.

"We know that the Keybearer's ship is headed for the Mediterranean," he hissed. "Yet your people have found nothing! Absolutely nothing! A hundred hover ships out searching, in the middle of taboo territory, risking discovery by the Spaniards! And what have they accomplished? Nothing! You are incompetent, Exikel! Do you know what that means?"

The pale Chief of Staff's face turned red and he doubled over as if in pain.

"Lord, no, I beg you, have mercy! I will repent! We will find him! We..." he stammered, then broke off abruptly as he was grabbed by an invisible force, lifted into the air, and hurled out the window of his office in a rain of glittering crystal shards. With a panicked scream, the man disappeared into the depths.

The blue-eyed man exhaled deeply, then chuckled.

"Ah, yes, that's better," he muttered to himself, as he walked over to the ruined window and looked down, smiling.

Resa stood there in a state of shock, frozen. An inner voice quietly told her to run as fast as she could. But where to?

It was already too late, anyway. Leisurely, the stranger turned around and seemed to notice her for the first time.

"Ah, hello!" he said kindly, smiling at her as his pupils shrank and the eyes under his bushy white eyebrows took on a human expression. "My name is Uriel. I am Chief Minister of this beautiful country. Unfortunately, there are too many incompetent officials here. I am working on a solution, as you can see."

He thought for a moment.

"Well, you may have witnessed a bit much. But I'm feeling generous right now. Plenty of killing for today. I think you'll make a good slave in the mines. Nice muscles."

He raised his right hand, the fingernails of which, Resa noticed despite her fear, were painted with blue glitter. It was strange how, in a situation like this, the senses were suddenly becoming aware of all sorts of insignificant details. Resa wanted to say something, to somehow placate this madman. But then her vision went black and her consciousness faded.

THE END

* * *

Kaura will return in ATTACK OF THE GODS, the second book in the six-part High Priestesses of Lemuria cycle. In a race against time, the Lemurian witch and her Scottish companions attempt to reach the ancient wizard city of Pyrrha before the Inquisition can seize it and enslave its inhabitants. Along the way, they must face the terrifying truth that some of the gods themselves are already on Gaia, wreaking havoc and plotting murder. Joe puts his life on the line to summon the only beings capable of taking on the invaders—and ends up on another planet...

* * *

The HIGH PRIESTESSES OF LEMURIA Series is an eclectic Fantasy-/ScienceFiction-Crossover inspired by the Indian Mahabharata Epic. Book 1 is set in an alternate Europe remotely similar to ours in the late 16th century. Book 2 explores the magical Portal City of Pyrrha, Atlantis and another Planet, Aalid. Book 3 is primarily set on Lemuria, in Siberia, the world inside of the earth, and in outer space. Book 4 moves between earth and other planets, while the final two volumes also cross between dimensions and realities.

* * *

Attack of the Gods
(Reading Sample)

The High Priestesses of Lemuria - Book 2 will be available in
Winter 2023/24.

* * *

Algiers, March 19, 1869 AB.

Three disparate figures moved through the colorful crowd that populated the winding alleys in the harbor district forming the lower
part of Algiers. Men and women wore wide, brightly colored shawls
or white and black cloaks. Many of the women and girls were
veiled, with only their sparkling eyes visible beneath the fabric.
Others walked with their faces uncovered–probably they came from
other lands.

Of the three companions, the one who seemed to fit the scene
best was named Kaura. Small, dark-skinned and with elegantly
flowing steps, she followed the almost two heads taller Headmaster
of the Scottish Lockwood Society through the crowd, whose blond
dreadlocks, interwoven with magical bells, now glowed orange in
the evening sun. The man's full name was Seneca Lumisworth, but
all who knew him called him 'Sen'.

Kaura and Sen were mages, as was the third of the group–
only five inches tall, blonde, with purple dragonfly wings and, as
she liked to point out with pride, a vast vocabulary of creative

profanities. Ariane D.H. Tinkerbell was a fairy—and, despite her diminutive size, not one to be disregarded.

The three were on their way to Egypt on their ship, the *Pride of Edinburgh*, in hopes of finding the ancient portal city of Pyrrha, accessible only to wizards and witches.

Although the Scottish merchantman had successfully slipped past the blockade of the Spanish-Ottoman fleet by way of a disguising spell created by Sen and his witches, it had subsequently suffered serious damage in a storm. They hoped to have the ship repaired in the North African port.

While the captain was arranging for the necessary repairs, Sen had agreed to show the other two around the city. They were mainly interested in the Djinn's famed magic district, *Mira'aleitha*. The Scottish wizard, who was about two hundred years old, had visited the city once in his youth, and it had obviously left a lasting impression on him. The enthusiastic expression in his eyes told the tale.

"You will be amazed!" the Scot enthused, winking confidentially at Kaura. "Mira'aleitha is better than any Oriental fairy tale. And the Djinn are amazing! Very courteous. Not to mention the excellent sweets they produce here! And the coffee is out of this world! Even you won't find anything wrong with it, Kaura!"

His companion had spent the last few years of her life as a young woman with no memory, living with a merchant family in the Baltic city of Inmarsund. Inmarsund was a trading center near the western border of the Mongolian Empire, known for the high quality of its tea and coffee.

It was only the night before, however, that Kaura had fully regained her memories—and surprised her fellow travelers with the revelation that she was an ancient Lemurian High Mage with a mission of utmost urgency for the fate of Earth. This made her journey to Pyrrha seem even more important than they had previously suspected.

Many of the passersby carried large Arabic scimitars, some Spanish rapiers, and Kaura saw a group of very dark-skinned men, probably from the interior of the continent, with quivers of glittering throwing spears slung over their shoulders.

There was a jumble of smells, sounds, colors, and other sensations that made the hustle and bustle of London, where they had started out on this mission, seem almost dull in comparison. No one seemed to be paying attention to the fairy as she fluttered confidently beside Kaura, though a few people gave her shy glances out of the corner of their eyes.

Sen tapped Kaura on the shoulder and pointed to the right.

"Here we are in Al-Wata, the lower part of the city. See that fort over there, up in Al-Gabal, the hill district? That's called the Kasbah, and it's right in the middle of the Medina, the center of the city. That's also where we'll find the streets of the Djinn, the magic district," he remarked with a sideways glance at Ariane.

The magician pulled Kaura with him into the dense maze of white, flat-roofed houses. Colorful linens and clothes were hung between them above their heads, on crisscrossed strings. The laundry was flapping in the warm breeze.

They walked up and down stairs for a good half hour, through souks with all kinds of offerings—once they passed through an alley where only gold jewelry was sold, and everything glittered brightly in the light of the torch baskets like a hundred thousand little suns—and past enormous, brick and whitewashed minaret towers. Then they reached a large square, behind which rose the massive dome of a mosque.

"The Square of the Roaring Lions," Sen told us. "Before the Spanish-Ottoman Treaty of Lepanto, this was the site where the large slave markets were held. European and African captives were auctioned off here. Since the two empires merged and both are ruled by our friend, the Sultan in Granada, this is said to have mostly ended. Or at least here."

He screwed up his face. "I suppose the Ottoman pirates still raid the Mediterranean. But they are probably now selling their 'wares' in less conspicuous places. And their new Spanish countrymen are meanwhile busy applying the same principle in West Africa, shipping people like animals to the New World to do slave work in their mines and plantations."

"I'm sorry, Kaura, I didn't mean to upset you," he said with a regretful glance to the side, where Kaura looked like she was about to throw up. "I know the subject weighs on you." Slavery was one of the few topics that the usually calm Lemurian could easily get into heated discussions about.

Sen turned around. "Come. Over there is the entrance to the district of the Shining Ones. That's where the magical creatures live."

Pigeons fluttered into the air in front of their feet as Kaura and Sen crossed the square with purpose. Ariane rode on Kaura's shoulder. She seemed to feel more and more comfortable there lately often preferring this mode of transport to flying herself. The muezzin had just begun to call to prayer from the minaret. A large number of passersby stopped. Many unrolled their colorful prayer rugs, knelt down, and turned to face the east.

But another part of the evening's street life just went on, and so the three of them continued through the exotic crowd.

At the opposite side of the square, they saw the entrance to an alley, marked by a large golden arch. They approached it from the side. The gilded stone arch was decorated all over with raised Arabic letters.

At the highest point, just below the roof of gleaming ruby-red glazed tiles, was a symbol that looked like a small, antiquated oil lamp.

"The Djinn's Alley," Ariane breathed in awe, moving over to Sen's shoulder, who was walking slightly ahead of Kaura. "I never thought I'd come here some time, to visit the Djinns, those old lampheads!"

But Sen's countenance had become very serious by now. He looked worried.

Ariane noticed his expression and fell silent. Then she saw for herself what made her companion suspicious. The alley behind the golden gate was dark and deserted. There were no torches, and the palm trees in the center of the street were withered and dry. They walked slowly, passing under the archway.

Sen lowered his voice.

"There should be a lot more going on here. Everything looks completely abandoned. And pretty run down. The last time I was here, fifty years ago, Mira'aleitha was the richest, liveliest, most opulent neighborhood in the entire city! I fear bad things have happened here."

He looked at one of the barricaded shops. "This one's been closed for a long time. A few years at least. Should the Spaniards..." he trailed off, turning to a boy of about twelve who was hurrying out of a side street into Djinn's Alley, headed for the square. The boy was well dressed, his white cloak looked freshly cleaned.

Sen waved to him.

"Salaam Aleikum, friend! God be with you! Do you know what has happened here? Where are the Djinn?"

The boy stopped and eyed the three travelers.

When he saw the fairy, his expression became hostile.

"Aren't your two slave girls enough for you, European? Do you need more?" He pointed at Ariane. His Atlantean was accented, but easily understood. "Too bad, my friend. There hasn't been a market here for years. All gone. The buyers have flocked to buy the slaves, especially the Djinn. The ones the Sultan's men didn't carry off with them to Granada, at least."

He spat at Sen's feet and turned away.

Kaura grabbed his sleeve and held him back. The boy stopped with a reluctant look on his face, apparently surprised that a slave would show so much initiative.

"You misunderstand us, friend. Ariane here is no slave. And neither am I. We're new in town, and we were looking for the Djinn."

"'Twere swell," grumbled the fairy between them. "Slave, my ass! That would be very unhealthy. For the buyer, I mean."

She thought for a moment, then shot like an arrow in front of the young man's face and stared at him with her violet eyes.

"Are you saying that they sold fairies as slaves? *Fairies*? That's impossible!"

Ariane looked completely puzzled. "How could anyone keep a fairy in bondage? After all, she can just wish herself away! Talk, boy! Have you seen this with your own eyes?"

The hostile look in the boy's eyes had given way to a sad expression. He nodded.

"Yes, unfortunately. Not a pretty sight. The strangers from Granada came with their own sorcerers. They put metal collars on the magical creatures, making their abilities accessible to no one but the holder. Only a few escaped."

He seemed to wrestle with himself for a moment, while Ariane felt her neck with a sour face. She probably imagined what such a collar would feel like. "I believe you. Sorry. I didn't see that you weren't wearing a collar at first," Ibrahim said then. "This one is with you, Exalted One?" he asked the fairy, pointing to Sen.

Ariane waved her hand magnanimously.

"Yes, we took him on shore leave. He needed some exercise."

She tried to giggle, but failed miserably. "No, seriously, this is Sen. I work for him, but not as a slave. This is Kaura, and my name is Ariane," she introduced herself.

"I am Ibrahim, mistress," the boy added seriously. "Come. I'll take you to the Mullah."

He turned and walked back in the direction he had come from.

Kaura and Sen exchanged a look and then followed him.

Through dark, winding alleys and stairs, Ibrahim led them deeper into the former Djinn district. Every few hundred yards, there seemed to be a shop or a small snack stand still open, filled exclusively with humans. Ibrahim seemed to know them all and greeted them friendly, but did not linger anywhere.

The outsiders were stared at curiously. Ariane received almost adoring glances. An old man playing chess with another in front of a shabby looking cafe stood up and bowed when he saw her fly by.

The guardian fairy blew him a kiss, hesitated for a moment, and then fluttered after her fast-moving human companions.

A short time later, they reached a small open bazaar that was filled with bales of cloth of all kinds and colors. Ibrahim motioned for the three to enter. Inside, they were greeted by an old, gray-haired woman whose face was wrinkled by thousands of deep laugh lines.

The boy hugged her and spoke to her for a moment in Arabic, pointing repeatedly at the fairy and the two humans. She asked him something, and he answered curtly. Then she smiled, pulled aside a thick curtain of heavy maroon silk, and made a welcoming gesture with her hand.

Behind the curtain, a medium-sized courtyard opened before them, like a living, plant-covered oasis between rough-hewn walls of shimmering reddish sandstone. Ferns, potted palms, and dense climbing plants were growing in pots suspended from the wall, and between them stood many small oil lamps in diversely sized and shaped niches in the wall, bathing the whole scene in a warm, flickering light.

In the courtyard, under the glittering stars of the North African night sky, about a score of tables were set up, around which sat, among some men and women, a few fairies and human-like beings with greenish skin and large, black topknots. They drank peppermint tea or coffee, ate small sticky sweets with their fingers, and talked in a low murmur that gave the scene a soft, cozy atmosphere. Some played chess or cards.

A few of those present looked up curiously, but turned back to their tables when they recognized Ibrahim. The boy led Kaura and Sen over to a slightly darker corner of the open area. There sat a white-haired man with a friendly, open face, calmly puffing on his pipe and taking in the scenery.

He watched the newcomers with interest. When he saw Ariane fluttering out behind Kaura, a friendly smile came to his face.

"This is the Mullah," the boy said, then turned to the old man.

"Master, I met these three outside the gate. They said they were looking for the Djinn. I think they are friends of our people."

The old man stood up and put his hand on Ibrahim's shoulder.

"You did right, my boy."

His voice was deep, and his Atlantean was completely unaccented. "Welcome to Mira'aleitha, the magicians' quarters!"

He made a small bow to Sen and Kaura, then laboriously went down on his knees in front of Ariane on the reddish, irregular slabs of sandstone and lowered his forehead to the floor.

"Welcome, *Sa'aleitha*, Great One. I am your most humble servant. My name is Abdel Naredhar. Envoy of the *Refuge*. You seek asylum for yourself and your two servants?"

Ariane looked at him thoughtfully.

"Thank you for the kind welcome. Now please get back to your seat, my dear, otherwise you'll scrape your knees or ruin your beautiful white nightgown! We wouldn't want that, would we? And then you'll tell us what's going on here."

A little later they were all settled comfortably on the oriental carpet around the small table. Ibrahim had just returned with a large pot of mint tea and a plate full of various sweet and sticky-looking pastries.

Abdel leaned forward a little.

"So, you don't know what happened here?" he asked.

Ariane, who had alighted in the middle of the table for simplicity's sake and was sipping peppermint tea from a delicate porcelain cup specially made to fit her size, shook her head. She felt instinctively that she could trust the portly Arab.

"We sailed here directly from Scotland and we're on our way to Pyrrha," she said without looking at Sen or Kaura.

The old man nodded, understanding.

"No request for asylum, then. Which is a pity. The Refuge could really use some younger fairies."

Interest flashed in Ariane's eyes.

"That means they weren't all captured. Good. But tell us from the beginning!"

The Arab bowed his head in agreement.

"Yes, Great One. As you have already seen, all non-human inhabitants of Mira'aleitha had to leave the city or go into hiding. Until six years ago, magical beings lived in Algiers largely undisturbed. This was despite the fact that all of North Africa had been formally part of the Spanish Ottoman Empire since the Treaty of Lepanto. However, the Spanish initially had an interest in maintaining the city's status as a free port. Today, many believe that this was simply to facilitate the recovery of hostages held by Algerian pirates. Occasionally, a rescue squad from Granada would raid the city. But they always left quickly. In short, people felt safe here, even the djinn, fairies, gnomes, and desert dragons. Too safe, as it turned out on that fateful day a little over six years ago.

He sighed heavily and continued. "At that time, there were several thousand djinn living in Mira'aleitha. In addition, there were wood elves, fairies, trolls, land nymphs, giants and centaurs who had come here from all over the world, as Algiers had become known as a safe haven for the persecuted Aleitha."

He furrowed his brow. "You must understand, the Siberian Witch Nations are not particularly attractive to many, even if they promise almost complete safety from the Inquisition. Too cold. Nine months of winter a year." He shivered. "There were many who were willing to accept the risk of being closer to the Emperor in Granada. Anyway, one day they were suddenly upon us. Hundreds of Inquisitors, accompanied by magical minions who had probably been enslaved like many of my friends here later."

His hand made a helpless gesture. "All entrances to Mira'aleitha were sealed within the hour, as were the harbor and the city gates. Anyone caught trying to escape was killed with witch fire if they resisted capture. The invaders were accompanied by light-skinned, white-haired people with strange metal machines that showed them the way to the djinns' and fairies' hiding places. There seemed to be no escape. We who lived in the quarters—at least those who were not found to have magical abilities—were allowed to move about freely and were not bothered, even if someone was caught harboring a magical being. That day, thousands of them were locked in cages, loaded onto Spanish galleons, and taken away. No one knows exactly why it was possible for sorcerers like you"—he nodded reverently at Ariane—"and the djinns to be captured so easily. Those who escaped reported that from one moment to the next, all magic spells in the district ceased to work. None of them had ever seen or heard of such powerful sorcery. There is no telling what happened to our friends in the ships. Several hundred they did not take with them, but put them up for public sale in a great slave market that lasted several days."

Abdels face betrayed his revulsion at the memories of that event. "Some friends of the djinns raised enough money to buy some of them, to give them back their freedom later. But there were still enough greedy rich people. They seemed to have been waiting for a chance to humiliate the djinns. Or perhaps they just wanted to use their abilities for their own purposes. The bids were astronomically high, so not that many could be ransomed.

He stared into the distance for a moment, then continued. "However, this anti-magic spell had yet another effect, and that was to save at least a few dozen djinns and a few fairies. You see, in Mira'aleitha, there is a sacred zone, a djinn temple, whose entrances are protected by magical weaves. At the time of the attack, these entrances closed automatically because the weaves lost their power, and all those who were in the sacred territory were trapped inside. When the Spaniards left a couple of weeks later, the gates reopened, and the meager remnants of Algiers' magical inhabitants set out to save what could be saved. Together with the few ransomed djinns, they began secretly tracking down the kidnapped slaves and liberating them by force. Since then, several hundred beings have returned to the former shrine and have built a small village community there. This is the Refuge."

"But," he continued, "no one has yet found a way to remove one of the bands of malleable metal from the neck of any of the former slaves. This means that they can only use their abilities when someone else is holding their leash and explicitly allowing them to do so. Not even the friends who have officially ransomed the djinns have been able to set them free. Some even took the question to the Ottoman-Spanish Inquisition in Granada. The answer they received was that the collars were meant to be a permanent solution, and that the contract of sale did not allow magical creatures to be returned their freedom. When they were no longer wanted, the 'material' would have to be resold or given to the Inquisition for 'further utilization'.

He fell silent. Ariane's face was a mask of suppressed anger. Joe and Kaura didn't look much different.

"Can we talk to the authorities of the Refuge?" asked Sen. "We have a psychomagician on board. Maybe my friend Simon can do something to help."

The old Arab shrugged.

"I am sure they will be happy to receive the Great One and her friends." Another reverent nod to Ariane. "But what a circle of thirteen powerful djinn cannot do, your expert will probably find difficult to solve. I do hope I'm wrong," he added.

Sen stood up.

"I want to try anyway. Can we come back tomorrow morning and bring Simon with us?"

Abdel replied in the negative.

"I need a day to clear you with the Refuge and get the consent of the elders. You can be back the day after tomorrow. Ibrahim will pick you up. What ship are you on?" the old Arab asked.

Kaura told him.

When they said their goodbyes, the envoy asked Ariane for a blessing.

With a gentle smile, the fairy pressed her small hand to his forehead, and a beatific expression appeared on Abdel's tanned, wrinkled face....

* * *

ATTACK OF THE GODS will be available in Winter 2023/24

Glossary and Personae

A Who's Who for the entire "High Priestesses of Lemuria" Saga

* * *

A'kaala Sect - Descendants of the former Lemurian ruling dynasty of Kal and its faithful, banished from Earth some fifteen thousand years ago for forgotten crimes.

Aaliyah Leivenstein - Matriarch of an Inmarsund Trading House.

Aalid - A planet in one of the central spiral arms of the Milky Way. Colonized by the Lemurians several decades ago, it became independent after the collapse of their empire as the administrative center of one of the more powerful planetary confederations.

Abigail Andrews - Head of the Nelson family's central trading office in London. Long-time lover of Joe Nelson.

Aleitha - A honorific used on Gaia for non-human magical beings.

Algiers - Independent city in North Africa. Formally part of the Spanish Ottoman Empire.

Amina - A fairy in the guard fairy contingent of the Lockwood Society, Oxford.

Amiro Tekanuata - A Lemurian politician, later head of the "Pure Hand of Reason".

Ar'ten - A city in southern Lemuria. Former center of the interplanetary Lemurian Empire. Location of the Wave Temple and starting point for pilgrimages to the "Sacred Island.

Ariane Tinkerbell - A member of the guardian fairy corps of the Lockwood Society, stationed in Westminster.

Arun - See Ömea VI.

Atam - A dog who survives a shipwreck together with Kaura as a puppy.

Atlantia - The capital of Atlantis, located on the South Continent. Location of the Crystal Temple.

Atlantis - Technologically advanced mini double continent in the Atlantic Ocean. For outsiders, access is strictly forbidden, except to a few trading ports, also accessible only with special permission, and the Irish peninsula in the east of the northern continent, which is de facto independent of Atlantis.

Aztec Empire - Empire in Central America loosely allied with the Atlanteans.

Mountain Elves - Mounted warrior race, common in the Lemurian Sima'ren Mountains.

Celia Ermigan - Lemurian doomsday prophet of antiquity. Various Lemurian doomsday sects refer to her, not least the "Pure Hand of Reason", although none of her writings survive and her prophecies have survived only through secondary literature in very vague form.

Cork - A port city on the Irish peninsula.

Cuauhnahuac - Cave System on Sacred Island in Rainbow Lake, Lemuria.

Diana Roseheart - Rosewinged Head of the Lockwood Society's Guard Fairy Contingent.

Dimension Gate - A discontinuity in the fabric of reality, situated on the planet Ömea VI and reason for its fame as the central spiritual hub of the Milky Way. Allows access to parallel worlds and realities.

Djinn - North African mage race with green skin and little body hair.

Eagle Gunnarsdottar - Witch of the Lockwood Society in Oxford. Originally from the north of Turtle Island (North America).

Edinburgh - Capital of the Scottish Empire. However, at the time of the events of this story, the queen lives mainly in her palace in Westminster, southern Scotland.

Ema-Lirel - Forest on fairy planet Sirius Q. Location of the tree of life.

Angel Fairies - Direct representatives of the Ix. Much larger than most other fairies and with gold feathered wings.

Earth - See *Gaia*.

Earth Magic - One of the four types of magic, primarily used by the Lemurians.

Fern temple - The seat of the Fern Priestesses in Ilkarion. More generally, used to describe the entire Lemurian priestly guild.

Fairies - Umbrella term for mostly winged gifted beings of wish magic with magic powers far superior to all other magic beings. There are two species on Gaia: Wish Fairies with direct descent from Sirius Q, and Forest Fairies symbiotically linked to the Sima'ren Mountains in northern Lemuria. Also known are angel fairies, wingless earth fairies (found only on Sirius Q), and the extremely dangerous dark fairies, which presumably resulted from genetic experiments of the "gods" with captured wish fairies.

Gaia - A planet in one of the outer spiral arms of the Milky Way. Known as the former center of the Galactic Lemurian Empire and the location of the "Magic Source" from which all magically gifted beings in the known universe draw their power.

Gan'olin - Originally from Ömea IV, high councilor of the portal city of Pyrrha, on Gaia.

Gar'akin - Omean monk on Arun, in the Order of the Dimension Gate Keepers. Former fellow student of Gan'olin.

George Papandreiou - Servant at the Nelson branch in Inmarsund.

Great Mother - Ambiguous. In European culture, name for the primordial source of reality. For the forest fairies of Sima'ren, it is the name for their central tree deity, an offspring of the Great Tree of Ema-Lirel, Sirius Q.

Grand Inquisitors - Magically gifted members of the Inquisition of the Spanish Ottoman Empire. Composed almost exclusively of Kai'Ala.

Great Mongol Empire - Empire founded by the Genghis Khan dynasty, stretching from Cipangu in East Asia to the Baltic Sea and the Danube, and encompassing almost all of Europe at its greatest extent. Known as technical pioneers, exporting their sophisticated

Ixchel'en - Spiritual center of Lemuria. Gathering place for the annual ceremonies. Under the pyramids of Ixchel'en are said to be the "ships of the ancients".

Jane Nelson - Mother of Joe Nelson. Together with her father Mercurio head of the Nelson merchant dynasty.

Joe Nelson - Globetrotter, merchant and youngest son of the Nelsons.

Kai'Ala - Blue-skinned, small-bodied, and minimally magically gifted aliens who appear on Gaia primarily in the role of Grand Inquisitors. Probably work for the "gods".

Kal Dynasty - Ancient Lemurian ruling caste. Banished from their home planet Gaia millennia ago due to a now unknown, but obviously extremely serious crime.

Kaura Alenu'ala - High mage and Supreme of the Lemurian High Priestesses. One of the four "Pillars of Life", responsible for Earth Magic (Emotional Magic), the main channel of the Lemurians.

Kerak - Tribal shaman of the Elm clan of mountain elves.

Monastery of Arun - Place of pilgrimage. The closest power place to the Dimension Gate, open to the public.

Control Device - Linen-like amulet developed by the chief scientist of the gods, Uriel, for controlling the will of mages.

Crystal Priest Guild / Crystal Templars - Religious elite of Atlantis. The Crystal Priests are mostly magically gifted, but rather more weakly than other European high mages and even averagely strong inhabitants of Lemuria, needing ritual to strengthen the effectiveness of their magic.

Crystal Rod IV - An expedition and combat ship of the Crystal Templars of Atlantis.

Lance d'Armancourt - Grand Master of the Knights Templar of Rhodes.

Pillar of Life - Lemurian honorific for four of the High Priestesses, who are supposed to channel the four known types of energy output of the magic source during a hitherto unknown ceremony. The title is bestowed–along with a near-immortality–by the Oracle as part of the priestly initiation in Ixchel'en. It is not known what exactly the role of the four "Pillars" will be, but tradition requires that they must always be prepared to fulfill it.

Lemuria - Continent in the Pacific Ocean, with an extension of over three thousand miles in length and one thousand in width.

Lockwood Society - One of the two most important mage guilds in the Scottish Empire, based in Oxford. Traces its founding directly to the mythical Merlin Silvercloak.

Lorenia - A Lemurian Fern Priestess, Friend of Kaura's.

Types of magic - Elemental Magic (Nature Magic), the art of communicating with nature spirits. Very rare. Spell Magic, the art of manipulating reality with words and sometimes through ceremony and ritual. Most common form of magic in European, African, and American cultures. Earth Magic (Emotional Magic), the influencing of reality by means of feelings, willpower, and visualization. Primary form of magic among the Lemurians. Wish Magic (Fairy Magic), especially widespread among fairies, partly also among the djinns.

Describes the ability of manifestation through focused attention and trust.

Magical Source - Sun of the inner world.

Maran - Inhabitant of Ilkarion. Friend of Irigenak.

Marie Deline - Young neo-French woman from Montréal in the key world, member of the high nobility in Robespierre VIII's empire.

Mea Lonu - Highest mountain of the Sima'ren Mountains. Here Kaura and her companions find the oracle for the first time.

Mera - Mountain in Sima'ren.

Mercurio Nelson - Jane Nelson's father, Joe's grandfather.

Mila Intan - Medieval Scottish travel writer, possibly a pen name. Author of the famous and widely translated book "Travels of Mila Intan".

Mira'aleitha - The "shining district", the quarter of the magicians in Algiers.

Mirafin - A Lemurian hover ship that likes hugs.

Mirkan (planet) - The main planet of the Mirkanese Confederation.

Mirkan (Confederation) - Second major planetary confederation that emerged from the former Lemurian Empire.

Moni - Large commercial space port on Illura.

Napoleon V - Ruler of one of the world empires of the key world.

Nature Magic - One of the four types of magic.

Nelson Trading Corp. - One of the most powerful Scottish trading companies of the nineteenth century after Buddha.

Nume'lin - Elder of the fairy community of Sima'ren.

Ojai - Deputy Director of the Alaris Spaceport.

Ömea - Sun of the planetary system with the same name.

Ömea IV - Main planet of the Ömea system. Inhabited by elephant-like intelligent life forms.

Ömea VI - Another name for Arun. Famous pilgrim planet.

Oracle - Spirit being that helps guide the destiny of the Lemurian settlers.

Oranga Mountains - Mountain range on Arun. This is where the Dimension Gate can be found.

Ormin - Forest fairy from Sima'ren.

Philip II of Granada - Sultan Emperor of the Spanish Ottoman Empire.

Pride of Edinburgh - Name of a trading galleon of the Nelsons. Commanded by Sir Elias McGregor.

Rashikam - Nomadic smuggler, operating mainly from Illura. Specializes in illegal cheese transactions.

Rau'atea - Ancient Lemurian base in the Western Pacific Spice Islands area.

Refugium - Refuge of the last mages and djinn of Algiers.

Rainbow Projector of Ar'ten - A kind of lighthouse in the former Lemurian capital. One of the seven wonders of the ancient world.

Rainbow Lake - A lake in southern Lemuria. Location of the mythical 'Sacred Island'.

Rainbow Valleys - Umbrella term for the scattered farming communities where much of the Lemurian population lives. More specifically, a region inland from Ilkarion, where this trend began several millennia ago.

Pure Hand of Reason - Religious sect, later political party in Lemuria.

Resa Leivenstein - Commander of the Baltic cog *Stralsund*, sailing on behalf of the Leivenstein family. Kaura's adoptive aunt and mentor.

Rhodes - Island in the eastern Mediterranean. Seat of the Knights Templar.

Rignar - Home planet of the A'kaala. The planetary capital is called Olympia.

Robbespierre VIII - Ruler of one of the two empires of the key world.

Red Wind - Extremely dangerous natural phenomenon of unexplained origin in the Sima'ren Mountains.

Scottish Empire - Island empire in Western Europe ruled by Queen Elizabeth I ("Lissy").

Selena - Lemurian high priestess from Ilkarion. One of the four pillars of life, responsible for elemental magic.

Seneca Lumisworth ("Sen") - High Mage. Headmaster of the Lockwood Society.

Sica - Hunter and guide in the Sima'ren Mountains. Sometimes works for the local representation of the Temple of Ferns.

Seven Wonders of the Ancient World - Crystal Temple of Atlantia, Rainbow Lighthouse of Ar'ten, Pyramids of Pyrrha, Golden Palace of Shamb'alla, Temple District of Tenochtitlan, Floating City of Pyrhe'in (Lemuria), Mountain City of Huang'shan (after Lemurian travel writer Ikel'in Urmailen).

Sillin - Mountain city on the extreme northern tip of Lemuria.

Simon Beauville - Young Psychomagician from Oxford.

Sirius Quinta (Sirius Q) - A planet in the solar system Sirius in relative proximity to Earth. Home of the fairies.

Skyölda - Young princess from the inner world. Member of the royal house of Merina.

Solaris Terza - Other name for Gaia, also called Earth or Terra.

Spanish-Ottoman Empire - World-wide empire of the conquistadors with its capital in Granada on the Iberian Peninsula, established after the Peace of Lepanto and the subsequent merger of the religions prevailing in the territory of the contracting parties. Dominated much of the Mediterranean, the Netherlands, parts of the Baltic coast, and made extensive territorial claims in Southeast Asia and the "New World." Led by Nazarite sultan-emperor Philip II. Magical talent is officially punishable by death in the s.-o. empire and is prosecuted by its own authority, the Holy Inquisition.

Spell Magic - One of the four classical types of magic, common on Gaia throughout Europe, Atlantis, the "New World," North Africa, and parts of Asia, and the most widely known form of magic among the general public worldwide. Spell magic uses rituals, potions, and words to influence reality. It is assumed that a total number of practitioners comparable to or even slightly larger than the Lemurian feeling magicians exists, with feeling magic occurring exclusively on Lemuria and partially in Pyrrha until the "Great Exile of the Pure Hand" in December of 1870 AD.

Knights Templar - Ruling Guild of Rhodes.

Tenochtitlan - Capital of the Aztec empire allied with Atlantis.

Temoz'pin - City in the Sima'ren Mountains, Lemuria.

Terra - Another name for Gaia.

Triabola - A female member of the A'kaala sect, charged with exploiting Gaia's magical potential.

Umari'en High Valley - Valley in Sima'ren Mountains.

Urg'ull - Mutant dark fairy and one of the leading personalities of the resistance on Rignar. Urg'ull is a vegetarian, which he tries to hide from everyone as it is considered the highest disgrace among his kind and is punishable by death.

Uriel - Chief planner and scientist of the A'kaala sect.

Ushanpur - Forest fairy name for the Red Wind.

Waipi'o - Island city off the East Lemurian coast.

Forest Fairies - Isolated for millennia from their origins on Sirius Q, a tribe of fairies native to Lemuria. Unlike their off-planet relatives, they have multicolored butterfly-like wings and uniform green eyes, as well as characteristics completely untypical of fairies, such as politeness and gentleness.

Western Kingdom - An unexplored area in the inner world. This is where magically gifted children are banished.

Wish Magic - One of the four types of magic. In it's pure form, it is common only among the fairies, although the djinns are also said to have parts of wish magic in their spellwebs.

Time calculations - On Gaia, a variety of methods are used to determine dates. The most common at the time of the events described in this book is the Buddhist calendar of the Mongols and their former European colonies. In the Spanish-Ottoman Empire, the former Christian calendar is officially in use - according to conjecture, because at the Peace of Lepanto, the one with the highest year was simply taken from the one used in the newly created empire, ostensibly to appear more 'respectable'. The most inaccurate is probably the current Lemurian calendar, which calculates only in family generations, seasons and moon phases and does not know any year counting anymore, although the ancient Lemurians, according to recently found written documents, counted the years as well until at least the disappearance of Celia Ermigan and the closing of the central library, probably from the first landing of a larger contingent of settler ships from the Pleiades system and the subsequent foundation of the Lemurian settler community.

Zika'dela - Lemurian hover ship commander.

Maps

The High Priestesses of Lemuria - Principal
Settings, Political and Geographical Overviews

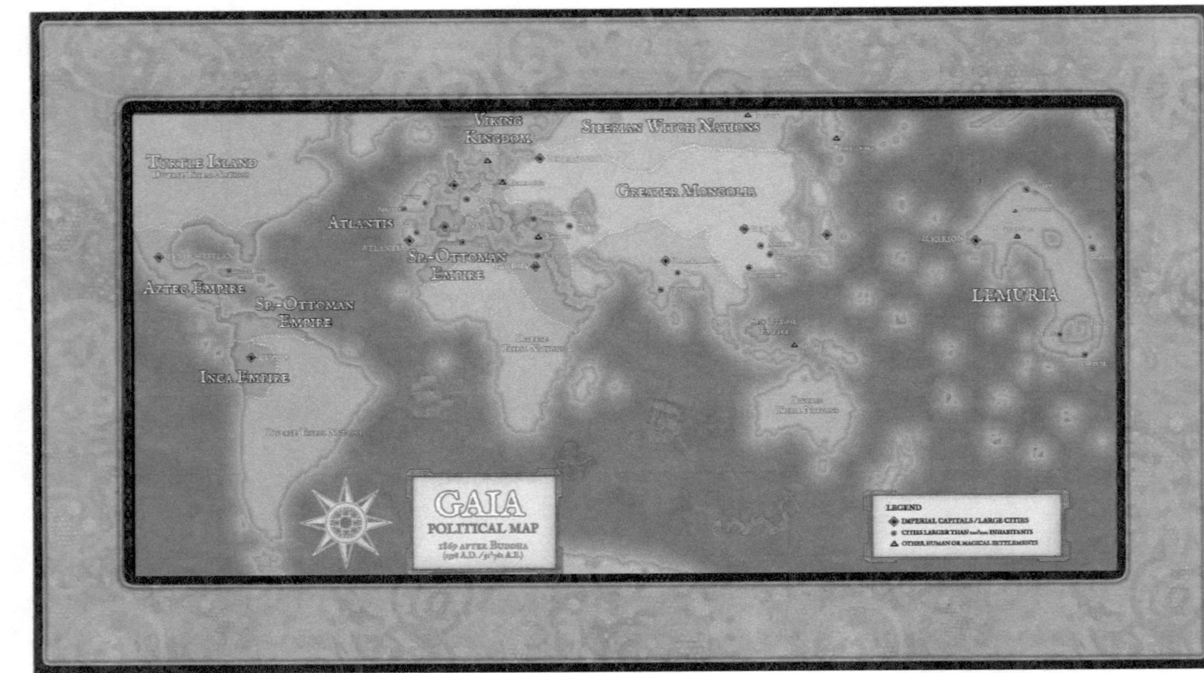

TURTLE ISLAND
VIKING KINGDOM
SIBERIAN WITCH NATIONS
GREATER MONGOLIA
ATLANTIS
SP.-OTTOMAN EMPIRE
AZTEC EMPIRE
SP.-OTTOMAN EMPIRE
INCA EMPIRE
LEMURIA
GAIA
POLITICAL MAP
1169 AFTER BUDDHA
(1298 A.D. / 5179 A.E.)
LEGEND
IMPERIAL CAPITALS / LARGE CITIES
CITIES LARGER THAN 100/000 INHABITANTS
OTHER HUMAN OR MAGICAL SETTLEMENTS

MAP OF
EUROPE &
ATLANTIS
NORTHERN ATLANTIS
SOUTHERN ATLANTIS
GULF OF ATLANTIS
EIRE PENINSULA
KINGDOM OF SCOTLAND
SPAN-OTTOMAN SULTANATE
MEDITERRANEAN SEA
Inverness
Gothenburg
Edinburgh
Copenhagen
Dublin
Oxford
Hamburg
Inmarsund
London
Cork
Paris
Venice
Rome
Constantinople
Athens
Granada
Cadiz
Algiers
Agadir
Rhodes
Alexandria
Pyrrha
Atlantia
Imelin
Avlin
Morania

CIPANGU
Edo
Kagoshima
Sillin
Sima'ren-Mountains
Temoz'pin
Ixche'len
Pyrhe'in
Ilkarion
Raia'tea
PAPUA
TERRA AUSTRALIS
PACIFIC OCEAN
HAH-NU-NAH (TURTLE ISLAND)
LEMURIAN OCEAN
Waipi'o
Ar'ten
Holy Island
Pape'ete
MAP OF LEMURIA
J.D. Uppender & Sons, London
A.R. 1880
1000
NAUTICAL MILES

GOLD OCEAN
BRETOHA
VENHEIM
THEKADA
KARALEN
PERAM
Russrot Giants
Emedam River
Ilodur Cascade
RIADURA
Rainbow Lakes
COBALT SEA
NEW ARTEN
Central Starseat Mines
ALARIS
Alar Mtn 36,243 ft
GULF OF TINTARA
AONOTAI
ASARI
ISTHMUS CITY
MACANIC OCEAN
MARACIA
NEW ILKARION
SHERKASIAN OCEAN
SHERKASIAN OCEAN
TIMARUA
RITENE
AALID
PLANETARY MAP
0   NAUTICAL MILES   5'000

Acknowledgements

THANK YOU

I would like to thank all the beautiful people in my immediate and wider surroundings who contributed to the creation of this book - through inspirations, ideas, readings, discussions, or simply by being there.

And also especially to the wonderful humans of Hotel OceanoMar in Mazunte on the Pacific Ocean, where the first draft of this book was written in February and March 2021, and to the inspiring energies of my changing homes, Sedona, Tepoztlán, and the islands of Hawai'i, Tenerife, and Tahiti, all of which somehow came together in the vision of Lemuria. Furthermore, I'm profoundly grateful to Damanhur Community and what it has taught me about my own past lifes and about unlocking my talents as an artist, as well as to all of the inspirations that have come to me through my own reading, not least, through the pirate pulp magazines I used to read as a teenager and which initiated a lifelong interest in the age of sail. This first novel in the series is also a tribute to the hardworking authors creating them. I hope you'll have as much fun with my novels as I had with theirs.

Andreas Farmann, Puerto de la Cruz, Spain, in March 2023

ANDREAS FARMANN

Andreas Farmann was born in the Swiss Alps in 1977 and now lives between Berlin, the Canary Islands and Hawaii. Since childhood he has been fascinated by the worlds of High Fantasy and Science Fiction.

"My work is inspired by classical sources such as the Indian epic Mahabharata and the Iliad, but also includes homages to my own favorite high fantasy authors, including J.R.R. Tolkien, Stephen King, Robert Jordan, and Tad Williams," says the author.

He has already finished writing the manuscripts for the six volume "High Priestesses of Lemuria" saga and currently works on another series set in Kaura's youth and the time when the Atlanteans arrived on Earth.

* * *

Andreas Farmann is also writing as Andreas Ziörjen

· CHAKRA SERIES ·
BY ANDREAS ZIÖRJEN

The Chakra Series is a sequence of practical guidebooks to awaken and harmonize your subtle energy centers. Some of the books are also available in the form of compact ten-day audio courses, making the chakra-energies more clearly accessible through guided meditation and introspection practices.

www.andreasziorjen.com

www.ingramcontent.com/pod-product-compliance
Lightning Source LLC
LaVergne TN
LVHW091402190726

843491LV00006B/1219